P9-ECO-183

Calculated risk

Encizo ducked back behind the cover of the van, aware that at least one opponent had yet to be taken out. His move was followed by the booming of the enemy shotgun, and a burst of buckshot peppered the van and raked the floor where he had been a split second earlier.

From his position, Manning followed the line of fire and saw the remaining IRA gunman huddled by the racks of spare parts and accessories. In a flash he also noticed that the man had broken open his side-by-side shotgun to reload. Seeing an opportunity to take a prisoner, Manning quickly rushed the Irishman's position. He reached the racks and aimed the Walther at the big guy with the sawed-off gun.

"Drop it," he ordered, training his pistol on the terrorist's face. "Give it up or you're dead."

The Irishman stared at Manning, then tossed the shells in his left hand aside and nodded to signal his surrender.

Suddenly he hurled his shotgun at Manning. The Canadian tried to dodge the unconventional projectile, but the heavy twin barrel struck his forearms and knocked the Walther from his grasp.

BOOKS 'N THINGS
3071 Robert Road
Suite F
Prescott Valley

Mack Bolan's

PHOENIX FORCE.

PHOENIX FORCE®

GAR WILSON

IRON CLAYMORE

A GOLD EAGLE BOOK FROM
WORLDWIDE®

TORONTO · NEW YORK · LONDON · PARIS
AMSTERDAM · STOCKHOLM · HAMBURG
ATHENS · MILAN · TOKYO · SYDNEY

First edition March 1990

ISBN 0-373-61346-6

Special thanks and acknowledgment to
William Fieldhouse for his contribution to this work.

Copyright © 1990 by Worldwide Library.
Philippine copyright 1990. Australian copyright 1990.

All rights reserved. Except for use in any review, the
reproduction or utilization of this work in whole or in part
in any form by any electronic, mechanical or other means,
now known or hereafter invented, including xerography,
photocopying and recording, or in any information storage
or retrieval system, is forbidden without the permission
of the publisher, Worldwide Library, 225 Duncan Mill Road,
Don Mills, Ontario, Canada M3B 3K9.

All the characters in this book have no existence outside the
imagination of the author and have no relation whatsoever to
anyone bearing the same name or names. They are not even
distantly inspired by any individual known or unknown to the
author, and all incidents are pure invention.

® are Trademarks registered in the United States Patent and
Trademark Office and in other countries.

Printed in U.S.A.

1

Shirley King inserted a sheet of paper into the Smith Corona and pressed the index button. The sheet rolled into position, but she barely glanced at the letterhead. It was official United States Embassy stationery with an address in London, England. Humming cheerfully, she set the margins on the DeVille 125 typewriter.

Shirley had been a secretary at the Embassy for six months. It was a wonderful job for a twenty-three-year-old Kansas woman, barely out of college and with limited work experience. She had worked as a secretary to support herself and to help pay for her education. Her employer knew she had trained in computer programming and that she was studying political science and international law. He also knew her secretarial skills were top-notch. When she had completed college, he'd contacted some friends in the federal government and had helped her get her present job with the American Embassy.

It was a wonderful opportunity for Shirley to see Europe and establish herself as an employee of the government. The work was not much different from what she had done in the past. Most of it was rudimentary, such as typing letters for the ambassador or simply stamping form letters with his signature and stuffing them in envelopes. The job was not very glamorous, but secretarial positions seldom are.

However, glamour had little appeal to Shirley. Her plan was to travel and see the world for a few years and learn more about foreign affairs and international law from firsthand experience. Then she would decide what new career decision to make. Maybe she would go back to school and try to get a teaching degree or get a job with the State Department. Somewhere along the way, Shirley intended to get married and have two, maybe three, children, but she had decided she was not going to rush into such a relationship. When it happened, it happened. In the meantime, she had other things in mind.

Shirley sat behind her desk and typed the letter, barely glancing at her dictation pad to consult the shorthand notes as her fingers flew across the keys. Molly, the senior secretary in the front office, had left to run an errand for the ambassador, and Shirley was alone in the office when a Marine corporal carried a package into the room. Dressed in a blue uniform and white gloves, service cap tucked under one arm and the package under the other, the young Marine walked to her desk and stood at attention until she looked up from the typewriter.

"Excuse me, ma'am," the lance corporal began, "this was hand delivered by messenger. He said the ambassador was expecting it."

"Oh?" Shirley raised her eyebrows with surprise. "He didn't mention a package to me. Of course, he's got a lot on his mind. Just leave it on my desk."

"Yes, ma'am," the Marine replied with a trace of relief in his voice. He felt slightly embarrassed at being made a delivery boy at the Embassy.

She thanked the Marine as he marched from the office, but she didn't feel any great sympathy at his discomfort. Shirley figured any Marine stationed in London instead of Beirut ought to consider himself lucky.

Shirley curiously examined the package on her desk. It was about the size of a shoe box, wrapped in brown paper with a label addressed to the ambassador, but bearing no return address. She frowned, knowing she couldn't give the ambassador a package without even knowing who it was from.

She took a letter opener from a desk drawer and slid the brass blade under the packing tape. When she had cut through those, she peeled off the paper. She laughed lightly as she stared down at the package. It *was* a shoe box. After clipping through some more tape, she pried off the cardboard lid with the letter opener.

Inside was a smaller box set in the middle of a nest of crumpled newspapers. A tiny metal replica of a sword was stapled to the lid of the second box. Smaller than her letter opener, the sword was entirely black, with a double-edged blade and a fancy handguard around the long handle. Shirley peered with puzzlement at its intricate design and detail. Odd little curio, she thought. A fancy letter opener or a memento of some sort?

Shirley leafed through the newspapers in the box to search for a card or letter. She found nothing, but noticed the papers were a week old and printed in Glasgow, Scotland. At last she reached in and raised the lid from the smaller box. The little sword added surprising weight to the lid. It was heavier than it looked.

Then, without warning, the box exploded. The blast struck her in the face and sheared off skin and hair in an instant. But she had no time to feel pain or fear as her skull cracked and popped apart, and her hand was torn off at the wrist. The ghastly corpse slumped from the chair and slid behind the desk.

The lance corporal and a Marine sergeant sprinted through the hallway when they heard the explosion. The latter man drew his sidearm as they approached the office. They were stunned to find Shirley's desk splattered with blood and glistening pieces of tissue. The Smith Corona had also been blown apart, and chunks of the typewriter lay scattered across the floor.

Part of a cardboard box lid was also among the debris. Torn and charred, it still held the miniature iron sword stapled in place.

GEORGE AND SUSAN MACKLIN stared out the window of the tour bus and admired the miles of green meadows and distant hills. It was beautiful and peaceful, a different world from the rat-race life they knew in Los Angeles. There were no traffic jams in northern Scotland. Even the cities of Aberdeen and Dundee have relatively light traffic, with far more bicycles and mopeds on the streets than cars.

The Macklins had planned their European vacation for nearly ten years. They had saved money for the trip and had researched travel brochures and issues of *National Geographic* to determine what they wanted to see and do in Europe long before they could afford the vacation. At last their youngest daughter had moved out, married and had a child of her own. George and Susan could finally take the burden of parental responsibility from their shoulders and take the holiday they had dreamed of for more than a decade.

"Yeh must be city folk," a young man in the seat across from the Macklins remarked.

The American couple turned toward the voice. The man smiled at the pair. His features were Nordic, with a strong lantern jaw, high cheekbones and shaggy blond eyebrows. A long mackintosh coat covered him from his neck to the top of his hobnail boots, and a tweed hat with a shapeless brim cast a shadow across his face.

"Well," George began, surprised by the stranger's remark. "Yes, we're from L.A. Uh, I mean Los Angeles. It's a city in California."

"Aye," the stranger said with a nod. "So yeh are Americans. I thought yeh be."

He rolled his "r"'s in the regional accent of the Central Lowlands and most of the west coast of Scotland. The Macklins knew that many Scots along the east coast spoke dialects they could not understand, and actually, some of the east coast Scots didn't seem to speak English at all. In fact, the farther northeast they traveled, the more they encountered locals who spoke a form of Scottish Gaelic and Buchan Doric. The latter language is barely comprehensible to other Scots, and English-speaking Americans are completely baffled by the Buchan tongue.

"My name is George Macklin, and this is my wife Susan," the American introduced himself and his spouse to the stranger. "We're pleased to meet you, Mr....?"

"Angus," the Scotsman replied. "Angus will be fine. Are yeh enjoying yer visit here in Scotland?"

"Very much," Susan said as she pulled back her head scarf to uncover her ear so she could hear the conversation better. A shock of gray-streaked red hair appeared from beneath the scarf. "How did you guess we're from a city?"

"Simple enough," Angus told her with a twinkle in his cobalt-blue eyes. "Yeh both been looking out the window at the countryside as if yeh ne'er seen grass nor lea before."

"Well, we've seen grass before," George assured him, "but we've never seen the Scottish countryside until now. When we planned our vacation, Scotland was a special place of interest to us both. We're of Scottish descent, you know."

"Aye," Angus said with a nod. "Visiting the country of yer fathers' fathers. The bus is going to the Castle of Cawdor. Does that be yer destination?"

"Oh, yes," George confirmed. "We're looking forward to it. You know, Cawdor Castle is mentioned in Shakespeare's *Macbeth*?"

"Macbeth, thane of Cawdor, murders King Duncan at the castle," the Scotsman replied with a nod. "With daggers, I believe. The murder is offstage, as I recall. Act II, Scene I, isn't it?"

"I'm really not sure," George admitted, slightly embarrassed that his knowledge of Shakespeare did not equal

Angus's. "I read the play back in high school, and that was . . . well, more years ago than I care to recall."

"I think Angus is right, dear," Susan stated, although she couldn't remember ever reading *Macbeth*.

"Cawdor might not be a grand and huge castle compared to some," Angus commented, "yet Cawdor be prettier than most. Many a castle was burned-out and looted long ago and ne'er recovered. Peasant uprisings claimed a number of manors in their day."

"That's interesting," George said, stroking his somewhat pudgy chin. "You seem to know quite a bit about the history around here."

"I be born here," Angus replied as if that should have been obvious. "The bus stops at Nairn before going to the castle. I know a shop or two yeh might fancy if yeh care to take a look."

"That sounds wonderful," Susan said eagerly. She loved to go shopping, and the quaint little places with unusual knickknacks and curios had a special attraction for her.

"We can take a look," George told his wife, but he was already beginning to worry that they might run out of money and traveler's checks before the trip was over. "You're sure this won't put you out of your way, Angus? I'm sure you've got things to do."

"Aye," the Scotsman said with a smile and a shrug. "I've many things to do, but this isn't a problem. Be me pleasure, I assure yeh."

The bus continued up the road, past more unfolding meadows and occasional herds of sheep and goats. Some small, shabby cottages dotted a line along the coast. "Butts and bens," Angus called them, and explained they were dwellings of the poor who made a meager living as fishermen in the treacherous North Sea. They could hardly compete with the big fishing industries, but they knew no other way of life. Little had changed for them in nearly a hundred years.

Nairn was a city that resembled a large village, a quality not uncommon in Scottish cities. Many buildings were two or more centuries old. Although most of the tourist trade is centered in Edinburgh, Nairn offered several fine hotels, tennis courts, two excellent golf courses and trout fishing in the area. It was, in fact, a favorite spot for visiting prime ministers and businessmen familiar with Scotland who desired privacy and a nice quiet stay before getting on with their affairs.

The bus rolled to a stop, and the passengers emerged. Most were tourists and stayed near the driver, who understood the Buchan Doric language as well as Gaelic. Actually they would have found little trouble communicating with the residents of Nairn. The people of a cosmopolitan city tend to learn the language best suited for successful trade. The Macklins separated from the group to follow Angus as he led them across a cobblestoned street to a row of small shops.

He guided the Americans to a tiny antique shop with the legend Red Stag printed on a wooden sign that was carved in the shape of a buck deer. Candlesticks, pewterware and other items were displayed in the window. George managed to suppress a groan. The shop looked as though it did little business, which meant the merchandise must be expensive. He didn't care for the idea of spending twenty or thirty British pounds sterling for something like a couple of old brass candlesticks.

The door opened, and a young man greeted them at the entrance. He was about five and a half feet tall, about seven inches shorter than Angus. Yet there was a striking similarity between the two Scotsmen. The shopkeeper also wore a mackintosh and tweed hat. His lantern jaw and blue eyes were identical to Angus's features, although the shopkeeper's bushy eyebrows were dark brown instead of blond.

"Yeh just caught me on me way out, Angus," he declared as he ushered the visitors into the shop. "Who yeh brought here, me lad?"

"These be the Macklins from the United States of America," Angus replied. "This is me younger brother William."

"Oh?" Susan said with surprise. "You didn't mention your brother owned the store."

"Nay, lassie," William said with a sly grin. "Ne'er been here till this day."

George glanced about the shop. It was filled with an assortment of antique bottles, kitchenware and clocks on shelves lining the walls. No one was behind the cashier box. William was still smiling as he pulled down the shade to the front window, and before George could even take it all in, Angus closed the door and shoved the bolt into place.

"George," Susan whispered to her husband with concern in her voice as she clutched his arm. She had also noticed the odd behavior of the two men.

"What are you guys doing?" George demanded, his stomach knotted with fear. Heck, he thought, as he considered that they came from L.A. to get mugged in the Highlands of Scotland.

Angus sighed and unbuttoned his coat, then withdrew a pistol from his belt. A metal cylinder was attached to the weapon's barrel. Angus pointed the pistol at the American couple and shook his head slightly.

"I do apologize for this," he stated. "Yeh seem decent folk, but some things has got to be done even if they mean decent folk has to suffer."

"What the hell?" George glared at Angus. "Now, you don't need that gun, fella. I'll hand over the money. No need for anyone to get hurt..."

"Folks get hurt all the time," William remarked as he stepped behind George. "Our folk have been choking to death on oppression, and our clan has been denied its proper place for too bloody long to endure.''

''My God!'' Susan exclaimed. Her eyes widened with fear as Angus pointed his pistol at her face. ''Are you crazy?''

''Act II, Scene I of *Macbeth*,'' Angus began as he reached to a shelf and picked up a small brass cowbell with his free hand. He shook the bell, and it clanged sourly. '''Hear it not, Duncan, for it is a knell . . .' ''

He squeezed the trigger. The silencer hissed harshly, and a 7.65 mm bullet crashed into Susan's skull. It struck the bridge of her nose and burned into her brain before she could hear the muffled report. George opened his mouth to scream as he saw his wife's head snap back from the force of the bullet. He felt her hands claw into his arm as she clung to him for protection even as her life vanished in a fraction of a second.

George lunged forward at his wife's murderer, but strong hands seized him from behind. William snaked an arm around the American's neck and held his neck in a viselike grip. Sharp steel plunged into George's right kidney, and his cry of agony was cut off by the choke hold. William stamped a boot in the back of George's knee, and the American's leg buckled as William forced him to the floor.

'''That summons thee to heaven or to hell,' '' Angus continued, completing the line from Shakespeare as he watched William raise the bloodstained dirk.

William drove the knife blade between George's shoulder blades, yanked it free and adroitly slit the American's throat. The murderer wiped the knife on his victim's clothing and rose from the floor. Angus nodded with grim satisfaction.

''Yeh didn't kill the shopkeeper, did yeh?'' Angus inquired.

''No, me brother,'' William replied, offended by the question. He slid the dirk into an ornate wooden scabbard on his belt and covered it with his mackintosh. ''Chap's tied up in the back room. Gagged and blindfolded, and I stuffed his ears with cotton so he heard nothing.''

''That's good, William,'' Angus said, and returned the pistol to his belt. He reached into a pocket as he added, ''There's to be enough bloodshed before this is finished. Don't be wanting any of it to be Scottish. Of course, sort of too late for that already.''

''What do yeh mean?'' William asked, puzzled by the remark.

''There be Scottish blood in the Macklins,'' Angus explained.

''They was Yanks,'' William said with a shrug. ''Whate'er Scot there be in 'em was polluted in America.''

''I hope yeh be right,'' Angus replied as he took a small iron object from his pocket and placed it on the lifeless chest of Susan Macklin.

He glanced down at the miniature sword on the dead woman's chest, shook his head sadly and gestured for his brother to follow him to the door.

2

Hal Brognola entered the Oval Office. He did not fit the usual description of VIP White House visitors. He was middle-aged, and his face displayed the deep-set lines and baggy eyes of a man who lived with nonstop pressure, high stress and enormous responsibility. His suit was old, ten years out of style, slightly wrinkled and permeated with the strong scent of cigar smoke. His striped tie, pulled down to half-mast, and the undone shirt button at his throat lent him a slightly rumpled air.

The President of the United States was sitting behind his massive desk. He looked up at Brognola, and quite unconsciously his lips tightened in disapproval as he noted the man's appearance. Brognola had to spend nearly all his time at Stony Man headquarters, where he handled operations assignments and details that ranged from Intelligence gathering to arranging for cooperation with foreign governments and forging passports. Brognola wasn't a public figure, and he had little concern about what he looked like. There was nothing polished or sophisticated about him. He was a federal agent with an impossible job, and he did it better than anyone else could have.

Politicians had to worry about how they looked in front of a camera, and they studied body language, voice inflection and color combinations for clothing to make good impressions. But Brognola couldn't care less about appearances. He dealt in hard reality every day. The Fed had little regard for show and ceremony. He was concerned with facts and actions that accomplished missions vital to the well-being of the United States of America, if not the entire world.

"Hello, Mr. Brognola," the President greeted as he peered over the top of his reading glasses to look up at his visitor. "We did meet rather briefly once before in this very office."

"I remember," Brognola assured him. "Congratulations on your promotion to President. I hope you're up to the job. A lot of people are going to be depending on you for the next four years."

The President took the glasses from his nose and stared at the Fed as if stunned. He had only taken office three days ago. Since the inauguration, literally thousands of people had congratulated him and welcomed him into the Oval Office. Yet none of them—not even members of the opposition party—had addressed him in this manner. Brognola had not wished him luck. He was telling the President not to screw up.

"Have a seat," the chief executive urged, and gestured toward a chair near his desk. "I think we'd better have a talk."

"Yeah," the Fed confirmed as he lowered himself into the chair. "I take it you made sure the room is secure?"

"You know my background well enough to know I'd make sure this conversation was absolutely top secret," the President stated. "You certainly know more about me than I know about you."

The President reminded Brognola of a high school principal, sitting behind his desk and staring at the Fed as if he was a naughty kid who'd broken one of the basic rules. Brognola was not sure what to expect from the new President. The man had run for office using campaign commercials that showed him dressed in the work shirt and denim trousers of an Iowa farmer. In actual fact, of course, this President was a long way from being "just-plain-folks," and Brognola knew it.

"I have to admit I was pretty surprised when my predecessor told me the details about you and your organization," the President began as he clasped his hands on the desk. "I'm really surprised he managed to keep all this stuff a secret, even from me. Turns out you're the highest ranking federal officer of any Intelligence or security organization in the country. Higher than the directors of the CIA, National Security Agency or FBI. There's no documentation of that fact or evidence that the Stony Man organization even exists, although it gets its authority directly from the White House. Right?"

"So far," the Fed agreed.

"Well, now imagine my surprise when I learned the Stony Man outfit had been set up along the lines of an antiterrorist unit with the assistance of Mack Bolan," the President continued. "The same Mack Bolan who was known as the Executioner. The fellow who waged a one-man war against organized crime a few years ago. A fellow who, according to virtually every reliable source, is officially dead."

"Those reports are greatly exaggerated," Brognola explained. "Mack Bolan is alive and well and carrying out very dangerous missions for the United States of America."

"Wait a minute," the President insisted. "The Executioner was a criminal. He was wanted by police in all fifty states and several foreign countries. According to what little I could learn about your career, you were one of the federal agents in charge of hunting down Bolan and bringing him to justice."

"That was a long time ago," Brognola stated. "A lot has changed since then. Besides, Bolan was never a criminal. I'm sure you must know he only struck at those whose inhuman actions proved them guilty many times over. He's still fighting them, whether they are criminal cartels, international terrorists, enemy agents and others of that ilk.''

"I still don't like the sound of it. Now, what about the two special commando teams that work with you and Bolan in Stony Man?"

"Able Team consists of three former comrades-at-arms who assisted Bolan during his war against the Mob. They generally handle missions within the United States. Phoenix Force gets the assignments abroad.''

"Phoenix Force?" the President repeated with a frown. "I'm going to ask you a straight question and I want a straight answer, Brognola. Are you people running some sort of assassination business that's been kept top secret all these years? Some people may have some big misconceptions about me, and if you think I'm going to approve of government-sanctioned death squads, you can just fold up your organization right now and tell your hired killers to find another country.''

"No, we're not assassins," the Fed assured him. "And before you decide to get rid of Stony Man, you'd better be damn sure you won't need us for the next four years. The last President considered dissolving Stony Man more than once. When a crisis came up that no one else could handle the way we can, he was always damn glad we were still available.''

"Tell me more about Phoenix Force," the President demanded. His voice was flat and hard, as if he wanted a straight answer right then. "Who are they and how do they operate?''

"Phoenix Force consists of five men," Brognola told him. "They were chosen from the best antiterrorist and elite combat units of the free world. Well, all except one who has an unusual background that includes special experiences and skills since the early 1960s when he was a freedom fighter pitted against Castro's regime in Cuba.''

"Before the Bay of Pigs or after?" the President asked.

"Before, *during* and after," Brognola explained. "The guy in charge as unit commander has a background that goes back to Word War II when he was a kid fighting the Nazis in Europe. Fifteen years old, and he was working with OSS and British Intelligence. The other three members of Phoenix Force are younger, but their track record is just as impressive. I'm unable to supply you with names or files. That's how Stony Man has managed to stay top secret. I won't even tell you details about who they are and exactly how they operate."

"How successful are they?" the President probed.

"One hundred percent success rate," Brognola stated. "They've never failed a mission. Unfortunately, though, one of the original members of Phoenix Force was killed in action during one mission. That sort of diminished the victory for us, but the terrorists were put out of action nonetheless."

The man behind the desk frowned. "Terrorists? Delta Force was created to deal with terrorism. CIA and NSA is concerned with it abroad, as well."

"Delta Force is a military outfit," Brognola explained. "Hell, Mr. President, you know that. The problem with an elite fighting unit like Delta Force is that it has to find the target first. NSA is almost exclusively concerned with gathering information and Intelligence, usually from electronic eavesdropping and spy satellites. Those tactics don't get too far with terrorists, or with a lot of other criminal organizations and clandestine conspiracy groups. You're more familiar with the CIA than I am, so I don't have to tell you the problems there."

"What problems are you referring to?" the President asked in a dry voice.

"To begin with, the Company has too many personnel who are inexperienced, and in positions they're not qualified for," the Fed stated. "At one time, the CIA recruited from the military Intelligence groups and other sources.

Now they get 'em right out of college or even from want ads in the newspapers. Of course, the biggest problem is security.''

"For Delta or CIA?" the President asked, obviously more interested in testing Brognola than really seeking an answer to something he didn't already know.

"Hell, after Watergate whatever security CIA had was pretty well ruined," the Fed said. "Congressmen and senators wanted to prove they could blow whistles on government cover-ups and wound up splashing details of Company operations all over the headlines. Didn't seem to bother them when at least two agents-in-place were killed because those politicians continued wanting to see their names in print while they were running for office. Delta Force has even worse problems. When network television news programs announce Delta Force's whereabouts off the coast of Lebanon, there's no way in hell they get in-country without everybody knowing they're there. Including the terrorists they were sent to deal with. NSA has still managed to maintain decent security, but their peeping and keyhole listening with fancy gadgets is useless when nobody knows where to start looking."

"But your Stony Man outfit is so secret only a small handful of people even know it exists," the President mused. "So you can still maintain security. Is that what makes your group so special?"

"They're special because they're the best," Brognola insisted. "A small team of highly professional experts with total authority and secrecy can accomplish things entire armies can't do."

"You say they've never failed, but they're so secret I'm not even sure they exist."

"You figure the former President was kidding about Stony Man?" Brognola inquired, tired of being grilled with questions that were verbal quizzes. "Okay. Let me give you a couple of examples. You seem curious about Phoenix

Force. Remember that business in Rwanda a few months ago?''

"I remember," the President assured him. "It looked like Africa was about to explode. Not just in Rwanda. Nigeria and some other countries seemed ready to throw Americans out and sever relations. Then it all worked out neatly and . . . I see. That was handled by Phoenix Force?''

"That was one mission," the Fed answered. "Phoenix Force has carried out others worldwide."

"Have they ever had an assignment in Scotland?" the President asked, and his tone revealed a trace of urgency.

"I thought you might want to talk about the bombing at the American Embassy in London," Brognola commented. "Stony Man has computer link-ups with the CIA and NSA, but I don't recall data indicating the bomb was connected with the events going on in Scotland. Of course, we get a lot of information rolling in all the time, and I can't really keep up with all of it."

"There's reason to believe the Embassy bombing is connected with the murders of two American tourists in Scotland," the President said grimly as he pulled open a desk drawer and removed a small plastic bag. "At the scene of each incident, one of these things was found. Sort of a calling card from the killers."

He placed the bag on his desk and pushed it toward Brognola. The Fed picked it up and stared at the object encased in clear plastic. It was a miniature replica of a sword. Brognola frowned and shook his head. "Well, it doesn't mean anything to me," he confessed, "but I can check with our records in the data banks at the War Room computer center. A couple of my guys are walking encyclopedias when it comes to various types of unusual knowledge. Maybe one of them can come up with something. You do want Stony Man to handle this matter, don't you?"

"I still have serious doubts about whether I should let you people continue the Stony Man outfit or order you to terminate it immediately," the President admitted.

"Actually we sort of hoped you'd have a better understanding of the need for covert operations than most politicians seem to have," Brognola remarked.

"Yes," the President began with a nod. "I realize there are times when matters have to be dealt with in a clandestine, even a violent, way. I am well aware of the threat of terrorism and organized crime. I also know the Cold War is going to continue regardless of *glasnost*. However, I don't know if it would be wise for me to allow your organization to continue to operate in the shadows."

"Stony Man is a small outfit," the Fed stated. "We have a few men who are directly involved with the missions. If we go public, we won't be able to function at all. It's that simple."

"What if somebody blows the lid off your organization?" the President asked. "Investigative reporters, senate investigations, one of your people decides to quit and blows your cover to the press..."

"None of my people would do that," Brognola said firmly.

"Maybe not," the President said, "but there are a hundred ways things could go wrong. Suppose one or more of your operatives is captured by an enemy force and made to talk. Torture, drugs—whatever the method—there are ways to break any man eventually. Then they know about Stony Man. They can expose the organization and exploit it for political reasons. They might get their hands on you. I'm sure you know a great deal that could jeopardize our national security if they got to you."

"Things can go wrong," the Fed agreed, "but that's conjecture, Mr. President. The facts are that Stony Man has a perfect record of success, and you'll have occasions in the future to need us or something like Stony Man. Frankly we're the best in the business. You can't get any better people than the men already with Stony Man.''

''You must realize I'm still closely associated with the previous administration,'' the President began. ''During the campaign, the Iran-Contra business was brought up again. I'm sure I haven't heard the last of it, and the opposition will be looking for any type of covert operations carried out during my administration.''

''So, you're concerned about your political career?'' Brognola snorted. ''Wouldn't you say that the safety of our country and the American people is more important? If you don't believe that, you shouldn't be sitting behind that desk.''

''My God,'' the President said, stunned by the other man's remark. ''Did you talk to the last President that way?''

''You'll have lots of people praising you and telling you you're always doing the right thing,'' Brognola stated. ''You don't need, and won't get, that from me. I just do my job, and that means trying to protect this country and everything it stands for. That's why Stony Man was created.''

''I'm still uncomfortable with this arrangement,'' the President confessed, ''but considering the most recent news from Scotland, I feel obligated to try any avenue that might offer the best solution. I think your Phoenix Force unit might be it.''

''I'll get them on it, sir,'' Brognola assured him.

''First you'll need to know the details about the most recent incident,'' the President told him. ''Have you ever heard of Daniel McGreggor?''

''Sure,'' Brognola answered. ''Millionaire industrialist. At one time, there was an effort to draft him into running for President, but he didn't seem interested. I seem to recall he was one of your supporters in the last election.

''That's right,'' the President confirmed. ''He also happens to be of Scottish descent. With a name like McGreggor, that's not much of a surprise. He decided to make a trip to Scotland. Wanted to visit his ancestors' homeland and begin plans to set up an automobile production plant with the cooperation of the British government. First time the English have been willing to consider such an offer by an American industrialist since that DeLorean deal that never materialized."

"DeLorean was supposed to set up a plant in Ireland," the Fed commented. "Economically depressed area in the north where a lot of Irish need jobs. I suppose parts of Scotland are in a similar situation. Too bad none of these generous and altruistic American industrialists show the same kind of interest in helping the economically depressed areas of the midwestern United States."

"That situation was caused by Congress," the President said, and when he noticed that Brognola was about to air his views on the subject, continued quickly. "But let's concentrate on this McGreggor business. He was kidnapped less than two hours ago. According to the information I received, the same 'calling card' was found next to the bodies of McGreggor's personal bodyguards. They had both been shot to death at close range. This time the killers also left a message. I have a copy of their letter. After you read it, I'm sure you'll agree the people behind this are either insane or egotistic enough to think they can get away with virtually anything."

"Could be a combination of both," Brognola remarked as he took a cigar from his coat pocket and stuck it into his mouth. He didn't light it, but chewed the cigar as he stared down at the sword.

"I'll get that letter for you," the President began. He wrinkled his brow as he looked at Brognola. "By the way, do you mind if I ask whether you're a republican or a democrat?"

"Independent," Brognola replied with a shrug.

"Well, I was just curious who you voted for in the last election," the President admitted. "For me or the opposition?"

"Hell," Brognola said with a weary sigh. "When was I supposed to find time to vote?"

3

"So, what do you think of the new President?" Yakov Katzenelenbogen inquired as he looked up at Hal Brognola at the head of the conference table. "More importantly, I suppose, what does he think of us?"

"Yeah," David McCarter added as he took a pack of Player's from the pocket of his wrinkled sports jacket and shook out a cigarette. "Did you call us here to give us the boot, Hal?"

The tall fox-faced Briton sounded worried. He had spent his entire life preparing for action. Formerly an SAS commando, McCarter had acquired a remarkable level of skill in small arms, hand-to-hand combat and virtually every form of warfare. He lived for excitement and felt most at home on a battlefield.

"I guess I'm like a lot of people right now," Brognola began, chewing a cigar butt as he spoke. "I'm not gong to form a solid opinion about the President until he's been in office for a while. All politicians make promises during their campaigns, but they don't keep most of 'em after they get in office."

"I didn't hear many promises made by the candidates during this campaign," Calvin James commented with a trace of disgust in his voice. "They spent most of their time bad-mouthing each other."

The tall, lean, black warrior had little tolerance for people who blamed others for what was wrong and failed to take action themselves to improve things. A product of the tough streets of Chicago's South Side, James had been born with a lot of obstacles to accomplishing his goals in life. He never gave up and eventually achieved most of his ambitions. Being a member of Phoenix Force was what he wanted to be, although he realized he probably would not live to retire from the unit.

"Right now the only issue we need to be concerned with is whether or not Stony Man will continue operations," Rafael Encizo stated. "What's the verdict, Hal?"

The tough Cuban was not one to mince words. Well muscled with dark, handsome Latin features and a natural charm that attracted women, Encizo was a veteran survivor since childhood. He hated to think that the new man in the Oval Office might do what thousands of terrorists, gangsters, enemy agents and assorted fanatics hadn't been able to accomplish—the destruction of Phoenix Force and Stony Man.

"Right now we're still in business," Brognola declared. "That might change in the future. The President has some doubts about us and he still might decide to terminate this organization. For the time being, he's reluctantly agreed to keep us going. The main reason seems to be terrorist activity in the United Kingdom."

"Your old stomping ground, David," Gary Manning said, and turned to face McCarter. "I just hope the terrorists aren't as crazy as you are."

"That's not very likely," McCarter replied with a shrug.

Manning suppressed a smile. The big Canadian occasionally questioned McCarter's relative sanity, but he also realized that so-called normal individuals would not be part of Phoenix Force in the first place. While McCarter regarded their missions as the opportunity to fulfill his thirst for adventure, for Manning they were his job—a very important job that he happened to be ideally suited for. Ruggedly attractive and physically powerful, Manning appealed to women who liked the strong silent type. Yet the Canadian was a workaholic, and his job was Phoenix Force.

"Okay," Brognola began as he took a seat at the head of the table and slapped several file folders on the counter. "We don't have much to go on so far. If you've been listening to the news, you may have already heard about the bombing at the American Embassy in London. We've got CIA, Scotland Yard and Interpol investigation reports on that incident. Two tourists were also murdered in Scotland the same day the bombing occurred. Now, this is what links the incidents."

He took the miniature sword in the plastic bag from an inner jacket pocket and placed it on the table. Katz picked it up and examined the object, a frown tugging the corners of his mouth. Katz had certainly acquired varied knowledge and experience, starting from his early days fighting the Nazis to his more recent involvement with Israel's Mossad.

"It's not a trademark of any terrorist organization I'm acquainted with," the Israeli admitted. "David, you spent some time in Northern Ireland with the SAS. This mean anything to you?"

Katz handed the sword to McCarter. The British ace looked at the replica and nodded slightly. The long double-edged blade with a wide, ornate handguard and hilt long enough to serve as a two-handed sword was distinctive and easily recognizable.

"It's a Scottish claymore," the Briton announced.

"Claymore?" James asked with surprise. "You mean like a Claymore mine? Sort of thing we used in Vietnam?"

"The mine was actually named after the claymore sword," McCarter explained. "Back in medieval times, the claymore was regarded as a real terror on the battlefield. A real claymore sword is about five feet long, but it was noted for being lightweight and very quick in the hands of an expert swordsman. Standard weapon for Scottish fighting men from the early 1500s to about the mid-1600s, I reckon."

"I'll be damned," Manning remarked. "How do you know about this stuff?"

"With the name 'McCarter' I ought to know a bit about Scottish history even if I was born in the East End of London," the Briton replied. "Give me a little credit for knowing a bit about my ancestors. Besides, I still got some relatives who live in Scotland."

"I figured your family members probably lived in a munitions factory," the Canadian said dryly. "The question is, what does the Scottish claymore have to do with terrorist activity in Great Britain?"

"A miniature replica of the weapon was found at the scene of each incident," Brognola explained. "The third and most recent incident is the kidnapping of Daniel McGreggor. Scotland Yard and the Security Intelligence Service is investigating the kidnapping, but it happened so recently—just a few hours ago—we don't have anything on it yet except the eyewitness account that's included in these files."

"McGreggor was one of the fat cats who supported the President when he was running for office," James commented with a grunt. "I don't want to sound too cynical, but it is sort of interesting that the President decided to keep us in operation because one of his buddies got grabbed by terrorists."

"Well," Katz began with a sigh. "Let's not base too many critical assumptions about the man on this. Besides, from our point of view it doesn't really matter if the President has any personal motives for sending us on the mission. The terrorists in the United Kingdom are obviously real. They're a threat to Americans associated with the Embassy and innocent tourists, as well as wealthy industrialists like McGreggor."

"Not to mention the fact they're probably also a threat to British citizens," McCarter added. "That might be a greater concern to me than to the rest of you blokes."

"You guys take care of the terrorists and you'll be doing a service for Great Britain as well as the United States," Brognola assured him. "Of course, you'll be working with the British authorities as well as the CIA."

"Any chance we'll have Colonel Hillerman on our team this time?" McCarter inquired. "Wouldn't mind working with my old SAS commander again. He was sure an asset for us when we had that mission in the Persian Gulf a while back."

"I already checked on that," the Fed replied. "Unfortunately, Colonel Hillerman is still stationed in Oman. In fact, he's the top case officer for British SIS in that part of the world now."

"That must be good news for Hillerman, but we sure could use someone with his experience and connections with both SIS and SAS," Encizo said with a frown. "Well, they've got a lot of good people in British Intelligence, and I'm not as worried about working with them as I am about the CIA. Whenever a new administration takes over, they put a new director in charge of the Company. That always means lots of confusion, changes in how things are done and who's in charge of different stations throughout the world."

"Yeah," Manning agreed. "Leave it to a bunch of terrorists to pull a stunt like this at such an inconvenient time."

"At least this time we'll be headed for a country that's on favorable terms with the U.S.," James commented. "I hate it when we have to sneak into a country where dealing with the government is almost as much of a problem for us as dealing with the terrorists we're sent after. The worst are the missions when the government *is* the bad guys we're after."

"Well, don't expect this mission to be easy," Brognola urged. He scoffed at his own remark and added, "Okay, I know none of them are easy, or we wouldn't need you guys to take care of them. What I mean is, the mission is sort of special due to our current status with the new President."

"You mean you want us to make a good impression?" McCarter asked with a grin. "What does he expect us to do? Catch up with the terrorists, ask them to kindly leave their weapons in the cloakroom and sit them down to tea and crumpets where we inform them they are under arrest and best come along quietly? Some of the blokes we go after are so crazy they'd set themselves on fire and try to jump in your lap before they'd surrender."

"I know you can't handle these suckers with kid gloves," the Fed assured Phoenix Force, "but I want you to pay even more attention to security and keeping a low profile. Try to avoid publicity. A shootout in front of television cameras, or blowing up a building in the middle of a major city— things like that are bound to get attention and wind up in UPI news coverage."

"We don't do that sort of thing unless there's no other way to handle a situation," Katz said with a sigh. "If you'll recall our mission in Czechoslovakia, we had to carry out a raid in broad daylight in Prague because the terrorists were about to launch a short-range nuclear missile."

"Yeah, yeah," Brognola agreed wearily. "I appreciate the fact there can be extraordinary circumstances, but I also know the President is still afraid we might be some sort of secret death squad or a gang of mercenaries that charge into missions like the proverbial bull in a china shop."

Manning groaned aloud. "Is that the man's opinion of Stony Man operations in general or just Phoenix Force?"

"He's not just picking on you guys," Brognola assured the Canadian. "It came as sort of a shock for him to discover Mack Bolan was still alive and working for the government. Actually I can understand his concern. After all, how will it look if the public learns a guy who was known as the Executioner and formerly led off the FBI's most wanted list is now one of our top operatives? People will want to know why we've been so secret if Stony Man is exposed. What are we trying to hide? Even the President can't give any details about who we are or how we operate. We seem to be an outfit that operates outside the law, without having to account to anyone for our actions. The President must view this as a potential scandal that would make Watergate dim by comparison.''

"So, this is the first mission authorized by the new President, and if we screw up, there's a good chance there won't be any more," Encizo said grimly.

"You got the idea," Brognola assured him as he reached for a file folder on the table. "Now, can I finish this briefing?"

"You have some more evidence for us?" Katz inquired.

"We sort of moved away from the subject of the mission itself to how it should be handled," the Fed explained. "Actually I was saving the most important piece of information for last. Guess I should keep away from high drama in the future. You see, when the terrorists kidnapped McGreggor, they also left a message."

He took a sheet of paper from the folder and handed it to Katz. The Israeli examined the copy of a letter that had been assembled by the process of pasting up words cut out from newspapers. Katz read the message.

To the United States of America,
We demand your government officially denounce the imperialist oppression by the dictatorship of Great Britain and the English ruling class. We demand the United States call a special meeting at the United Nations and reprimand Britain and its oppression of Scotland, Ireland and Wales. We demand the United States sever all political and trade relations with Great Britain until the above-mentioned countries are granted full independence of British rule and British armed forces are withdrawn from these lands. We demand the

right to full self-government and recognition in the
United Nations as independent and sovereign nations.
Finally, we demand recognition of the King of Scot-
land as the rightful, legal authority of this land.

If these demands are not met, McGreggor will die.
Many others will die, and the United States will suffer
for its association and support of the British tyrants.

The message wasn't signed. Katz passed the letter to
McCarter. The British ace looked as if he had swallowed a
mouthful of sour milk as he read the message. He shook his
head and handed the letter to Encizo.

"These buggers sound like a lot of crazy bastards," he
remarked. "They really think the United States government will go along? And what's this rot about 'the King of
Scotland'?"

"It suggests they won't kill McGreggor," Encizo commented as he handed the letter to James. "Not right away,
at least. I suppose the President will be happier with us if his
industrialist pal can be rescued and brought home safe and
sound."

"That'd be nice," James agreed, "but I wouldn't count
on it. Any bunch of nut-cases who'd come up with the rest
of this stuff have to be regarded as pretty damn unstable."

"Maybe this is the IRA operating in Scotland," Manning suggested after reading the letter. "Perhaps they figure it will be more effective if they can convince people they
have widespread support in Scotland as well as Ireland."

"Of course, there's no way the U.S. is going to agree to
any of these demands," Brognola stated. "Uncle Sam isn't
about to break off relations with our strongest ally in Europe just to please some murdering fanatics. However, the
last part of this letter is accurate. A lot of people will probably die if these terrorists aren't stopped."

The Fed pushed the rest of the file folders to Katz and took out the well-chewed cigar from the corner of his mouth as he surveyed his trusted Phoenix Force.

"And that, gentlemen, is your mission."

4

Daniel McGreggor felt as if he had followed Alice through the looking glass and taken a wrong turn into a nightmare realm of madness. The American industrialist sat in a heavy antique armchair with a large pewter goblet of ale within easy reach on the small table to his right. He had been offered a plate of roast mutton and sweet potatoes, as well as cigars, but accepted only the ale as he watched the contest in the middle of the great hall.

McGreggor's captors had not mistreated him. In fact, they seemed to be pretending he was the guest of honor. But McGreggor had seen the kidnappers gun down his bodyguards in cold blood before they'd abducted him, and he realized the two brawny young men who stood near his chair would pounce on him if he tried to leave the great hall. McGreggor also knew that the man at the opposite end of the hall could order his execution at any time, and he would be killed quickly and ruthlessly.

The man called himself Andrew Robert Bruce. He occupied an ornately carved armchair with inlaid gold designs on the arms and backrest. Elevated on a raised stone platform at the opposite end of the hall, the chair served as a throne. Dressed in cotton trousers with a frilled white dress shirt and goatskin boots, Bruce displayed an odd combination of upper-class finery and peasant garb.

A large man who had once possessed a muscular physique, Bruce had suffered from the toll of more than sixty years of great hardships and sacrifice. His weather-worn face and deep-set blue eyes revealed some of the harshness he had known. A mane of white hair and a full beard framed his rugged features. His left arm was partially paralyzed and lay across the armrest of his throne like a dead animal. In his right was the knobby head of a black thornwood walking stick.

Behind the throne hung three portraits. One painting was immediately recognizable to McGreggor as a portrait of Robert Bruce, crowned King Robert I in 1306. McGreggor suspected the artist had used a well-known eighteenth century engraving of Robert Bruce as a model for the painting, because the portrait also depicted the Scottish king clad in armor, battle axe in hand and beard fluttering in the wind.

The second portrait was that of David II, the son of Robert I. The painting depicted a young man without a beard, his features grim and determined. A scarlet cape draped the boy king's shoulders, but an armor breastplate and chain mail was visible beneath the cowl.

The third painting was a portrait of Andrew Robert Bruce himself. Clad in a red robe with a white fur collar and a golden crown atop his snow-white head, Bruce seemed a wise and majestic figure in the painting. Indeed, he was an impressive and charismatic individual in person.

"With Scot blood in yer veins, yeh might find this of interest, Mr. McGreggor," Bruce stated as two young men stood in the center of the great hall, face-to-face and twelve feet apart. "Me eldest son, Angus, and me youngest, Malcolm, will demonstrate the fighting art of the claymore."

Bruce's sons swung their swords in wide circles in the air. McGreggor guessed that to be a warm-up exercise. He never had much interest in physical combat to begin with, and he regarded fencing as one of the most absurd forms since he considered such weapons obsolete in the twentieth century. Still, McGreggor pretended to be interested in the mock duel because he thought it wise to humor old man Bruce until he could figure out how best to handle the situation.

Angus was taller and more muscular than his brother. He held his claymore with both hands fisted around the long handle swooping the four-foot blade gracefully in a series of figure eights. Malcolm swung his claymore faster, but the motion lacked the skilled ease displayed by his brother.

Both men wore armor breastplates that covered the torso from the neck down. There was a metal codpiece for extra protection of the crotch, and they wore pads on their knees, elbows and wrists. Their heads were covered by brass helmets with grille-work face guards. The·sword blades were copper-alloy, not steel, and were unsharpened with blunted tips. Yet the contest was still potentially dangerous and required the protective gear they wore.

"Begin," their father announced.

Malcolm attacked first. He shouted a battle cry and swung his claymore in a frenzied series of overhead chopping strokes. Angus raised his sword and blocked the attacks with apparent ease. The blades clanged three times. Frustrated, Malcolm swung a wild roundhouse stroke at his brother's head. Angus ducked under the sword blade and delivered a fast cross-body cut to Malcolm's breastplate.

The younger brother hissed angrily and swung a sideways sword stroke at Angus. The blades clanged once more as Angus chopped his claymore across his opponent's weapon and forced his sword to the floor. Angus delivered a quick stab before Malcolm could raise his claymore. The blunt end of Angus's claymore jabbed Malcolm in the breastplate and made him stagger.

Malcolm roared and lunged with his sword as though it were a lance. Angus parried and sidestepped the attack, making Malcolm's forward momentum carry him past. Angus stepped behind his sibling and chopped his claymore across Malcolm's armor-plated back. Malcolm swayed forward and buckled to his knees on the hard stone floor.

Angus stepped back and lowered his sword, but Malcolm jumped to his feet, spun about and raised his claymore for another attack. But before they could tangle again, their father shouted for them to halt. Both brothers froze in place.

"The contest is over, lads," Bruce announced. "Yeh can't attack yer brother again, Malcolm. He's already killed yeh at least twice."

Malcolm threw down his sword. It clattered loudly on the stone floor as he pulled the helmet from his head. The younger brother shared the family features, with his lantern jaw, blue eyes and bushy brows. His blond hair was a lighter shade than Angus's, and he wore it longer. The few yellow whiskers on his upper lip were a feeble imitation of a mustache.

McGreggor's attention shifted to two men who were approaching the center of the hall. The taller of the pair was built like a professional wrestler, with a broad, powerful chest and limbs that bulged with thick muscles. His shaggy brown hair was untidy, but the beard along his strong jaw was neatly trimmed. McGreggor guessed he was yet another son of Andrew Robert Bruce.

But the man beside the muscle-bound figure did not look like a typical Scot. He was thin, with black hair and a drooping mustache, and he appeared amused as he approached Malcolm. The big man stooped to pick up the discarded sword and shook his head sadly. Malcolm unfastened the buckles to his breastplate and glared at the black-haired man.

"Yeh find me amusing, Douglas?" Malcolm demanded, and tossed the helmet to the dark man. "Think it funny, do yeh?"

The breastplate fell to the floor with a clatter. Malcolm's hands suddenly streaked to the big buckle of a belt around his narrow waist. The leather was wide and studded with heavy brass rivets. The belt came free in an instant, and

Malcolm lashed out with it. Douglas tried to raise his arms to fend off the attack. Studs banged against the brass helmet in his hands as the belt struck. The buckle whirled around the helmet to catch Douglas above the left eyebrow. The skin split open, and blood trickled into his eye. Douglas yelped with pain and doubled up, raising the helmet to protect his head and neck.

"Laugh now, Douglas!" Malcolm snarled, and again flogged the belt across the man's back and shoulders.

Douglas dropped to his knees. Malcolm was raising the belt again when his father shouted his name, but Malcolm ignored him and swung the studded leather across the fallen man's back. Douglas groaned under the lash, and Malcolm's eyes shone with cruel glee as he raised the belt once more.

Large, powerful hands seized Malcolm's wrists. The big, muscular man had stepped behind the youth and grabbed him from behind. He pulled Malcolm away from Douglas and held his wrists. Malcolm's arms were spread wide, as if in imitation of crucifixion. Then the hand around his left wrist squeezed harder, and Malcolm's fingers popped open to drop the belt.

"Damn yeh, Duncan!" Malcolm shouted, helpless and frustrated in the grip of the powerful man. "Leave go of me!"

"Yeh be the son of a king," Duncan stated in a firm, hard voice. "Yeh best be acting like it, lad."

The big man quickly wrapped his powerful arm around Malcolm's waist and set his shoulder at the small of the other man's back. With ease Malcolm was hoisted into the air, and he gasped as he found himself slung across Duncan's shoulder. The man locked his fingers together at Malcolm's abdomen, shoulder firmly planted under the youth's back. Malcolm struggled weakly as the breath was squeezed from his lungs, and the pressure at his spine nearly paralyzed his ability to move.

"Put him down, Duncan," Andrew Robert Bruce ordered. "Yeh do not want to harm yer brother."

Duncan lowered Malcolm to the floor and released him. The youth breathed deeply and rubbed his midsection to try to recover from the untender embrace. Angus helped Douglas to his feet and examined the gash above his left eye. He spoke some words of comfort or apology and sent the fellow off to have the wound tended to.

Angus glared at Malcolm as he scooped up the youth's belt. "T'wasn't right what yeh done to poor Douglas," Angus declared. "Yeh know he can't strike back at yeh 'cause yeh be a prince and he be a commoner. 'Tis not right to abuse yer authority and status in such manner, Malcolm."

"He mocked me," Malcolm replied. "A bleeding commoner with the look of a Jew about him had best not be making sport of me. Maybe I'll ne'er match yeh with a claymore, but I can flog me belt with the best of strappers."

"Yeh had no call to use a strap on that lad, Malcolm," Angus insisted. "Not the proper way for a noble blood to behave."

"Aye," Duncan added. "If yeh lead men, yeh need be an example of strength and courage, not a bully boy."

Malcolm snatched his belt from Angus and angrily marched from the hall. Duncan prepared to follow him, but with a glance his father detained him. Andrew Robert Bruce lowered his gaze to the floor, embarrassed by Malcolm's behavior.

"I regret yeh had to witness me son's shameful temper, Mr. McGreggor," Bruce said sadly. "He's still quite young and short of wits. Since he be a wee lad he's been a problem. Trying to live up to being as good as his brothers, I reckon. Don't think he'll e'er manage."

McGreggor suspected Malcolm had been told all his life that he was not as good as his older brothers, which was probably why he was a bad-tempered, violent young man. The American kept his opinion to himself and nodded in mock agreement.

"I've got three kids myself," McGreggor declared. "They can bring you a lot of grief. I worry about my girls a lot. One of them is married now and has a child of her own, but I still think of her as my little girl."

"I don't have a daughter," Bruce stated. "All me children were boys. Four fine strapping lads. Angus be eldest, then Duncan and William and finally Malcolm. It is good to have sons. Someone to carry on yer family name. Continue yer bloodline. The blood of Robert Bruce runs in our veins."

McGreggor did not reply. He doubted that the man was really descended from Robert I or any other king, but he was equally certain Bruce believed his claim. McGreggor had had enough experience in dealing with people and had developed a well-honed sense of who was sincere and who was trying to peddle manure disguised as roses. It was clear that Andrew Robert Bruce really believed he was a direct descendent of Scotland's most famous king.

"I've got grandchildren too, Mr. McGreggor," Andrew Robert Bruce continued, tilting his head toward the two sons in the hall. "Angus and his wife have blessed me with two grandsons and a wee granddaughter. Only six months old she is, but the infant lass and her brothers had to go with their mother off to the Inner Hebrides. 'Tis a harsh place in the northern islands. Duncan's wife and his lad are there, too. A hard sacrifice for their womenfolk and children, yet it has to be as long as their husbands fight in our war of independence."

"I see," McGreggor remarked, although none of it made much sense to him. "But I don't understand why you want me? If you wanted a ransom to help finance your activities, I might understand."

"We've no quarrel with yeh," Bruce assured him. "No true quarrel with yer country except it's an ally of the English. The Brits are no longer an empire. They stopped being a real power at the end of the Second World War. Without the aid of America, England is nothing but a heap of pompous Brit scum with so wee manhood they need a woman to lead them."

McGreggor glanced about the great hall. It was a grim setting with high, gray, stone walls. Naked light bulbs burned from outlets attached to cords along the ceiling. A few hunting trophies decorated the walls, along with two crossed claymore swords with black iron blades mounted on the wall opposite the stag.

"Admiring the family coat of arms?" Bruce inquired. "The iron claymore has become the symbol of our struggle. The Bruce family and our brave followers are all part of the Clan of the Iron Claymore."

"The Iron Claymore?" McGreggor asked, astonished that there should be such an organization. He wondered how a man whom he considered to be a lunatic had managed to recruit enough followers to carry out his insane scheme. "You must think I'm far more important than I am if you believe the United States will change foreign policy because you're holding me hostage."

"'Tis more here than yeh," Bruce stated. "Yer country must come to realize England is no friend. 'Tis in the best interest of America to cut relations with the Brits. England has become a parasite that relies on America for protection and support. All we're doing is making it more difficult for yer country to continue dealing with the Brits. When Washington and yer president realize their embassy in London isn't safe, nor tourists nor traveling businessmen like yerself, they'll have to take a long, hard look at their relationship with England."

"And you think America will support your group instead?" The American shook his head. "They're not going to reward you for this sort of behavior."

"America will have no choice if it agrees to our demands," Bruce said with a shrug. "If yer government goes to the United Nations, reprimands the British oppressors, demands that Scotland become an independent nation and recognizes the rightful king of Scotland as legal ruler—well, when all that be done, yer country can't turn around and condemn us without looking to be fools. When Scotland has its own vote in the United Nations, America will learn we're better allies than the spineless Brits e'er were."

"I know the President," McGreggor told him. "I was a major supporter when he ran for office. He'll never give in to this sort of blackmail. You won't make any of these changes you're talking about. Not this way. If you think you have a legitimate complaint against Great Britain, you should go through legal channels."

Duncan Bruce had been quiet, but looked eager to join the conversation. "Legal channels?" He snorted with contempt. "What do yeh suggest? Go to the Security Council of the United Nations? They're supposed to be concerned with maintaining world peace, ain't they? They wasn't much good in Vietnam or the Middle East. Ethiopia has been having a civil war for more than twenty-five years. Angola near as long. The Security Council ain't no good at maintaining peace. What chance have we that it would help us be free of British rule in Scotland?"

"You can try the United Nations," McGreggor insisted. "Take your complaints to the International Court of Justice, not the Security Council. That's the branch concerned with administering international law . . ."

"Yeh think we haven't looked into that possibility?" Angus Bruce said with a sigh. "Aye, we considered it. That is, till we discovered who the judges be in Hague. Fifteen men, including an American and a Brit. They don't give a damn about us Scots. There's also a Russian, a Chinese and a judge from Brazil, but they're not about to recognize our plight. Their governments oppress people and they wouldn't wish to give their disgruntled masses cause to hope for change. The other judges be from Japan, Norway, Italy, some African countries thrown in to make it seem fair. None of them will do a thing to help Scotland.''

''But instead of fighting England by terrorist activity...'' McGreggor began desperately.

''Don't yeh dare call us terrorists!'' Bruce warned in an angry voice. ''We're fighting for freedom and independence from England. Yer country fought the Brits for self-rule. I had hoped an American of Scot blood would understand us better than yeh.''

''Hey,'' McGreggor responded, his tone more cross than he intended. ''I saw your people gun down my bodyguards. They stuffed me in the back of a van and hauled me through the streets to where another truck was waiting. I was handcuffed and blindfolded and had a gun shoved in my ribs with the threat of death if I tried to get away or cry for help. Just how goddamn sympathetic do you think that makes me, Mr. Bruce or your highness or whatever the hell you want to be called?''

''Still yer tongue if yeh want to keep it,'' Angus warned, and pointed the blunt tip of his practice sword at the American.

''Easy, Angus. Mr. McGreggor don't understand Scotland. He knows only what he's been told and he was brung here under unpleasant circumstances that would leave a bad taste in any man's mouth. In time, we hope yeh will see what we see, my American friend.''

Three men entered the great hall with a clatter of boots and strode determinedly forward. The one who led the trio was average in height and build, but his manner suggested he was accustomed to command. A mop of unruly red hair and a jaw of untended whiskers hinted at his lack of concern for personal grooming. He wore a military-style field jacket, wrinkled jeans and combat boots, and his Sten Mk. 2 submachine gun hung from a shoulder strap. His hard, dark eyes turned toward McGreggor with anger.

"What's he doing here, your highness?" he asked Bruce with an Irish brogue that accented his words. "This is no way to handle a prisoner."

"We're hoping he'll understand why he's here," the self-proclaimed king replied.

"It's a breach of security," the Irishman stated. "I need to talk to you and I don't want that Yank bastard present."

"Aye," Bruce agreed. He gestured for the men guarding McGreggor to escort him from the hall. "Yeh excuse us, Mr. McGreggor. 'Tis business. Duncan, go with our guest and see to his comfort."

"Aye, Father," the muscular son replied with a nod.

GARRETT O'FLYNN WATCHED Duncan and the two guards take McGreggor from the hall. The Irishman bit his tongue to keep from exploding into a burst of verbal accusations. O'Flynn struggled with his temper a moment or two before he turned to face Andrew Robert Bruce.

Talking to the old man was always a frustrating chore for O'Flynn, in whose opinion Andrew Robert Bruce was mad as a hatter. Bruce thought he was the King of Scotland, and everyone was supposed to kiss his arse. Damn old fool. Yet O'Flynn reckoned that the Scottish madman indirectly fought for the same goals as the Irish Republican Army, which had O'Flynn's allegiance. He would tolerate Bruce if the Scottish war for independence would aid Ireland's struggle, as well.

"Yeh seem distressed, Mr. O'Flynn," Bruce observed. He leaned forward, his good right hand clutching the top of his walking stick. "Mr. McGreggor was here to see a bit of claymore sword-fighting by me sons."

"McGreggor is a prisoner," O'Flynn reminded the Scot. "He's not a willing guest. The Yank's not your friend. He's part of the capitalistic industrialist complex that runs the bloody United States of America. Same sort as the Brit bastards what controls England. They're all in bed together, your majesty."

"I know many of yeh IRA fellers have socialist or Marxist notions," Bruce said with a sigh. "That's fine if that be what Ireland wants. Our politics are a wee bit different, although we share the same goals, me lad."

"Well, might I remind you the reason I'm here?" O'Flynn began in a weary voice. "The IRA has been conducting guerrilla warfare against the English for centuries. We're experts at fighting the Brits."

"Yeh haven't driven the British soldiers from Northern Ireland," Angus Bruce declared, staring into the face of the tough Irishman. "Our ancestor, Robert I, defeated the British at Bannockburn in 1314 and won independence for Scotland in 1328."

"Scotland didn't keep its independence, now did it?" O'Flynn replied, meeting Angus's gaze without flinching. "Ireland is still saddled with a semi-autonomous government—and Ulster is just a figurehead run by London—but that's still more independence than Scotland can claim. Sure, it's not enough, but it's still proof we Irish have been pushing the Brits a hell of a lot more than you Scots have for a very long time."

Angus stiffened, and his grip on the hilt of his claymore tightened. But O'Flynn wasn't afraid of Angus. He carried a Sten chopper and figured any contest between a sword and a submachine gun could only end one way. Besides, Sean and Jamie were with him. Even if the so-called prince managed to strike the Sten from O'Flynn's hands with his silly claymore, the other two Irishmen would take care of the fiery Scot.

However, O'Flynn did not want to fight the Bruces or the other Scottish rebels. Taking out Angus would accomplish nothing except the senseless deaths of O'Flynn and every IRA member attached to the Iron Claymore clan. The Scots at the castle outnumbered the Irish four to one. O'Flynn figured his IRA soldiers were better trained and more experienced than the Iron Claymore lot, but the odds were still too great to take on.

Besides, the IRA troops were in Scotland to assist the Claymore clan. They were supposed to be at war against the English, not each other. If Scotland could achieve independence from Britain, Ireland would have a strong ally to help in its own struggle for liberation. That was the theory, at any rate, but O'Flynn knew better.

With a flourish, O'Flynn spread his arms wide and smiled disarmingly. "Sure, this is an exercise in blarney which would have the Brits grinning ear to ear," O'Flynn stated, arms spread as he rolled his eyes toward the ceiling. "Scot and Irish about to come to blows over which has been the biggest enemy against the English. We need to be united against our common enemies."

"Aye," Andrew Robert Bruce agreed with a nod. "That's been the plan from the start. We do appreciate the help yeh IRA lads have given us. Together we can beat the Brits and drive 'em from our land. Eventually both Scotland and Ireland will be free of English rule."

"Not if we don't keep the front lines active," O'Flynn stated. He fished a pack of cigarettes from his pocket and shook one out. "I know you're king of Scotland, but only a few people acknowledge that. Until we force the Americans to recognize your right to rule Scotland and thus make Britain do likewise, you'll have to remain in hiding and stop treating a prisoner like he's your long lost brother."

"But after things change," Bruce began, "Mr. McGreggor will understand why we had to abduct him, and he'll become a strong supporter of Scotland's new order..."

"Don't be getting too fond of McGreggor," O'Flynn warned. "If things don't work out the way we hope they will, we'll have to terminate Mr. McGreggor. He knows who you are and has a pretty fair idea where this castle is located. In fact, we may have to execute the Yank even if you do succeed at getting the desired recognition with the United Nations. Southern Ireland has a vote in the UN, but they are only independent as long as they obey London. That doesn't mean a fiddler's damn. England might try to give you the same sort of meaningless recognition. All well and good for you to play king, but the Brits will still try to run Scotland. Then, if evidence comes out linking you and your sons to kidnapping and murder, they put you in prison and reclaim full possession of this country."

"But yeh told us me father needed recognition as king," Angus declared. "Yeh even suggested we use the symbol of the iron claymore to let the Brits know who they was up against."

"Yes," the Irishman admitted. "I also told you it may be necessary to deny any knowledge of the Iron Claymore clan. You may have to denounce your own people for the actions you ordered them to carry out."

Bruce frowned. "Betray our people? Ne'er will I do such a thing."

"You may not have a choice, unless you want to have the shortest monarchy since the regime of Lady Jane Grey," O'Flynn cautioned. "You'll find there's some ugly realities in this sort of warfare—things the IRA learned long ago. When you catch Irish girls, Catholic or Protestant, getting involved with Brit soldiers, you have to make an example of 'em. Maybe they was just talking to the enemy troops, or maybe they will go for more sport. One would lead to the other in time unless you show 'em that can't be tolerated."

"So yeh tar and feather the girls," Angus commented with disgust.

"Yes," O'Flynn said with a shrug, "or give them a good taste of a riding crop across the back and buttocks. Sometimes we have to kill a few Irish civilians to blow up some Brit soldiers. We have to punish informers with a power drill through the knee caps. Doesn't bother me to punish the Protestants. I reckon they're not true Irish, anyway... But no offense meant. You Scots are mostly Protestants, aren't you?"

"Presbyterians," Bruce said stiffly. "The official state church of Scotland. Some of our followers are Episcopalians. Mostly from the northeast coast. The only Catholics among us be yeh Irish."

"Well, this ain't about religion," O'Flynn said, wishing he hadn't brought up the subject. "The Irish and the Scots will be free to worship as they please after the revolution."

Angus snorted sourly, but did not comment. He didn't like O'Flynn and considered the IRA agent to be a ruthless manipulator and opportunist. The British had not enforced any restrictions on Scottish or Irish churches for more than a century. O'Flynn was promising them something they already had.

"Yeh mentioned the front lines," Angus said at last. "What do yeh mean by keeping them active?"

"Continued attacks on the enemy, of course," O'Flynn answered as if that much should be obvious. "The Brits and the Yanks."

"Can't say I care much for killing American tourists," Angus confessed. "William and I had to kill a middle-aged American couple that trusted me like I be a blood relative."

"Did it bother William?" O'Flynn asked, aware that the younger Bruce brother was a natural-born killer. Angus and Duncan were more intelligent, more courageous and highly skilled fighters. Malcolm, the youngest, was very dangerous, but too emotional and short-tempered. Only William was a true killer—one who enjoyed taking life.

"I didn't ask him," Angus replied grimly. "But I killed the woman, because William likes to use the dirk. I was not about to stand by and watch him stab that woman to death."

"I admire your morality," O'Flynn said, and there was a trace of sarcasm in his tone. "If it bothers you, I suggest you don't go in the field any more. Let your brothers or the other followers do it. After all, you're a prince. No need to dirty your hands."

"I'm a warrior prince," Angus responded angrily. "Descended from a warrior king. I've no intentions of ordering others to do what I can't stomach meself."

"That's up to you," O'Flynn told him, "but we have to continue operations."

"It's a true shame innocent people must die so our countries can be free," Andrew Robert Bruce said sadly.

"I'm not sure anyone is innocent," O'Flynn replied as he puffed on his cigarette and tapped some ashes onto the stone floor. "But a lot of people will have to die before this is over. Best get yourselves prepared for that. Things have just begun."

5

Eugene Henderson recognized Phoenix Force immediately when they disembarked at Heathrow airport. This was not difficult, because the five men deplaned from a military C-130 and they matched the descriptions of the elite team of "experts" from the United States. Henderson shook his head when he saw the long aluminum carrying cases and black briefcases in the visitors' hands. Gun cases, Henderson guessed. Trick valises with gadgets and weapons, as if designed for James Bond movies. Americans, he thought with frustration—they think technology and money can solve anything.

Henderson had been in British Intelligence for twenty-two years. He didn't think much of American CIA. The Company seemed to train their agents from textbooks and taught them to play with computers and fancy electronic eavesdropping devices. But they did not understand people, in Henderson's opinion, and people are what espionage is really about.

The five arrivals did not look like Company men. They seemed tougher, less polished or neat. They appeared to be alert, aware of everyone and everything around them. Their clothing was loose fitting and practical. Physically they seemed to be totally different types, but Henderson suspected that perhaps they had more important things in common than age, skin color or national origin.

"Hello," the British agent greeted as he approached the men on the ramp. "I'm Henderson, Euro-American Chemicals Limited, Research Division."

"Pleased to meet you," Katz replied with a nod. "I'm Grey. These are my companions Mr. Black, Mr. Blue, Mr. Brown and Mr. Green—in alphabetical order."

"We're a colorful lot," David McCarter added with a grin.

"Pleased to meet all of you," Henderson assured them. "Come along. We have a car waiting for you."

They passed customs without being stopped. A tall man in a dark green raincoat and cloth hat exchanged nods with Henderson and signaled the customs officials to let the visitors pass. He joined the six-man group and walked them to the nearest exit.

"I take it you cloak-and-dagger chaps exchanged passwords and all that rot," the man commented gruffly as they stepped outside.

"Yes," Henderson replied. "Oh, this is Inspector Fellows, Scotland Yard."

"I'm attached to Interpol," Fellows grunted. A dark gray scrub-brush mustache concealed most of his mouth, and since he barely moved his lips when he spoke, his voice seemed to be dubbed in through a hidden tape player. "Pretty straightforward police work most of the time. Can't say I care much for this sort of business with spies and such."

A limousine minibus was parked at the curb. It was more than large enough to accommodate seven passengers. Fellows pulled open the sliding doors, and they climbed inside. The driver glanced over his shoulder at the men in the back of the vehicle and waited until the doors were closed before he started the engine.

"Are you sure no one had a chance to plant any bugs on this limo?" Gary Manning inquired as he shoved a long aluminum case into the overhead storage rack.

"We took every precaution," Henderson replied, and lowered himself into a seat. It was hardly large enough to hold him, since he weighed more than three hundred pounds. Less than six feet tall, he was nearly a yard across. "Guarding against eavesdropping devices is naturally part of that. Standard for SIS."

"Do you have a special reason to suspect someone might plant a listening device on us?" Fellows asked with a frown. Quite the opposite of Henderson, the inspector was a slender athletic man. Although he was at least fifty, the man from Scotland Yard obviously devoted considerable time and effort to staying in shape.

"No," Manning answered. "We didn't have any reason to expect it on our last mission, either, but it happened anyway."

"Well, we're not dealing with the bloody KGB," Fellows stated. "These bastards are terrorists. Gangsters with a lot of fanatic political nonsense."

"Actually, the KGB has been involved in quite a bit of terrorist activity in the past," Katz replied. "Numerous terrorist groups have been controlled, manipulated or at least influenced by Soviet Intelligence. It's not surprising when one notices that the majority of terrorist outfits are left-wing. However, the KGB has also assisted several right-wing groups such as the Turkish Gray Wolves."

"Why would they do that?" Fellows asked, surprised by Katz's statement. "Helping right-wing groups is sort of helping anticommunism as well as terrorism."

"The purpose of terrorism is to create chaos," Katz explained. "It doesn't matter whether the terrorists call themselves right-wing or left-wing—the methods and results are pretty much the same. The Soviets don't support a terrorist group because they think the terrorists will actually overthrow a government and take over. Unless you're talking about a small country with a very large number of terrorists, that's not likely to happen. Usually the goal is social unrest, fear, domestic turmoil within a nation. When the KGB wants to weaken a country from within, sponsoring terrorism serves its purpose.''

The limo pulled away from the curb and joined traffic on its way from Heathrow. Dozens of vehicles struggled for space in the narrow roads.

''Well, the Irish Republican Army is probably behind this business in Scotland and the bombing at your Embassy,'' Fellows declared. ''Either that or it's some fanatic splinter group of the Scottish Nationalist Party.''

''The SNP is a major political party in Scotland,'' Henderson explained. ''Founded in 1934, its primary purpose is to strive for total self-government in Scotland.''

''That doesn't seem like an unreasonable request,'' Rafael Encizo commented. ''Scots wanting to run their own country makes sense to me.''

''I hope you know what side you're on, Mr. . . .'' Fellows said, his eyes hard as he stared at the Cuban.

''Mr. Brown,'' Encizo answered. ''And I'm never on the side of terrorists, even if they do have a legitimate complaint. Murdering innocent people is not excusable conduct for any reason.''

''Well, it may disappoint you, Mr. Brown, but the majority of Scots want British control,'' Fellows stated. ''The subject of independence for Scotland was put on the ballot back in 1979, I believe. The majority of Scots voted to remain part of the United Kingdom under British rule. So, you see, we Britons really aren't oppressing those poor valiant Scots, regardless of what the bleeding SNP might claim.''

''Inspector,'' Katz began. ''We're not here to argue about England's relations with Scotland. The terrorists are calling for Scottish independence, so this is obviously a motivation factor. Although it is possible they're being manipulated by individuals with other goals in mind.''

''KGB?'' Henderson asked doubtfully.

"Too early to rule out anything at this point," the Israeli explained as he took a pack of Camels from his pocket.

"You mentioned the IRA," McCarter remarked. "Why do you think they might be involved?"

"Judging from your accent, you sound like you're British," Fellows commented. "You ought to know the answer to your own question. The majority of terrorism in the United Kingdom is connected to the IRA. Besides, the terrorist tactics fit the damn Irish bastards. Kidnapping, bombs, shooting unarmed people, all the sorts of things the IRA does on a regular basis."

"But there's no proof, right?" Calvin James inquired.

"Not really," Fellows admitted. "You chaps probably know as much as Scotland Yard, so far. The only real clue we have that links all three terrorist incidents together is the little iron claymore calling card left at each scene."

"You might be able to answer one question we don't have an answer to," Manning ventured. "McGreggor's bodyguards were shot to death. What sort of firearms were used by the terrorists?"

"Interesting question," Fellows mused as he reached for a briefcase under his seat. "I have some copies of reports on the killings here. Ballistics is here, too."

He opened the case and leafed through the papers. "Here it is," the inspector declared. "McGreggor's bodyguards were killed by 9 mm parabellum bullets, 115-grain NATO hardball ammunition. Each man was hit by half a dozen rounds point-blank in the chest. Cartridge casings were all over the ground. Dented up rather badly. Weapons were full auto with a very high rounds-per-minute cycle. It seems plausible that the weapons used were two machine pistols of American manufacture, known as Ingram M-10s or MAC-10s."

"The good old Ingram," McCarter commented. "Not a usual weapon for the blokes in the IRA to have."

"Oh, they get arms shipments from the States," Henderson said. "Generally from Irish-American sympathizers."

"By the way," Fellows continued, checking the reports. "Mrs. Macklin was killed by a single 7.65 millimeter bullet—same as a .32 auto round—fired between the eyes. The reduced velocity of the projectile suggests it was fired through a silencer. No one reported hearing gunshots, so this makes sense. Ballistics says the murder weapon was a Hungarian Model 37 semiautomatic pistol."

"World War II vintage," Katz remarked. "Model 37 was very popular among members of the Third Reich stationed in Eastern Europe during the war. There are still hundreds of them scattered across Europe and the United States. Mostly war souvenirs brought back by Allied soldiers."

"MAC-10s and fifty-year-old pistols," James commented. "That's an interesting combination."

"Mr. Macklin was stabbed to death," Fellows added. "Double-edged steel blade, probably a Scottish dirk."

"As long as you've got the sheets out," Manning began, "what do you have on the bomb used to kill the lady at the Embassy?"

"It was a simple spring-loaded trigger mechanism with a mercury detonator and special blasting cap," Fellows said, skimming over a report form. "The explosive was an improvised version of RDX. An ammonium-nitrate-based explosive. The sort of thing sometimes referred to as a 'fertilizer bomb' because they usually get the substance from fertilizer. Once again, this is a standard IRA tactic."

"Hell," the Canadian said with a shrug, "that sort of bomb is made all over the world. I was fifteen when I put together my first fertilizer bomb."

"A misspent youth?" McCarter inquired with a grin.

"Look who's talking," Manning replied dryly. "As a matter of fact, my uncle supervised my work on that ammonium nitrate explosive after I expressed interest in homemade bombs with compounds from common fertilizer. He figured it would be better if he helped me do it safely than blow myself up fooling around with dangerous materials.''

''Your uncle sounds like a helluva guy,'' Calvin James remarked.

''He was,'' Manning confirmed with a nod. His expression softened slightly as he recalled his Uncle John.

Manning's uncle had been one of the best demolitions experts in Canada. When still a teenager, Gary Manning had been fascinated with his uncle's profession and had badgered John to teach him about explosives. At last Uncle John agreed and reluctantly introduced his nephew to the precarious world of demolitions.

''Let's not discuss events from our personal histories, Mr. Green,'' Katz advised, his voice soft with a slight edge of reproach. Manning had not revealed enough about his background to jeopardize his identity or the security of the unit, but Katz felt it wise to remind him to be careful of what he said even in the company of allies.

''Actually,'' Henderson began, tapping his pudgy fingers together in a thoughtful manner, ''Inspector Fellows's suspicions about the IRA shouldn't be dismissed entirely. Some radical elements in Scotland—mostly fringe groups of the SNP—have associated with the Irish extremists in the past. There's relatively little terrorist activity in Scotland—until recently, of course—but there have been a few incidents in the last few years. Oil pipelines near the North Sea were sabotaged, and a couple of political murders in the past were probably the work of such an unholy alliance of Scottish and Irish fanatics.''

''We're not dismissing any possibilities,'' Katz assured him as he fired up a cigarette with his battered Ronson lighter. ''Where are we headed?''

''To a safehouse,'' Henderson answered, absentmindedly waving the drifting smoke away from his face. ''Davis, the CIA man from the Embassy, is waiting for us there. You chaps aren't with the Company, are you?''

"No," Katz replied, his cigarette held between the steel hooks of his prosthesis. "I thought you'd been informed that we have White House authority and we'll be in full command of this operation."

"Well," Henderson began awkwardly, "I rather suspected that was sort of a stunt by this new President you have in the States to try to impress us."

"Check with the prime minister's liaison, and you'll find this is no stunt," McCarter told him.

"My superiors told me I'd have to take orders from you Yanks," Fellows said grimly. "I can't say I care much for it. The superintendent of the constabulary in Edinburgh has been working with the Yard on this matter, and I doubt he'll care much for this business about a bunch of Americans being in charge of these investigations."

James was muttering and shaking his head. "This stuff should have been taken care of before we got here."

"Great way to start a mission," Encizo added with a sigh.

DAVID MCCARTER PEERED OUT a window as the limousine rolled across Albert Bridge. He smiled, pleased to be back in the city of his birth. London was still McCarter's home, although his missions with Phoenix Force left little time to relax at his flat or take a pleasant stroll in Hyde Park. They probably would not be in London long, but it was good to come home even for a brief visit.

They had arrived in the evening, and darkness masked the Thames. Just as well, McCarter thought. The river was a mess last time he saw it in broad daylight. The top of Big Ben was visible to the east. The 320-foot clock tower is probably the best known feature of London. He saw Victoria Tower, which is also located at the houses of Parliament, but he couldn't see if the light shone from the tower. When the members of Parliament are in session, a flag flies from Victoria Tower by day and a light shines at night. Cynical about politicians of any sort, McCarter thought it was just as well that the light wasn't shining that night.

The limo passed the Chelsea Old Church as they drove west on Cheyne and turned right on Beaufort. Any city as old as London is filled with history, and Chelsea had its share. Sir Thomas More had lived there, Henry James had died there, and Oscar Wilde had been arrested in Chelsea. For movie buffs that part of London was memorable as the setting of British films about the "mod generation" of the sixties. Chelsea always had a reputation for being a bit flashy, though some even accused it of being vulgar and crude. Chelsea had always been one of McCarter's favorite parts of London.

Cars, lorries and the famous double-decker buses rolled through the streets as the limo headed east on King's Road. Eventually they reached the large array of shops and restaurants, popular with tourists and locals alike. The driver pulled into the driveway of a posh restaurant, then the vehicle came to a halt and Henderson announced they had reached their destination.

"This is the safehouse?" Encizo asked with surprise as he carried his luggage from the limo.

"Not the restaurant," Henderson explained. "The pub on the corner. Don't want a limo pulling up in front of it."

They walked to the Black Wolf. It was a rather plain-looking pub with a wolf's head sign, which was black with the legend written in bright yellow paint, above the door. The shades were drawn and a sign in the window declared the pub was closed, yet amber light within suggested the place was not empty. Phoenix Force hoped someone would open the door and let them in. The winter chill cut through their clothes and peppered their skin with goose bumps. They had neglected to unpack their winter coats before getting out of the limo. Katz was the only exception. His camel-hair greatcoat admirably protected him from the cold.

Encizo's teeth chattered as he anxiously watched Henderson knock on the door. The Cuban hated cold weather. He had tried his best to avoid it. Accustomed to a Caribbean climate as a youth, Encizo had spent most of his adult life in southern California, Florida and Texas. The majority of missions with Phoenix Force had been to warm climates, but the occasional assignment to Alaska or Finland had been unpleasant for Encizo.

The door opened and they entered. The pub was warm and comfortable with leather-bound chairs and oval-topped tables. A heavy set man with a shaggy rust-colored beard stood behind the bar. He seemed to be protecting the beer taps as he watched the newcomers file into the barroom. The bartender looked at them as if he figured they were there to rob the place.

A man in a single-breasted gray suit had opened the door. He wore a pale blue shirt and a red-and-white-striped tie. A tan and professionally styled hair labeled him as an American with an above-average income. Phoenix Force knew the guy had to be Davis, the CIA case officer, before Henderson introduced him.

Another figure sat at the bar. Six foot three and less than a hundred and eighty pounds, his tall lean frame was garbed in a khaki uniform. A sand-colored beret was stuck under the epaulet at his left shoulder. His face was unpleasant—long, with pinched cheeks and small green eyes bisected by a ski-slope nose. He wore the insignia of a major and a button-flap holster on his hip.

McCarter and the major locked eyes. Their gaze contained mutual hostility. The rest of Phoenix Force knew why. They also recognized Major Geoffrey Simms, although he did not recognize them. The men of Phoenix Force had been wearing gas masks when they'd encountered Simms four years ago outside the Mardarajan Embassy during a previous mission in London.

"Oh, Christ!" Simms exclaimed. "What the hell are you doing here, McCarter?"

"I'm on a bloody mission, Simms," McCarter answered angrily. "And the name is Black, you arse."

"You two know each other?" Henderson asked with surprise.

"Unfortunately," Simms replied sourly, "This fella Black or whatever name he wants to use this time has worked with me on a previous occasion or two."

"You served in the Special Air Service, Mr. Black?" Fellows asked. His tone suggested he admired SAS and would be pleased to hear an affirmative reply.

"Let's just say we know each other well enough not to like each other much," McCarter replied. "I'll grant you Simms is fairly good at maintaining security, and he's willing to make sacrifices in order to accomplish a mission. A little *too* willing to make sacrifices—usually with somebody else's life."

"I get results," Simms stated with a shrug. "Mc-Mr. Black doesn't like my methods at times, but he's not generally squeamish, and I can't accuse him of being a coward. I have to admit that he's a bloody good fighting man, but not a very good soldier."

"Sounds like a contradiction," Davis, the CIA man, commented. "How can he be a good fighting man and a poor soldier?"

"A good soldier follows orders," Simms answered, his eyes narrowed as he stared at McCarter. "This one has a maverick streak in him. Oh, he's good in a brawl and handles a gun like he was born with one in his hand, but he doesn't have proper respect for authority. Likes to do things his own way. Fact is, I'm surprised he hasn't gotten himself killed by now."

"A lot of blokes have tried," McCarter told him.

"All right," Katz announced sharply as he unbuttoned his camel-hair coat. "We've got a personality clash between the Major and Mr. Black. That's something that has the potential for hurting our mission. Unless there's a very good reason for Simms to be part of this, he's out of the mission as of now.''

"What the hell . . .'' Simms began, outraged by the statement.

"We are in charge of this mission, Major,'' Katz stated. "We have absolute authority in this matter. Now, why are you here?''

"I can answer that,'' Henderson volunteered. "Major Simms has extensive experience in antiterrorist tactics and urban guerrilla warfare against the IRA and similar subversives in Northern Ireland. Last few years he's been involved in similar duties in Scotland.''

"No wonder there's an increase of anti-British sentiment there,'' McCarter muttered.

"Please, Mr. Black,'' Katz insisted. "Major Simms must be familiar with Scotland and knows more about the radical elements among the SNP and other groups than we do. Although you don't like him, Simms is a veteran SAS officer and he hasn't been assigned to this mission because he's a fool.''

"Does that mean I stay here or not?'' Simms demanded.

"You're still in unless Mr. Black feels he can't deal with associating with you during this mission,'' Katz replied.

Simms glared at McCarter. "*He'll* decide?''

"We're in command of this mission, Major,'' Katz informed him. "I don't care if you have a field-grade rank in the military. My team and I will decide what to do, when to do it and how it will be done. Your own definition of a good soldier is one who respects authority and follows orders. If you remain with this mission, we'll expect you to be a good soldier.''

Simms turned from McCarter to Katz. "All right,'' he said with a sigh. "Where do we start?''

"I suggest we start with the weapons," McCarter announced. "The gunmen who killed McGreggor's body-guards used American Ingram M-10 machine pistols. They must have gotten those firearms from the black market. I know someone involved in the gunrunning business here in London."

"Doesn't surprise me," Simms muttered.

"Get off your high horse, Simms," McCarter snorted. "This fellow generally sells overseas to legitimate freedom fighter organizations. Does business with anticommunist resistance groups in Vietnam and Cambodia. He's also been selling arms to a group that is opposed to the current dictatorship in Albania and hopes to eventually set up a parliamentary government similar to Britain's and establish new relations with Yugoslavia and Western Europe. The bloke has also supported groups such as the Afghan *mujahedin* and Savimbi's Unita in Angola."

"So he's particular about who he sells to?" Davis inquired. "I thought gunrunners didn't care about politics."

"Some do and some don't," Encizo said with a shrug, speaking from personal experience. Of the many arms dealers he had known in the United States and Central America, some had principles and some were amoral, apolitical scum. "We met the guy you're talking about on a previous occasion, didn't we?"

"Yeah," McCarter confirmed. "You'll recall he helped us then and did more than he had to because he believed in what we were doing. He's reliable."

"He's still a bloody criminal," Inspector Fellows commented. "I'm not about to associate with local gangsters because we're after villains in Scotland."

"You won't have to associate with him," McCarter replied. "For obvious reasons, this fellow wouldn't appreciate having a chat with a police inspector, anyway. Best if I contact him on my own and find out if he has any idea who may have sold those Ingrams to the terrorists."

"I don't have anything against that idea," James remarked as he took a seat at the bar and looked at the man behind the counter. "Do you actually serve drinks, fella?"

"I own this pub," the bartender·replied dryly. "I also happen to be with the SIS, and we use the place for meeting, safehouse operations and the like. You want a drink, gov?"

"Yeah, a beer..." James said, but as soon as he said it, he changed his mind. "On second thought, this is England. I'll have a Scotch and water instead."

"We've got some cold beer," the bartender told him. "I knew there'd be Yanks here, so I put some on ice."

"Scotch will be fine, thanks," the black commando assured him, and turned toward the others. "As I was saying, checking out the arms dealers is fine, but I sort of lean toward the basics of investigations. Start at the scene of the crime."

"We've already done that," Inspector Fellows explained. "Scotland Yard, SIS, CIA, the local authorities and God knows who else have been involved in investigating all three incidents. I don't know what you people intend to find that the rest of us overlooked."

"I don't know, either," James assured him as the bartender placed a glass of amber liquid on the counter. "I'm sure you guys all did a good job, but it never hurts to crosscheck. Can't look at evidence too hard, in my opinion."

"Fifty pence," the bartender declared.

"Huh?" the American replied.

"Oh, just give me a dollar," the bartender grunted, but looked a lot happier when James hoisted his glass and said "Here's to England."

6

Felix Holmes owned a bicycle shop called Spokes Unlimited, a simple little store that officially made a modest profit. On the surface, Holmes was barely able to get by from year to year, since half his income was consumed by Britain's hungry tax system. However, his other business was a secret matter, far more profitable than Spokes Unlimited, and didn't share the fruit of its efforts with the government.

Holmes welcomed David McCarter into his shop and shook his hand as if trying to pump his arm loose from the shoulder. Holmes's hand was large and strong, but it suited his six-and-a-half-foot bearlike physique. A dense black beard and long, shoulder-length hair framed his pale features. Though he resembled Rasputin, he tended to be jovial and pleasant.

"David!" Holmes declared as he shook hands, simultaneously pushing the door shut and shoving the bolt into place with his free hand. "Good to see you. It has been a while. Care for a spot of brandy to ward off the chill? Getting terrible cold out, isn't it?"

"I'll pass on the brandy," McCarter said. "Actually the weather doesn't seem too bad this year. Not much snowfall, near as I can tell."

"It's been one of those on-and-off-type winters," Holmes stated. "Snow flurries in most of December, but this month isn't bad. February? I think it will be a bastard."

"Reckon the weather's the same up in Scotland?" McCarter inquired.

"I imagine so. Haven't been up that way for a while. You're not much for social visits, David. What's on your mind, lad?"

"Information," McCarter explained.

The gunrunner sighed with disappointment. "Oh, I rather hoped you might be here to take an order. Got some nice merchandise. Well, come on. Let's talk."

He led McCarter past shelves of handlebars, bike frames and wheels. Various designs of bicycles were in the shop: British models and imports from France, Japan and Germany. Different parts for hundreds of models were also available.

Holmes took his visitor to the back room and offered him a seat at a card table. McCarter sat and removed a pack of Player's cigarettes while Holmes set a teakettle on a hot plate.

"You know some of the other arms dealers in the United Kingdom," McCarter began as he lighted a cigarette. "Any involved in trade with terrorists or extremist groups?"

"Well, there are unprincipled men in my profession, just like in any other," Holmes answered. "We talking about terrorists in the U.K. or abroad?"

"Scotland," McCarter answered. "Maybe Ireland."

"That narrows the field a bit," the gunrunner stated. "You see, one doesn't dirty his own nest if he's smart. Some of the villain types sell arms to German Red Army Faction, Italian Red Brigade, that sort of trash, but they don't do business here. Gangland types usually buy guns from small dealers in Soho. Revolvers, shotguns, maybe a rifle or two. The IRA gets weapons from various sources. They trade with other European terrorists and sympathetic Irish-Americans, and a few Brits of Irish blood supply them with weapons. A number of them apparently don't even charge for the guns. They give the bloody IRA free firearms with the notion that they're helping to liberate Ireland."

"Somebody sold certain terrorists at least two Ingram M-10 machine pistols that were used to kill the bodyguards with that American industrialist who got kidnapped a couple days ago. Man by the name McGreggor."

"Heard about it on the telly," Holmes confirmed as he poured some hot water into a teapot. "Ingrams, eh? Well, American full-auto weapons aren't that common with gunrunners in the U.K. I'm one of the few that handles such merchandise..."

He paused to turn and stare at McCarter. "I say," Holmes began with alarm. "You don't think I'm selling arms to these buggers?"

"Of course not," the Phoenix pro assured him. "I've known you for some time, Felix. Never had any reason to doubt you. I remember the time you helped my mates and me when we launched that raid on the Mardarajan Embassy."

"I liked those chaps," Holmes said with a smile. "You still working with them?"

"We're still in touch," McCarter replied. "The Ingrams?"

"Oh, yes," Holmes said with a nod. "I know a bloke named Thornwood who has access to American military arms and has done business with Irish extremists in the past. He's just the type to sell those guns to the bastards you're after."

"Thornwood," McCarter repeated thoughtfully. "Know where we can find him?"

"I know where he operates from," Holmes replied as he finished brewing the tea and poured a cup for McCarter and one for himself. "Sorry I don't have any Coca Cola for you. Still, I doubt even you would prefer a chilled soft drink to hot tea on a night like this."

"Tea is fine," McCarter assured him as he accepted a cup. "So, what's Thornwood's address?"

"I'll have to look it up for you, but it's along Aldgate East not far from the Whitechapel Art Gallery," Holmes answered, taking a seat across from McCarter. "Figures a lowlife like Thornwood would feel at home in the old stalking grounds of Jack the Ripper."

"I was born in the East End," McCarter reminded him.

"I've had my doubts about you from time to time myself," Holmes said with a grin. "So, can I count on you putting Thornwood out of business?"

"Not sure yet," the commando stated as he ground out his cigarette in a glass ashtray, "but I'd say the odds are pretty high. Any objection?"

"For getting rid of some competition and lowlife competition at that?" Holmes chuckled. "You'll be doing me a favor, mate. Blokes like Thornwood give my trade a bad name."

"I hate to disappoint you, Felix," McCarter said, "but gunrunners don't really have a good name under any circumstances, anyway."

"Come now," Holmes said defensively. "I'll have you know I've done business with certain individuals in government. Chaps in Intelligence and such."

"Yeah, but they'd never admit they had anything to do with you," McCarter said with a grin.

"They know I'm discreet," the gunrunner replied, shrugging.

"Are you sure you know what that word means, Felix?" McCarter inquired. "Discreet isn't another way of saying 'illegal,' you know."

"Technicalities," Holmes said with a sigh. "Tell me, you still carry that outdated 13-shot, single-action autoloader?"

McCarter patted his coat at the bulge of the Browning Hi-Power 9 mm pistol holstered under his left arm. "Never leave home without it," he confirmed.

"You ought to try some of these double-action automatics in 9 mm caliber, David," Holmes stated. "This is the latter part of the twentieth century. Pretty soon that Browning is going to be like carrying a musket into combat. Walther, Beretta, Smith & Wesson, SIG-Sauer—all make good double-action 9 mm pistols with 15-round capacity."

"I'll stick with the Browning," McCarter insisted.

He had heard the argument before. All four of his fellow Phoenix Force commandos carried double-action 9 mm autoloaders, but McCarter had stubbornly kept the Browning as his standard side arm. He had been a member of the British pistol team in the Olympics and had scored high marks with a Browning. McCarter was in the SAS at the time and he was assigned to Oman during the Olympics, so he never actually tested his skill against pistol marksmen from other nations in official competition. However, he had used the Browning hundreds of times in actual combat. He had no reason to fault the weapon's performance in a life-or-death situation.

McCarter had fired numerous D.A. pistols at the Stony Man firing range. The Briton thought many of these weapons seemed reliable enough and he had yet to see one of his partner's D.A. autoloaders jam in combat. Nonetheless, McCarter simply did not trust double-action autos. To him, it was an unnecessary feature in a semiautomatic pistol, and he figured it was just one more thing that could go wrong with a gun. Perhaps his concern was needless, but he still intended to stick with the Browning Hi-Power, which had proved dependable for so many years in the past.

"Well, if I can't interest you in buying any firearms," Holmes began, sipping his tea before he completed his comment, "then would you happen to know about any nasty little wars that might be a marketplace for my services?''

"Sorry, Felix," McCarter replied. "All my wars are private matters. I can't invite anyone who isn't already involved."

"Pity," Holmes said with a fatalistic shrug.

INSPECTOR FELLOWS STARED grimly through the windshield of the Saab as he drove past the Monument. The two-hundred-foot tall memorial was never referred to by any other name. All Londoners knew the Monument was a reminder of the Great Fire of 1666. Fellows barely glanced at the Monument as he steered onto Gracechurch Street. The windshield was fogged despite the car heater, and the wipers slid to and fro across the glass as half-frozen sleet descended from the night sky.

"I didn't expect your friend to come up with information of this sort so quickly," the inspector admitted. He did not sound very pleased about the recent turn of events.

"Mr. Black's contact was available and gave us a clue about who may have sold the Ingram machine pistols to the terrorists," Yakov Katzenelenbogen commented from the back seat. He placed a briefcase on his lap and opened the lid. "He even managed to arrange a meeting with that Thornwood character at midnight. I'd say that's pretty fair progress, considering we've only been in London a few hours."

Fellows grunted sourly. The fact that Phoenix Force had already uncovered a potential lead in the investigation stuck in his craw. But Katz didn't harp on the matter. Fellows was a proud man; there was nothing to gain by embarrassing or belittling him, and there was no justification for it, either. Thornwood might know something about the terrorists or he might not. Their lead might be a false hope. Besides, McCarter's information had come from Felix Holmes, and Scotland Yard probably did not even know who he was and wouldn't have gotten the gunrunner's cooperation if they did.

Geoffrey Simms sat next to Katz and peered into the open briefcase on the Israeli's lap. The SAS major was surprised to see an Uzi submachine gun in the valise. He watched Katz expertly cradle the Uzi with his prosthesis and slide a fully loaded magazine of 9 mm parabellums into the well at the bottom of the pistol grip. The Phoenix Force commander kept the muzzle pointed at the ceiling of the car as he shoved back the cocking knob, chambered a round and pressed the safety catch.

"Think we'll need that much firepower?" Simms inquired. He had only brought his side arm and doubted that he would have to resort to it at all.

"If we don't need it," Katz replied, "I won't use it."

Gary Manning sat in the front seat with Fellows. The Canadian was a man of few words and had not contributed to the conversation—he saw no reason to do so. Manning checked a city map and glanced out the window at a street sign with the legend Fenchurch. It would lead to Aldgate Street. Manning picked up a two-way radio and pressed the transmit button.

"Unit One, this is Unit Two," Manning spoke into the mouthpiece. "Do you read me? Over."

"Unit One," Encizo's voice replied from the radio. "Read you loud and clear. Over."

"We're heading for the destination and will be there in a matter of minutes. Two or three. Five if the traffic gets heavier."

"Glad to hear it," the Cuban's voice replied. "We're already at the site. Ready to go as soon as you can join us."

"I can hardly wait for that," Manning said dryly. "Okay. Over and out, Unit One."

He put the radio on the floor between his feet and leaned back in the seat. Closing his eyes, he inhaled slowly through his nostrils and breathed out through his mouth. Already he could feel the familiar tension of combat. It might be a false alarm, though. He had gotten incorrect signals before, and the so-called sixth sense was far from infallible—if, indeed, it even existed beyond his imagination.

The Canadian was taking advantage of the chance to relax in preparation for possible trouble ahead. Manning was very experienced in dealing with tension. He had served in Vietnam as a "special observer" attached to the 5th Special Forces, where he perfected his ability as a combat demolitions expert and sniper, and he had spent two years in West Germany with the elite GSG-9 antiterrorist squad pitted against the Baader-Meinhof Gang and 2nd June Movement fanatics. Added to his missions with Phoenix Force, it amounted to a great deal of experience.

"Are you all right?" Inspector Fellows inquired when he noticed Manning's deep, methodical breathing.

"I'm fine," the Canadian assured him. He opened his eyes and glanced out the window. "Is this Aldgate Street?"

"That's right," the man from Scotland Yard confirmed as he watched for the Jacoby Garage among the buildings along the street. "I hope you chaps aren't planning to charge in with guns blazing. This is London, you know. Perhaps they don't mind having bullet-riddled corpses littered about the streets in New York and Chicago, but people take a rather dim view of that sort of thing here."

"If all goes well, there won't be any shooting," Katz said with a sigh. He was a bit tired of Fellows's attitude. The inspector seemed to regard Phoenix Force as a team of trigger-happy Neanderthals Washington had sent to the United Kingdom expressly to slaughter British citizens.

Fellows grunted in reply. He felt a cold shiver creep up his spine when he spotted the Jacoby Garage. It was a drab building with gray walls and a pair of dark green bay doors. A sign outside the closed doors listed the services offered by the garage. Auto repairs, parts and tune-ups were the official business of the building, which still bore the name of its previous owner. Lloyd Thornwood had purchased the garage after Oscar Jacoby's death and had added a new, secret trade to the activities at the auto shop.

Scotland Yard had a file on Thornwood. He had a criminal record, which began when he'd been a youth in Liverpool. Thornwood had served five years in the army in the early seventies. The police were unable to learn details about Thornwood's military career, but his rank was still private by the end of enlistment, which suggested he had been demoted more than once during his time in the army. In 1977 he was arrested for peddling marijuana and had received a fine and a thirty-day sentence. In 1980 Thornwood was convicted for fencing stolen goods and had spent two years in Her Majesty's Prison Wormwood Scrubs.

But Thornwood hadn't been in trouble with the law since, and civil servants assigned to check on the ex-convict were convinced he had reformed. Apparently Thornwood simply hadn't been caught indulging in his most recent criminal activities. Of course, Scotland Yard hadn't suspected Thornwood had turned to illegal arms trading. Inspector Fellows still had some doubts about the mysterious five foreigners he had been ordered to work with, yet he had to admit they had uncovered a proper villain when they came up with Thornwood's name.

Gary Manning spotted the battered gray van across the street from the garage. That was the Unit One vehicle, with Encizo, James and McCarter inside. The black commando and the British ace emerged from the rig as the Saab approached. As the pair headed for the Jacoby Garage, Fellows drove past the building. He glanced out the window and saw McCarter and James standing by the door of the garage.

"Turn at the next corner and park out of sight of the building," Katz instructed. "The last thing we want is to make Thornwood suspicious. We need to check the back of the garage, anyway."

"Do you plan to enter from the rear of the building?" Simms inquired as he drew a Glock 9 mm pistol from his holster and jacked the side to chamber the first round. Because the Glock has no safety catch, he returned it to the holster.

"Well, we'll have to see what's back there first," the Israeli answered. "Besides, we don't know how many people Thornwood has inside. I doubt he's alone. If things go wrong, they may start bolting from exits front and back."

Fellows nodded in silent agreement. He steered the car around the corner and searched for a parking space. Manning's radio crackled, and Encizo's voice spoke from the machine. The Canadian picked up the radio.

"Our friends are inside," Encizo declared. "The wire is working. Everything seems okay so far."

"It's early," Manning replied. "Keep us posted."

"Don't go to sleep out there," the Cuban's voice warned. "Over and out."

As Manning returned the radio to the floorboards between his feet, Fellows located a blank section of curb to park the Saab. The street lighting was poor, and the surroundings were cloaked in shadows. Shops and homes were crowded together into long files of nondescript buildings. The rooftop of the Whitechapel Art Gallery towered above shorter structures in the distance. The gallery was several blocks away, but it seemed closer due to the size of nearby shops and pubs.

"What does he mean by 'the wire is working'?" Major Simms inquired.

"A 'wire' is a hidden microphone worn by a person to allow others to eavesdrop on conversations," Manning explained. "The term is really a misnomer, because the mike or transmitter is actually wireless. In this case, Mr. Blue is wearing a miniature transmitter concealed in a jacket button. Mr. Brown has the receiver unit in the van hooked up to a tape recorder, so we'll have the conversation on record in case it has to come to court."

"English law is similar to American law when it comes to this sort of thing," Fellows commented. "I'm not sure evidence acquired by these methods would be admissible in court without the proper warrants..."

"Mr. Henderson has already seen to that," Katz assured him. "The SIS didn't have much trouble getting authority from three different judges. We have the necessary warrants, each dated five days back to ensure that everything is technically legal."

"You chaps don't miss much," Simms remarked.

"We try not to," Manning replied. "This business doesn't leave much room for mistakes. Make one or two, and you're dead."

"Let's just hope our friends in the garage don't make any," Katz added in a serious tone, "or that's exactly how they might wind up."

7

Lloyd Thornwood stared at the visitors, his dark eyes filled with distrust. The thirty-eight-year-old gunrunner was suspicious of virtually everyone. He trusted the trio of burly young men, who were posted at strategic points in the bay area, more than most. One henchman stood behind Thornwood, another was stationed by the door and the third stood eight feet to the right of David McCarter and Calvin James.

"You're Murphy?" Thornwood asked as he folded his arms on his narrow chest and gazed up at McCarter. The arms dealer was five foot three and weighed about a hundred and ten pounds. Perhaps he hired muscular brutes to compensate for his short stature and skinny physique.

"That's right," McCarter replied, and a slight Irish brogue colored his cockney accent. "Least that's the name I'm usin' tonight."

"You didn't mention your friend would be a burr head," Thornwood remarked as he turned toward James. "I don't generally do business with you coloreds."

"I bet you take my money just as quick, mon," James replied, doing a convincing imitation of a Jamaican accent. "Don't be so hostile. I am not here to marry your sister, mon."

"I don't have a sister," Thornwood stated. "Thank God. If I did, she'd probably be like half the other sluts in England these days. Spreadin' their legs for Africans and Pakistanis and every other sort with dark skin and a throbbing willy.''

"We gonna talk skin color or guns and money?" James said with a weary sigh.

"We might not talk at all," Thornwood replied. "Nigel, pat these blokes down. Ron and Greg, keep alert in case there's a problem."

Nigel, the big guy closest to the Phoenix Force pair, stepped forward. He looked like a beer barrel that had grown arms and legs, and his pitted face seemed incapable of expression. His eyes revealed no more emotion than the orbs of a corpse as he reached with both hands toward McCarter's chest.

But the Briton had already raised his arms. "Save ya a bit of trouble," he offered. "There's a revolver holstered at the small of my back."

Ron and Greg watched carefully as Nigel plucked the 5-shot Smith & Wesson snubnose from its hiding place at the base of McCarter's spine. The henchmen opened their jackets to openly display the pistols they carried in their belts. A bulge under Thornwood's left shoulder suggested that he also carried a gun beneath his tweed sports coat. McCarter offered no resistance as Nigel confiscated the revolver and frisked him for other weapons.

James also told Nigel of the gun holstered at the rear of his right hip. Since neither Phoenix commando carried other weapons, they were completely unarmed. Thornwood could have become suspicious if his customers had not been armed, so the pair had brought handguns generally used for backup weapons in actual combat. McCarter and James did not want to risk losing their 9 mm autoloaders if circumstances did not allow them to retrieve the confiscated weapons.

"This is it," Nigel announced as he handed Thornwood the two revolvers. Those were the only words uttered by any of gunrunner's henchmen since the Phoenix pair had entered the garage.

"American," Thornwood remarked as he examined the guns, one in each hand. "Very good quality. Colt and Smith & Wesson are among the leading manufacturers of firearms in the United States."

"What do you think of Ingram?" McCarter asked. "The M-10 machine pistol, to be exact."

"M-10s?" Thornwood frowned. "That's a curious subject to bring up. Why ask me about them?"

"You deal in guns, don't you?" James inquired.

"I wasn't talking to you," Thornwood replied sharply, then turned toward McCarter. "Who is this bloke and what's he doing here?"

"Best let up on your prejudices," McCarter suggested. "My companion is with a syndicate that's making a very large profit in Soho these days. They've got a lot of money and they'll need guns to help keep it. You don't want to lose potentially profitable customers, do you?"

"Won't be usin' our guns on you white fellas, mon," James said with a shrug. "We'll just kill other coloreds and wogs. I was born in 1954, so I consider myself to be a British citizen. I still think like one."

"Cheeky," Thornwood said with a chuckle. "I still don't see how you two got together. Common interests, I suppose."

"What the hell?" McCarter said sharply. "My mates told me they got some Ingrams from you. You want a bloody biography, go to the library. You want to do business, then let's get on with it. How much for the bloody Ingrams?"

"Well, what did your mates say they paid for their M-10s?" Thornwood asked. He still held the two revolvers in his fists and glanced down at them as he spoke.

"They didn't mention a price," McCarter answered. He sensed something was wrong by the inflection in the gunrunner's voice. "Said they bought the guns from you recently. My cell needs weapons of that sort for the campaign we're conducting at a different front.''

"Oh, I see," Thornwood commented with a slow nod. "Nigel, I think it's time to get our other guests in here."

Nigel nodded and headed across the bay area. He stepped out of view when he walked around a four-door sedan with both front tires removed, the hood raised and the front end propped up by a jack. The sedan was the only car in the garage, but several rows of metal shelves contained plastic bins filled with parts for various types and models of automobiles. Some shelves contained tools and car batteries, and tires were stacked up like giant rubber doughnuts.

The Phoenix pair heard a door creak open and realized Nigel had entered another room. Thornwood and his other two henchmen kept their eyes on James and McCarter. The gunrunner slowly raised his arms, the revolvers in his fists, and menaced the pair with their own guns. An unpleasant smile crept across the man's face as he pointed the revolvers at them.

"Hey, mon," James began, and slowly started to raise his hands. "Careful with those things. They be loaded, mon."

"You'd better remember that," Thornwood replied. He glanced at the cylinders of each revolver. The brass butts of cartridges were visible at the rear of the chambers.

"What's this crap?" McCarter demanded, hands raised to shoulder level. "If you're upset because we didn't bring any money, it's out in the car. We didn't know how much the guns would be and . . . well, neither of us have ever dealt with you before."

"You knew enough to call my private line and give the proper passwords to arrange this meeting," Thornwood began. "I wouldn't have any doubts about you, except you're claiming to be connected with the IRA cell that purchased thirty-five Ingram M-10s from me. Of course, you didn't know that particular group and I have a different, individual set of passwords for phone contact."

"The passwords Murphy used were those my syndicate learned about," James said quickly, thinking fast and hoping the button transmitter was still working.

"Really?" Thornwood raised an eyebrow. "And how did your band of Jamaican baboons find out about me? Don't even bother to answer that. Murphy is the one who claims to be associated with my clients. Claims he knew about a sale of Ingram M-10 machine pistols. So he ought to know my old mate Kevin Dwyer."

Nigel returned with three more men. A pug-faced guy with muttonchop sideburns walked beside the big Briton. As he approached, followed by two other men, his lips curled into an ugly sneer. A large fellow with a handlebar mustache had a cut-down double-barrel shotgun canted across a shoulder. The third man was long-haired and creepy looking, with a boxlike machine pistol in his fists. McCarter immediately recognized the weapon. Compact, with a stubby barrel, a charging bolt on top and a long magazine that extended from the butt of the pistol grip, the M-10 was very familiar to McCarter. The Ingram used to be his standard assault piece.

"This the bastard who claims he's one of us?" the pug-faced character asked, his gaze fixed on McCarter.

"That's right, Kevin," Thornwood confirmed. "Ever met him before?"

"I told you I'm with a different cell," McCarter said. He felt a cold knot of fear in his belly. The bluff wouldn't get far, he realized, but perhaps he could stall them for a minute or two.

"Damn liar," Kevin Dwyer cursed as he pulled an old Webley revolver from his belt. "No one outside our group knew where we bought our guns. No other cells knows any details about what we're doin'."

"One way or another, somebody did manage to find out," Thornwood commented. "Put your gun away. We don't want any shooting here. These two aren't armed, and we've got them covered already.''

"What are we going to do about this, Lloyd?" Dwyer demanded as he shoved the Webley back in his belt.

"We'll make them talk," the gunrunner replied. "Ron, fire up your torch for these lads."

Ron nodded and headed for the car propped up on a jack. He was slightly smaller than Thornwood's other two thugs, but still big enough to knock down the average pro-football player. He shoved out a dolly from behind the sedan. A tank with a welding torch attached was mounted on the cart. Ron's broad, toadlike face glowed with cruel pleasure as he turned on the torch and held a flame to the muzzle. A jet of bright blue fire burst into life from the torch.

"Do you have any idea what a welding torch can do to human flesh and bone?" Thornwood inquired. "I saw them work a fellow over with a torch once before. Always figured I had a cast-iron stomach until I witnessed that. Made me vomit, it did. When they start to work on you two, I'm afraid I'll have to leave the room."

"Can we be excused, too?" James inquired. His sarcastic request was made with a stress-strained voice, and he had unintentionally dropped the phony Jamaican accent.

James had good reason to find the threat of torture terrifying. He knew the reality of the systematic administration of torment from a previous mission. Ironically, he and Encizo had been tortured in the Vatican by a gang of terrorists who had seized control of the holy city. The tip of James's little finger on his left hand had been brutally torn off by the torturer's pliers. The session in hell had left no other permanent physical damage, but the abbreviated finger was a constant reminder of that incident and the monstrous acts of savagery man will inflict on his fellow man.

Ron held the torch in a gloved fist and pulled the dolly closer. The flame hissed like the blue tongue of a demon serpent. Ron's eyes widened as he examined the torch. He seemed eager to use it on the prisoners. Nigel shook his head. He didn't seem to share the other man's enthusiasm for torture, but he did not look like he was ready to leave the bay area, either. Greg, the third member of Thornwood's hoodlum trio, smiled. His eyes were concealed by the wide brim of a checkered cloth cap, but James guessed the man's expression was probably identical to Ron's.

"Wait a minute!" McCarter urged, trying to keep his own terror under control. "You blokes are making a big mistake. There's no need for this sort of thing—"

"Shut up!" Thornwood snapped. "You're going to tell us who sent you here, or you'll be turned into crippled, blind and burned globs of charred flesh, praying for death to end your pain."

"If they're peelers or government agents, they didn't come here alone," Dwyer declared. "There are probably a dozen coppers or two dozen Brit soldiers outside."

"I'll watch the front," Nigel volunteered, eager to find an excuse to avoid participating in Thornwood's plans for torture.

"Cover the back," Dwyer told his companions.

The Irish flunkies nodded and headed across the bay toward the metal shelves while Nigel walked to the front door. Ron's twisted, malevolent features were illuminated by the welding torch flame. Greg stepped toward McCarter and flexed his thick fingers. Thornwood faced the Phoenix pair and continued to cover them with the confiscated revolvers in his fists.

"Before things get really ugly," the arms dealer began, "I'll give you a chance to tell me who you really are and how many of your mates are outside."

"We're with the People's United Liberation Front," McCarter declared, making up the organization as quickly as his imagination allowed. "It's a new movement to free the people of the United Kingdom from the oppressive regime of Great Britain."

"That's right, man," James added, going along with his partner's fiction. "We've got all kinds in the movement—blacks from Africa and Jamaica, Pakistanis, whites from slums here in London and other cities where the ruling class keeps its boot on the throats of poor people regardless of color or background."

"You don't sound like a Jamaican anymore," Thornwood said with a frown. "You're a Yank. A goddamn American burr head."

"Hey, pygmy brain," James replied as he glared at the gunrunner, "I'm a veteran urban guerrilla since my Panther days in the sixties, man."

"I don't believe any of this verbal dung," Thornwood said grimly. "You two are going to burn."

"Look, I told you I was with a cell of the IRA because I'd heard you'd sold weapons to them before," McCarter insisted. "Seemed to me you'd be more inclined to deal with us if you figured we belonged to an established outfit rather than a group you never heard of..."

"A multiracial group that includes non-whites and folks of non-British origin," James added quickly. "After all, it turns out you are a damn racist, and for all we knew you might object to selling guns to an organization devoted to overthrowing the British government..."

"Ron! Greg!" Thornwood angrily declared. "Burn 'em! Start with the nigger!"

The roar of an engine and screeching tires startled the men inside the garage. One of the doors suddenly burst apart and hurtled across the bay area. The rear of the gray van surged through the gap. Rafael Encizo had driven the vehicle backward and used it as a battering ram to smash through the bay door.

"Christ!" Dwyer exclaimed as he jumped behind the stationary sedan to avoid being slammed by the hurtling van.

The Irishman drew his Webley and fired at the vehicle. Glass shattered from a rear window, and a second revolver slug punched a hole in the metal skin of the van. Nigel had also drawn a weapon and triggered two rounds. Bullets smashed the front window by the driver's side. Encizo clenched his teeth as he ducked low behind the steering wheel and felt broken glass shower across his arched back.

The back door suddenly exploded from the opposite side of the bay. The blast tore it off the hinges and smashed the lock, propelling the door into the rows of metal shelves. Plastic bins fell and spilled auto parts across the concrete floor. Dwyer's gun-toting partners ducked instinctively and jumped for cover along the racks.

Gary Manning rushed across the threshold, knees bent, head low and a Walther P-5 pistol in his fists. The Canadian dashed for cover behind a pile of rubber tires. The IRA trooper with an Ingram triggered his weapon. A flurry of 9 mm bullets pelted the tires. Slugs tore into rubber and ricocheted against the stone wall behind Manning, but none struck him.

Yakov Katzenelenbogen appeared at the doorway and fired his Uzi. Braced across his prosthetic arm, the submachine gun spat a lethal 3-round burst. The 115-grain 9 mm slugs slammed into the chest of the Irish gunman before he could retreat behind cover once more. As the impact drove him backward, he fell against another rack. A crimson stain blossomed on the left side of his shirtfront. The Ingram blaster fell from his grasp, and he slumped to the floor.

The Irishman with the sawed-off shotgun pointed it at Katz. The Israeli jumped back outside and behind the doorway as the 12-gauge cannon roared. Buckshot hammered the door frame and slashed across the threshold. Inspector Fellows and Major Simms were also standing outside the back entrance, and the Scotland Yard man hissed with pain as shotgun pellets tore into his coat sleeve and creased the skin at his upper arm. Fellows retreated from the doorway and clutched his wounded limb.

Simms pushed the inspector aside and poked his Glock around the edge of the doorway. The SAS officer fired two pistol shots into the garage without exposing his head or face to the line of enemy fire. Blindly he fired another shot and swung clear of the doorway.

"Stop!" Katz hissed, his eyes ablaze with anger. "You might hit our people with a stunt like that!"

"Calculated risk," Simms replied simply. "The mission comes first. All of us are expendable..."

"Try that again and I'll kill you myself," Katz told him in a firm, serious voice.

Simms tested the Phoenix commander's gaze and realizing Katz was not bluffing, he nodded in silent agreement. The major had agreed to follow orders and he would do so until the foreigners pushed him too far. Simms had his own ideas about how to deal with terrorists and so-called urban guerrillas: bloody trash that deserved to be wiped out like the vermin they were. He knew McCarter well enough, and he had some vague suspicions about the others. Professionals, Simms realized, but they might be a bit soft when ruthless methods were necessary.

Major Geoffrey Simms was an expert in ruthlessness. If he felt such tactics were needed to accomplish the mission, he would use them regardless of what the others thought. He had personal reasons to want to succeed in this operation. No one had better get in his way, Simms thought grimly. No one.

McCarter and James had immediately taken advantage of the distraction when Encizo smashed through the bay door. The black commando swung a crescent kick to Ron's forearm above the welding torch. The unexpected blow deflected the flame away from James, but failed to strike the torch from Ron's gloved fist.

James instantly closed in and swung a hard left hook to his opponent's jaw. His right hand grabbed Ron's wrist behind the torch, pushing the flame away. The thug struggled and raised his other hand before he realized where the torch was pointed. The concentrated blaze burned into the base of his left thumb. It cut through flesh and sheared the bone joint in less than a second.

Ron screamed as the thumb dropped from his hand and blood dribbled from the charred stump. His other fist opened and dropped the torch. James hit him under the jaw with the heel-of-the-palm stroke. Ron's head snapped back from the blow, and he stumbled backward, his damaged hand cradled in his trembling right palm. James slashed a cross-body karate chop and slammed the side of his hand under the other man's heart. Ron moaned and crumpled to the concrete.

Greg pulled a .45 Colt autoloader from his belt, but McCarter pounced before the henchman could use his weapon. The Phoenix pro grabbed his forearm with one hand and closed the other around the frame of the pistol in the hood's fist. He shoved down hard and raised a bent knee to smash the wrist. Fingers popped open, and the .45 fell to the floor.

"Goddamn it!" Thornwood bellowed as he pointed the two confiscated revolvers at James and McCarter.

He pulled the triggers simultaneously. The .38 S&W and the .357 Magnum clicked. Hammers snapped into firing pins and the cylinders turned, but the cartridges did not respond. Thornwood threw down the revolvers and reached inside his jacket for the SIG-Sauer P-230 pistol in shoulder leather. But he was a step behind.

"Eat this!" Calvin James shouted as he delivered a fast straight-kick.

The heel of his boot crashed into the point of Thornwood's jaw. The kick lifted the arms dealer off his feet, then after a brief flight dropped him unconscious on the concrete floor. As James quickly bent over to scoop up Thorn-wood's .380-caliber handgun, he saw Nigel approach from the front of the building, pistol in hand. James started to swing the confiscated SIG-Sauer toward the thug, but Nigel's weapon was already pointed at the black American.

Two shots snarled, and Nigel stopped in his tracks. A 9 mm parabellum had shattered his breastbone and drove the thug back two steps even as the second bullet struck left of center to punch into his heart. James glimpsed Rafael Encizo crouched at the open door at the driver's side of the van, a Heckler & Koch P-9S pistol in his fists. The Cuban fired a third round and watched the henchman collapse in a lifeless heap.

Although McCarter had disarmed Greg, the big hood-lum grabbed the Phoenix fighter by the lapel and shoved him toward the sedan. The commando held on to the larger man, and both stumbled across the bay area. Greg snatched the cloth cap from his head and clenched it in his fist, the wide bill aimed at McCarter's face.

Born and raised in the East End of London, McCarter knew why Greg had grabbed the hat. As a youth, the Phoenix veteran had encountered street fighters who sewed razor blades in the brim of a cap's bill. It was a favorite weapon among the more vicious brawlers in London.

McCarter grabbed Greg's wrist above the cap, holding the unconventional weapon at bay as they staggered into the side of the sedan. Greg shoved McCarter back against the frame of the car and seized the commando's throat with one hand as he tried to press the cap closer to McCarter's face.

The fight had turned into a deadly wrestling match. Greg was larger and heavier than McCarter, and he was also about ten years younger and probably stronger. McCarter felt the constriction at his throat as his breath was cut off by Greg's grip. Light glittered along the steel edge of a razor blade at the rim of the hoodlum's hat.

McCarter had to act quickly if he wanted to survive. His right hand streaked to Greg's face, and clawed fingers hooked onto the man's left ear and pulled hard. His thumb slid across the thug's cheek to dig into Greg's eye. The hood howled and tried to shake off McCarter's gouging hand, but the firm grip on Greg's ear held fast and the thumb threatened to poke the eyeball from its socket.

Greg released McCarter's throat to bat aside his opponent's hand with a forearm. The Phoenix pro immediately snapped his head forward and butted his forehead into the thug's face. The man's head was severely jarred by the blow, and McCarter hit him with a solid right cross. Greg stumbled backward, and McCarter assisted him with a shove to make him fall against the open hood of the car.

McCarter quickly slapped a palm on the hood and slammed it down on Greg's head and shoulders. The henchman groaned and slumped into a seated position on the floor. Blood trickled from a scalp wound and a broken nose. His head slumped forward, and he slid to the floor.

Kevin Dwyer swung his Webley revolver toward McCarter. The British ace dropped low behind the sedan before the Irishman triggered his weapon. The shot roared dramatically, but the .38 bullet simply burned air above the hood of the sedan and passed more than a foot above McCarter's prone form.

Encizo moved around the front end of the van and had a clear view of Dwyer poised by the tool racks. The Irishman wasn't likewise aware of Encizo, and this allowed the Cuban the luxury of half a second to choose his target, take careful aim and squeeze the trigger of his H&K pistol.

A 115-grain Silvertip hollowpoint round smashed into Dwyer's right kneecap. Bone and cartilage burst apart. The Irishman shrieked as the leg shot out from under him and dumped him to the floor. The Webley skidded across the concrete as he grabbed the wounded limb with both hands.

Encizo did not congratulate himself on his marksmanship. He ducked back behind the cover of the van, aware that at least one opponent had yet to be taken out of the battle. Encizo's experience and instincts saved his life. The enemy shotgun boomed, and a burst of buckshot peppered the van and raked the floor in the position Encizo had been a split second earlier.

Manning had seen the remaining IRA gunman duck for cover by the racks of spare parts and accessories. He also noticed the man had broken open his side-by-side shotgun to reload. The Canadian saw an opportunity to take him alive and quickly rushed to the Irishman's position. When he reached the racks, he pointed his Walther pistol and demanded surrender. "Drop it!" he ordered. "Give it up or you're dead."

The terrorist stared at Manning as he held the shotgun in one hand and two shells in the other. He could not shove the shells into the open barrels, close the shotgun and hope to aim and fire the weapon before Manning could simply squeeze the trigger of his pistol. He tossed the shells aside and nodded as if to signal he agreed to surrender.

Suddenly he hurled the shotgun at Manning. The Canadian tried to dodge the unconventional projectile, but the heavy twin barrels struck his forearms and knocked the Walther from his hands. The Irishman rushed forward and swung a left hook, but the Phoenix pro weaved away from the attack, and the terrorist's fist whistled inches away from his face. Manning's left hand shot out in a fast jab to the chin, and his right followed with a hard cross to the side of the jaw.

Stumbling from the blows, the terrorist fell against some shelves of tools. He grabbed a tire iron from a shelf and charged. Manning jumped back as the iron swished through the air, making the Irishman miss and slash a vicious backhand sweep. Manning continued to retreat from his attacker until he backed into a stack of tires.

He seized a tire and pulled it from the pile. The terrorist swung the tire iron, and Manning blocked with the tire in his hands. Iron bounced on rubber. The Phoenix warrior turned the tire slightly and thrust it forward like a battering ram. The hard rubber rim slammed into the opponent's chest and drove him backward. The IRA man grunted and swung his iron once more. Manning blocked the blow again.

The Irishman tried to kick Manning in the groin, but his ankle bounced against the hard rubber. The Phoenix pro delivered another thrust as the tire iron was swung toward his arm. The tire struck the IRA goon's wrist and knocked the iron from the man's hand. Manning shoved the tire in a downward diagonal stroke and rammed the edge into his opponent's abdomen.

The terrorist doubled up with a groan, and Manning quickly slipped the tire over his head and shoulders, pinning the man's upper arms to his chest. Grabbing the man's hair and yanking his head forward, Manning plowed his fist into his jaw, and the contest was over.

Manning had just shoved the inert figure away when he heard a voice. "You dropped this." It was the Israeli, holding the Walther P-5 out to Manning, who nodded and accepted the handgun.

"Our people all right?" he asked.

"Fellows suffered a flesh wound, but it doesn't seem serious," Katz answered. "I'm not sure how many opponents we managed to take alive, but none got away."

"Who the hell fired a pistol from the doorway?" Manning asked. "Scared the hell out of me. I thought another gunman had gotten behind me, and it almost drove me out from cover before I realized the shots came from the door and were fired without being aimed."

"That was Simms," Katz replied. "I'm glad he didn't have any grenades. He didn't seem very concerned about possible risk to anyone on our side."

"Great," the Canadian muttered. "Maybe we should see about getting rid of the bastard. You remember what McCarter told us about Simms's actions when they were in Northern Ireland?"

"I remember," Katz assured him. "Though we may end up still having to work with Simms, I'll see if we can get a more agreeable replacement."

David McCarter approached the pair. He had retrieved his .38 Smith & Wesson and was examining it as he walked toward Katz and Manning. McCarter pressed the cylinder catch, opened it and dumped the cartridges from the chambers into the open palm of his other hand.

"Thornwood tried to shoot us with our own guns," he said with a wolfish grin. "Quite a surprise when neither would fire."

"Loading the revolvers with dummy ammo instead of live rounds was a good idea," Katz remarked approvingly.

"Since we knew they'd confiscate the revolvers, it didn't make much sense to give them extra guns loaded with live ammo. On the other hand, Thornwood would have been suspicious if the revolvers had been empty," McCarter said with a shrug. "By the way, one of Thornwood's flunkies fetched those Irish blokes from a room concealed behind these racks. Reckon that's where they keep the illegal arms supply."

"Good," Katz said. "All considered, it went pretty well."

"You chaps cut it a bit close," McCarter complained. "Poor Cal and I were about to dirty our trousers when the bastards got that welding torch ready."

"Sorry," Manning said. "Rafael needed time to get the van into position to ram the door, and I had to measure and set the plastic explosives to blow the back door—"

The conversation ended abruptly as Major Simms came up to join them. Simms took a pack of cigarettes from his jacket and looked at the trio as if he knew some great secret joke he refused to share with the others.

"Fellows is doing his policeman bit," Simms announced. "Officially placing the survivors under arrest. I suggest we take these scum before he hauls them off to Scotland Yard."

"We must interrogate them before the police take over," Katz confirmed. "Better round up the prisoners and check the arms room for any evidence we might need. I'll talk to Fellows."

"Have to do more than just talk if you expect to get the least bit of information from any of these blackguards," Simms commented.

"Looking forward to using a cattle prod like in the good old days in Belfast?" McCarter asked dryly.

"You can't handle people like these with kid gloves," the SAS major replied, casting a disgusted glance at McCarter. "I would have thought you had learned that by now."

"We don't use your methods, Major," Katz told him. "Don't worry. They'll talk."

"I just hope they have something to tell us that will make this little raid worthwhile," Manning said, summing up the situation for all of them.

8

"I need a doctor, you bastards!" Kevin Dwyer said as he lay on a cot in a subterranean cell located beneath the Black Wolf pub. "I've got rights, damn it!"

"Not right now you don't," Calvin James replied. The black commando sat on a stool by Dwyer's side. He held a hypodermic syringe in one hand and a sterilized cotton ball in the other.

Dwyer's eyes widened with fear. Leather straps across his chest, wrists and ankles secured him firmly to the cot. He tried to struggle, but there was little he could do as James plunged the needle into his arm. Yakov Katzenelenbogen and David McCarter stood near the heavy door of the cell and watched James deliver the injection.

"You black son of a bitch!" Dwyer exclaimed. "What have you done to me? What was in that syringe?"

"Scopolamine," James answered as he placed two fingers at Dwyer's wrist to take his pulse. "Truth serum. You're in good enough shape to handle it. Don't worry about your leg. Bullet went through the kneecap. Busted it up pretty bad, but it can probably be reasonably repaired with enough operations."

"You won't be running around much in prison, anyway," McCarter stated. "That's where you'll spend the rest of your life, so just relax and let the scopolamine do its job."

"I'm a soldier in the Provisional Irish Republican Army!" Dwyer cried. "This is a war crime against a legitimate freedom fighter trying to liberate Ireland from British oppression . . .''

"Save it for your press conference," McCarter snorted. "I've heard all this IRA war-for-liberation business before. You blokes claim you're so concerned about getting independence for Ireland, but every time someone offers terms to grant Ireland greater autonomy, the IRA responds with escalated violence. Remember the Fitzgerald Plan in 1977?"

"It was unacceptable," Dwyer replied in a slightly slurred voice—evidence that the scopolamine had begun to take effect.

"And to protest the Fitzgerald Plan the IRA murdered Lord Mountbatten by blowing up his fishing boat in Donegal Bay," McCarter stated. "You figure that sort of behavior is going to convince Britain to pull out of Ireland? You think that's the sort of action that proves the IRA would help set up a fair and just government in Ireland?"

"We'd establish an Irish government run by Irishmen," Dwyer insisted, but his words were less clear and he was obviously struggling to stay awake.

"The leader of the Sinn Fein, O'Bradaigh in 1979, publicly told the world what sort of government the IRA favors," McCarter reminded the prisoner. "Sinn Fein is the officially accepted 'legal' spokesman arm of the IRA, so O'Bradaigh was one of your boys. He said the IRA would accept nothing less than 'domestic socialism,' roughly based on Marxism. He also claimed any opposing political parties would not be tolerated. In short, the IRA wants to establish a one-party republic that would have more than a slight similarity to a Communist dictatorship."

Dwyer muttered something totally unintelligible. James peeled back an eyelid and examined the Irishman's pupil. He took Dwyer's pulse again and consulted his wristwatch to time the beats.

"Bloody IRA tried to assassinate Prime Minister Thatcher in 1984," McCarter continued. "In 1985 they killed nine police officers and civilians in Ulster when they attacked the police station. *Irish* civilians. The IRA never shows much concern for the Irish people they claim to be fighting for when they lob grenades into crowded pubs or booby trap dead British soldiers. Irish civilians have been killed or maimed when they found those corpses. Irish children have been victims of the IRA's 'war for liberation'..."

"Hey, knock it off," James told him. "This guy's gone under, and it's time for us to question him about events in Scotland, not Ireland."

"Sorry," the Briton said with a shrug. "Guess I got on my soapbox a bit."

"That's all right," Katz said patiently. "You spent enough time stationed in Northern Ireland to have some strong feelings about the IRA. For that reason, I think Cal and I had better handle this interrogation."

"Maybe you're right," McCarter agreed with a sigh. "I'll go see if I might be more useful doing something else."

"Just don't get into a confrontation with Simms," Katz warned. "I spoke with Henderson, and he says Simms has more experience concerning SAS activities in Scotland than any military officer currently on active duty. We're going to have to work with him, and we don't need any more friction than we already have."

"I'll steer clear of him as best I can," the Briton assured the Phoenix Force commander.

McCarter left the cell. Katz and James spent the next three hours questioning Dwyer under the influence of the truth serum. This method of interrogation could prove frustrating on occasion, because the subject was in a drug-induced trance and sometimes failed to understand questions or answered in a mumbling, slurred voice. However, Dwyer was unable to resist the effects of scopolamine and answered all questions honestly.

To be certain, James had attached a polygraph machine to Dwyer. Under normal circumstances, a person can beat a polygraph, but the scopolamine reduces one's ability to trick the lie detector. Besides breaking down conscious efforts to control pulse rate and physical signs of stress, scopolamine is potentially dangerous. However, the polygraph served double duty by registering heart, pulse and respiratory functions, so James could monitor the subject's physical condition during questioning under the influence of the drug.

There were possible pitfalls. Post-hypnotic suggestion would result in false information being relayed under the influence of the truth serum, but James did not see any evidence that Dwyer had undergone such sophisticated programming. In some cases, schizophrenics have such a distorted view of reality that they don't know the difference between the truth and a lie. But even a schizo is aware of certain facts, events, names and places.

Dwyer answered questions and told them he belonged to a radical cell of the IRA headed by Garrett O'Flynn, and he and his men had been delivering arms and supplies to O'Flynn's contacts in Glasgow, Scotland. However, most of the contacts appeared to be Scottish instead of Irish. Dwyer wasn't in possession of any further details about the Scots or what O'Flynn was doing in Scotland. Of course, he suspected they were responsible for the McGreggor kidnapping, but he had no information about the incident.

The prisoner also told them about a prearranged meeting site in Glasgow to deliver the weapons. He could add little more except the names and locations of a handful of other IRA operatives scattered across London and other parts of England. O'Flynn clearly followed the age-old rule of Intelligence operations and kept his field agents on a need-to-know level of information. Dwyer was aware that O'Flynn's cell was acting independently of the mainstream of the Irish

Republican Army and that Sinn Fein had no knowledge of O'Flynn's activities in Scotland.

Dwyer had no knowledge of the Iron Claymore clan or the demands issued by the kidnappers of Daniel Mc-Greggor. Katz and James cross-checked information by asking the questions again and later interrogating the other IRA captive, Thornwood and Greg. They did not get many answers, but Phoenix Force had discovered the name of a terrorist leader and the next site for their mission.

CLOUDS DRAPED the early morning sky above Glasgow. The sun was a circle of light behind a gray veil as the Churchill 15 transport circled a small airfield outside the Scottish city. The Churchill was a new British-designed military transport aircraft, similar to the American C-130, but capable of carrying more cargo or passengers and equipped with larger fuel tanks that increased its range. The British plane could also be converted into a hydrofoil to allow it to take off or land on water.

The first impression of Glasgow from the air was that of a busy, industrialized metropolis. Not the general image usually associated with Scotland, but this description aptly suited Glasgow. The third-largest city in the United Kingdom, Glasgow is also the center of industry in Scotland. Dozens of factories and mills are located in the city. Phoenix Force and the others aboard the Churchill gazed down at the steeple of Saint Mungo's Cathedral, the world-famous University of Glasgow atop Gilmore Hill and the great towers and stone ramparts of Crookston Castle.

The castle seemed an anachronism, surrounded as it was by numerous modern structures and factories. The traffic was light, but that was due to the early hour. Glasgow has a population of a million residents, and the streets would soon be crowded with motor vehicles, cyclists and even a few horse-drawn carts.

The Churchill flew over Glasgow International Airport, located about eight miles from the heart of the city, not far from Crookston Castle. The airport is the second largest in the United Kingdom—London's Heathrow is still the largest—but the small and obscure airfield better suited their needs. The plane descended on a runway while British soldiers and Royal Marines stood by and watched the landing.

The airstrip had been converted into a liaison point for the British military and government authorities. Cooperating with the Scottish constabulary, the troops had recently increased in number and activity in Scotland due to the McGreggor kidnapping.

Phoenix Force and Major Simms emerged from the plane. Frost crunched underfoot as they drew closer to the soldiers. The wind slashed at them like the chilled breath of an invisible ice dragon. They were grateful for their topcoats as they carried their luggage from the plane. A smattering of large, white snow flakes swirled in the cold northern wind.

A large man dressed in SAS uniform and tan beret stamped his feet and stood rigidly at attention, his gloved hand raised in a crisp salute. McCarter groaned when he recognized the handlebar mustache, stiff with excessive hair wax, and the name Hutton above the soldier's breast pocket. The British Phoenix Force pro had met Sergeant Hutton once before. The NCO was Major Simms's toady. A pit bull that walked on two legs, eager to attack at the command of his master.

"Good morning, sir," Hutton greeted.

"No saluting, Sergeant," Simms instructed with a curt nod. "That's the reason we're in civilian clothes. Don't want to draw any more attention than necessary. These gentlemen are a team of special operatives from the States. They're using cover names. You will address them by those names or as 'sir.' Understand?"

"Yes, sir..." Hutton began. His gaze fell on McCarter, and the sergeant's eyes widened with surprise. "Isn't that...?"

"Black," McCarter said sharply. "You can call me 'sir' if you like, but don't blow my cover or I'll yank your tongue out, Hutton."

"I'd like for you to try," Hutton replied with a cruel smile. "Maybe after this is over. Sort of figured that other bloke would call himself Black."

"Little too obvious," James said with a shrug. "If I said 'I'm Black,' you'd figure you can see that for yourself. So he gets to be Mr. Black. Goes along with the color of his heart. I'm Mr. Blue. You know, singing the blues?"

"We're all turning blue in this weather," Encizo commented. The Cuban turned up the collar of his coat and glanced at the falling snow as if witnessing an invasion of giant albino germs.

"Sutherland is waiting for you inside," Hutton stated. He seemed to address Simms directly and all but ignored the five men of Phoenix Force—aside from his obvious dislike for McCarter. "I think he was expecting that Scotland Yard gent."

"Inspector Fellows will probably join us tomorrow," Yakov Katzenelenbogen explained. "Let's discuss this inside. Somewhere with better security."

"This base is secure," Hutton assured him.

"Really?" Gary Manning inquired, his tone doubtful as he stared at a line of pine trees about half a mile from the airstrip. "Then you know who those people are?"

Hutton turned and stared. At first glance, the sergeant saw no one, but movement behind some shrubbery between the trees drew his attention. He caught a brief glimpse of somebody poking his head out from the bushes. Whoever it was retreated quickly behind the foliage and vanished from view. Simms had also seen the incident and grunted with disgust.

"You havin' a nice holiday here, Sergeant?" the SAS officer asked dryly.

"We didn't have any reason to think anyone would be spying on us," Hutton replied lamely. "I'll get some men and check it out immediately."

"Don't jump to any conclusions one way or the other," Katz warned. "The locals are no doubt suspicious and curious about what's going on here. It's understandable if they want to take a look from time to time. No law against taking a stroll in the woods."

"At six-thirty in the morning?" Simms commented.

"Some people wake up earlier than that," Manning countered. "Nothing sinister about that, but I think we should try to keep track of who might be watching us."

"Take care of it, Sergeant," Simms instructed. "I'll take the others in to see Sutherland."

"Yes, sir," Hutton replied, and came to attention before he remembered Simms had told him not to salute.

The sergeant turned and marched to the uniformed troops. Several soldiers and Royal Marines carried FAL assault rifles or Sterling 9 mm submachine guns. Katz sighed and hoped no one would start shooting without good cause. He knew the SAS and the Royal Marines are among the best-trained elite fighting men in the world, but even the best have a few bad apples in the barrel from time to time. The Israeli did not have a high opinion of Major Simms, and Hutton didn't seem any better. Katz found some comfort in the knowledge that the troops were probably more professional than their commander and the NCO.

Although it seems an inconceivable paradox, highly competent personnel are often controlled by less competent leaders. Katz recalled several world leaders—prime ministers, chancellors and Presidents—who had been incompetent despite their high office. Giant corporations had folded because the people in charge arrogantly refused to listen to the advice of the more knowledgeable individuals on their payroll. The same thing happened in the military. Veteran professionals were under command of higher-ranking persons who had been promoted to important positions due not to their ability but to family ties, political affinities and the like.

"Maybe a couple of us should go along with the troops," James suggested. "Keep Hutton from screwing up if there's still somebody out there."

"Hutton isn't—" Simms began.

"Good idea, Mr. Blue," Katz declared, ignoring the major. "Mr. Green, perhaps you'd go along, as well."

"Right," Manning agreed with a nod.

"If Hutton steps out of line, put him out of commission to make sure he won't be a problem in the field for the rest of this mission," Katz added in a firm voice.

"Hey, can I go with them, too?" McCarter volunteered.

"What the hell—?" Simms began, enraged by Katz's instructions.

"Your man had better behave like a professional and in a responsible manner, or he's out," Katz told him. "We'll make sure of it if we have to. That applies to you, as well, Simms. Nobody is going to foul up this mission."

"Does that include your fellow teammates?" Simms demanded.

"I don't have to worry about them," Katz answered. "They don't open fire around doorways without aiming when they know they might hit someone on our side."

"That reminds me," Manning said as he glared at Simms. "Don't ever pull a stunt like that again or you'll spend the rest of the year on crutches."

The Canadian was not the sort to make idle threats. Simms suspected that and took Manning's remark seriously. A quiet man seldom says anything he doesn't mean. Manning and James handed their luggage to the other members of Phoenix Force and headed toward Hutton and the troops.

Simms marched stiff legged to one of the hangars. Katz, Encizo and McCarter followed him to the wide sliding doors, which were open just enough to admit the men in single file. The interior was warm and well lit by a skylight in the roof.

The hangar was spacious, virtually a garage for airplanes, but there were no aircraft inside. A man waited by a workbench, surrounded by mechanic's tools on tables and hung on the wall. He wore a wrinkled mackintosh and an old fedora with a battered rim. His face appeared as worn as his clothing, the skin scored by exposure to extremes of weather and hardships. The bags under his eyes suggested he hadn't slept much in the past few days. He frowned as the three Phoenix pros and Simms approached.

"Police Superintendent Sutherland," Simms began. "These are three members of the special team the Americans sent us. Call themselves Gray, Brown and Black. They consider they're in charge 'cause their President gave them authority."

"It was an American kidnapped," Sutherland replied with a nod. "And others killed by the terrorists. Still, the kidnapping of Mr. McGreggor happened in my jurisdiction. That gives me some cause for concern."

"We'd like to work with you, Superintendent," Katz assured him. "I understood the kidnapping occurred near Edinburgh?"

"Aye," Sutherland confirmed. "That's my jurisdiction. Inspector Fellows told you that, did he not? Where is he, by the by?"

"The inspector was wounded during a gun battle last night," Katz explained. "Not seriously, though. Fellows was lucky to be wearing a heavy coat, and he was only grazed by shotgun pellets. Still, he needed some rest and has to make a report to Scotland Yard. A few other details he has to look after, but he'll be along later, unless something unforeseen detains him."

Encizo placed an aluminum suitcase on a table and opened the lid. Sutherland glanced inside, surprised to see a compact submachine gun with three long curved magazines stored in the case. The weapon seemed vaguely familiar to the Scot, but it was not a British Sterling or Sten. Sutherland thought the gun might be an Uzi, but it did not look like the photos he had seen of the Israeli assault weapon.

The submachine gun was a Heckler & Koch MP-5, Encizo's favorite assault piece. The Cuban considered H&K firearms to be the best in the world, and used the German-made weapons whenever possible. Like the P9-S pistol, the MP-5 was a 9 mm parabellum weapon. But instead of taking the subgun from the case, Encizo removed a small transistor radio from a pouch in the lid and extended the antenna.

He raised an index finger to his lips to signal for the others to be quiet. He began stalking around the hangar, with the radio antenna pointed before him like a divining rod. Sutherland looked at Simms and raised a thick sandy eyebrow. The major shrugged.

"Were there any witnesses to McGreggor's abduction?" Katz inquired.

"Should I just nod?" Sutherland asked with a sigh, frustrated and confused by the actions of the newcomers.

"Please answer," the Israeli urged. "The report Inspector Fellows showed us was a bit sketchy."

"Aye," Sutherland confirmed. "There were several witnesses, but the terrorists wore masks. Pullover types. Sort of thing skiers wear. All the witnesses could say was that these men gunned down McGreggor's bodyguards and forced him into a dark blue car. In fact, we found a car fitting the description about two miles up the road. Obviously they'd abandoned the car and spirited poor McGreggor away in another vehicle."

"No tire prints?" McCarter asked. "Nothing that could help identify the second vehicle?"

"Tracks were left by a lorry," Sutherland answered. "I think you call 'em trucks in the States. Medium-sized lorry of the sort used by farmers and fishermen throughout east Scotland. Pulled off the dirt road onto a highway near Inverness. No way to track it from there, not without some better idea about make and color and such."

"Okay," Encizo snorted. "No bugs. We can talk."

"Bugs?" Simms snorted. "You mean electrical listening devices and that rot? I could have told you not to worry. My men have been here for the last two days."

"Just a precaution," Encizo assured him. "That's why I scanned the place with this detector. Standard stuff."

"We'd talked a bit before you scanned for bugs," Sutherland stated with a thin smile. "Wee bit careless?"

"Not really," Katz assured him. "If the enemy did have the hangar wired, they would have already learned everything we discussed and probably a good deal more. Of course, Simms had opened his mouth about who we are and why we're here, but the terrorists would have already suspected that if the men in the woods are their agents doing recon here."

"You saw men in the woods?" the Scot inquired.

"I saw one man," Simms declared. "And we don't have any proof he's working for the terrorists. Probably just some bloke out walking his dog."

"Don't assume anything and don't underestimate the enemy," Encizo warned as he returned the radio to the case. "So far, they're still two jumps ahead of us."

"Only two?" Sutherland asked with surprise. "I figured we be further back in the game than that."

"We have a lead that might change that," Katz explained. "Last night we caught some people connected with the terrorists. Lucky hunch that paid off. An IRA member named Dwyer gave us information about a delivery point here in Glasgow for guns going to a terrorist cell leader named O'Flynn. Fellows and Henderson are looking into records to see what Scotland Yard, Interpol and SIS might have on O'Flynn.''

"I'm not surprised the IRA is involved," Sutherland stated. "Northern Ireland is right next to us, you know. Across the North Channel. The Irish coast is about as close to Glasgow as Edinburgh. Many an Irishman crosses the channel and tries to find work in this city. Glasgow has more job opportunities than you'll find in most of Scotland and far more than available in Ireland."

"More Catholics in the west portions of Scotland, too," Simms added gruffly. "IRA come from the Irish Catholics. Figures they'd fit in better among those of that same religion."

"Religion doesn't have anything to do with it, Simms," McCarter growled. "The bishop of Londonderry publicly denounced the IRA and condemned its actions. The majority of the Catholic community in Ireland is opposed to the IRA's tactics—including those who want Northern Ireland to be free of British rule. Hell, you were stationed in Belfast same time I was. You know it's the truth."

"I wouldn't count on the IRA dealing exclusively with Scottish Catholics," Katz warned. "Terrorists don't seem to care about religion when they seek out allies. People who use violence as a primary political tool aren't apt to be choirboys. We'll learn more about them as the mission progresses. Speculation is never as good as facts."

"Most important fact we have so far is that Dwyer's people are supposed to meet some terrorists from O'Flynn and the Scottish radicals working with them."

"Are you sure Scots are involved?" Sutherland asked, taking a black briar pipe from his pocket. "Maybe leaving that list of demands about the United States breaking relations with England and recognizing the King of Scotland is a smoke screen to draw attention away from the IRA."

"Some of the terrorists are Scots," Katz insisted. "We questioned Dwyer and another IRA member under the influence of truth serum. Besides, it's very unlikely the Irish terrorists could conduct major actions in Scotland without the assistance of locals who know the country. The need to supply the terrorists with more weapons suggests O'Flynn couldn't arm all those involved with his own cell's supply."

"Well, we've been keeping tabs on the more radical members of the SNP and a couple pro-Marxist outfits," Sutherland remarked. "Hauled in a few leaders for questioning. No luck so far, but we still hope to get something by watching the fringe groups and leftists. That seems to be the way Scotland Yard has been going, as well. Those are the most likely groups to be responsible for this mess. Wouldn't you agree?"

"Not really," Katz replied. "Apparently the demands for recognition of the King of Scotland are genuine. Marxists might work with the IRA, but I can't imagine them trying to establish a new monarchy instead of a socialist state. I can't claim to be very knowledgeable about the Scottish Nationalist Party, but I don't think they've ever endorsed anyone for king."

"The SNP wants Scotland to be independent," Sutherland said with a shrug. "They feel the British have exploited our country."

"Scotland is part of Great Britain," Simms stated.

"We Scots don't consider ourselves Englishmen," Sutherland replied. "Although Scotland and England officially merged back in 1707, some things never change."

Manning and James appeared at the doors of the hangar. Sergeant Hutton followed the pair as they entered and approached the others. The NCO's expression suggested he was very unhappy with the situation since Phoenix Force had arrived. But Hutton appeared none the worse for wear, so he had not been a serious problem for the Canadian and the black warrior.

"There was somebody in the woods," Manning announced as he took a flannel plaid cap from his head and shook snow from it. "They took off before we could get a decent look at them. There's a road along the opposite side of the woods, and we heard a car engine, glimpsed a vehicle streaking away, but the trees blocked our view. It was dark green, but I can't say what kind of car it was, let alone give you a license plate number."

"I only saw the outline of a man's head and shoulders," Simms remarked. "Are you sure there was more than one?"

"Two sets of footprints in the immediate area where we saw someone by the tree line," Manning replied with a nod. "There's frost on the grass and bushes, so the prints were very clear and easy to distinguish from tracks made before this morning. Both individuals wore boots, one pair with waffle-style rubber soles and the other with wavy-patterned soles. Waffle-foot is probably about six feet tall and more than two hundred pounds. The other guy is probably around five-eight and weighs approximately one-hundred and fifty pounds."

"You could tell that by the footprints?" Sutherland asked, surprised by Manning's statement.

"I've been a hunter all my life," the Canadian explained. "Stalked deer and men. Learned to read signs of either. By comparing how deep the prints are and the stride between them with my own on the same area, it gives me a pretty good idea about weight and height. Of course, that doesn't include stuff like backpacks, which might add another ten to thirty pounds, or someone with abnormally long or short legs, but it's still a fairly reliable system. Unfortunately I can't tell you anything else about them except some of the tracks were partially covered with frost, so they'd been there for a while. At least three hours."

"They didn't leave anything except footprints," James added. "No cigarette butts, gum wrappers, conveniently discarded map to the bad guys' headquarters, nothing."

"I still think they were just a couple of poachers," Hutton said with a shrug. "Poachers sometimes creep around forest areas in the early morning to search for grouse sleeping in high grass and bushes. They wring the birds' necks, stuff them in a burlap bag and sell them to unprincipled grocers or restaurant owners."

"Poachers wouldn't be standing around those little woods for three hours, hunting grouse that aren't there," Sutherland replied.

Simms sighed before speaking. "This is fruitless supposition. There isn't any proof one way or the other. Any idea how we can find out the truth?"

"For now it's best we assume they were from the enemy camp," Katz answered. "O'Flynn and whoever else is involved must have an Intelligence network. Whether crude or sophisticated, the most fundamental activity of any intel outfit is to gather information by watching enemy sites. The terrorists may regard this airstrip as an enemy base, since there are uniformed British soldiers here."

"But there hadn't been any reports of terrorist activity here at Glasgow," Sutherland declared. "There was no reason to believe we couldn't operate fairly openly here."

"Well, no sense worrying about what's already happened or whether it should have been done differently," Encizo said with a sigh. "But we have to assume the terrorists saw us arrive and suspect we're connected with the search for McGreggor and those involved in the kidnapping."

"Which means our cover ain't so good now," James added. "Might screw up any chance of meeting O'Flynn's people for the gun deal."

"Perhaps," Katz said thoughtfully. "Tell me, Superintendent, do you think we can find a hotel with enough vacancies for the five of us?"

"A hotel?" Simms said with surprise. "I thought you'd stay here at the base."

"We're supposed to be a group of American business-men," Katz explained. "It suits our cover if we stay at a hotel rather than here. Maybe our cover isn't blown, and we can still play out our roles. Even if the terrorists observed us, they'll be less suspicious if we go to a hotel. They may guess we received a military escort due to the new threat of terrorism and we're not connected with your mission here in Scotland."

"But if they reckon you fellas be American agents," Sutherland began, "you might be the next targets."

"It'll save time if they come to us instead of us having to go after them," McCarter remarked with a sly grin. "And we think that's just fine."

9

William Bruce sat on a crate and stroked the steel blade of his dirk across the oil-slick surface of a whetstone. Joseph Kehoe watched the Scot and wondered, not for the first time, whether Garrett O'Flynn had made a monstrous mistake by joining forces with the Bruce family and the Iron Claymore clan. Kehoe had virtually been born into the IRA, the son of a Provisional IRA zealot, and he had met many an Irish fanatic, but none quite like the Scottish followers of the self-proclaimed king and his four warrior sons.

Kehoe considered William Bruce to be the worst of the lot. William wasn't as unstable or short-tempered as Malcolm, but Kehoe figured William was the most sadistic one. The Scot seemed unnaturally fond of his dirk. There was a strange smile about his mouth as he sharpened the double-edged blade, and he often talked about how he enjoyed the feel of plunging the knife into living flesh. William spoke of stabbing victims and hot, gushing blood with more enthusiasm than most men express about sex. Kehoe was far from squeamish, and he had been responsible for many more deaths than William, but he had never found such pleasure in the taking of life. Besides, the Irishman was sickened by the idea of killing another human being with a knife.

"I was afraid this assignment to Glasgow would be far from the action we seen in the east," William remarked, and smiled at Kehoe. "Now it seems the enemy has delivered themselves into the mouth of the lion."

"Before we take any action, we ought to check with the home base," Kehoe began, worried that the bloodthirsty Scot would order them into a rash attack without authorization from O'Flynn, whom he still regarded as the real leader of the operation. "They may just want us to observe the strangers..."

"I remind yeh I be the son of King Andrew Robert Bruce," William declared as he pointed the tip of his dirk at Kehoe. "A Scottish prince can make command decisions in the field."

Kehoe nearly laughed out loud. Scottish prince! They were huddled in the basement of a camera shop owned by one of the Iron Claymore sympathizers. William's "command" consisted of eight demented Scotsmen and four IRA members. The terrorists hadn't established a major operation in Glasgow, because their primary targets were supposed to be Americans, and both tourists and visiting diplomats prefer Edinburgh to Glasgow. Besides, O'Flynn had been opposed to setting up a large number of their men in Glasgow, since it was too close to Northern Ireland. The British would almost certainly suspect the IRA when the terrorist strikes began in Scotland, and an unusual number of Irish strangers would immediately attract attention.

William had probably been sent to Glasgow because the commanders of the movement didn't trust him in Edinburgh. He was more competent than Malcolm, though. The youngest Bruce brother hadn't been permitted to join his siblings in the field and had to stay at the castle headquarters. Nonetheless, William was clearly less reliable than the two elder brothers, Angus and Duncan. The knife-loving Scot was too fond of bloodshed, but there had been little chance of William finding an excuse to carry out violence in Glasgow.

Until now, Kehoe thought grimly.

The door to the dark room opened and MacDonald emerged. The shop owner carried several freshly developed photographs in his hand and nodded at William, ignoring Kehoe. His allegiance was to the alleged descendants of Robert Bruce, and he considered the Irishman to be a low-ranking foot soldier in the movement.

"Did the photographs come out all right?" William asked eagerly as he reached for the photos.

"Most of them," MacDonald replied and handed the pictures to William. "The recon team took the shots from a long distance and they weren't professional cameramen. Still, I gave 'em the proper lenses, and the photos came out better than I would've hoped from such amateurs."

William examined the prints. They were a bit grainy and two were out of focus, but there was no doubt seven men had deplaned from the Churchill at the airstrip. Two were familiar faces to the terrorists—Superintendent Sutherland and an SAS major. The other five were strangers.

"They said one of these bastards be a blackie," William announced cheerfully. "Another looks to be a Mexican or somethin' of that sort."

"I'm not so sure," Kehoe said with a frown as he peered over William's shoulder. "The fella's got a dark complexion, but he could be of Mediterranean descent. Might even be a Turk. Hard to say from these pictures. Other one is black, but that doesn't mean they're Americans. Lots of blacks live in Great Britain these days. Even some here in Scotland."

"They're Americans," William said with conviction. "CIA specialists sent to work with the Brits."

"Those metal suitcases look like the sort of thing they tote special weapons and gear in," Kehoe admitted. "Still, I don't see any cause for alarm . . ."

"Dwyer and his men haven't reported back from London, and no one has been able to contact Thornwood," William reminded the Irishman. "Yer mates and the gunrunner disappear last night, and these five gunmen for the

Yanks arrive this morning. I do not think this be happenstance, Kehoe.''

"You're jumping to conclusions," the IRA man warned.

"We'll see about that," William declared with a sly grin. "Me lads spotted these five headed into the city. Tailed 'em to the Kentigern Hotel on Rottenrow. Most tourists favor the Albany or the Grosvenor when they visit Glasgow. Yanks on a low budget and little imagination usually stay at the Holiday Inn. The Kentigern is small and not as well-known. Better suited for the needs of spies like this lot."

"Doesn't prove anything, William," Kehoe said with a sigh.

"Aye," the Scot insisted. "It does, and with a wee bit of encouragement, I'll prove it beyond any doubt even for yeh. Better yet, I'll also lure these sons of Yankee trollops into a trap not a one shall live to tell of, me fine Irish friend."

Kehoe sighed and reluctantly asked, "So, what's the plan?"

GLASGOW HAS A REPUTATION for friendliness and fine seafood. Phoenix Force discovered both to be well-founded. The locals were generally pleasant and polite. The majority of people Phoenix Force met during their first few hours in Scotland impressed them as honest, hardworking and honorable.

Their dinner at the Kentigern Hotel proved Glasgow's reputation for superb seafood to be equally accurate. Phoenix Force rarely had the opportunity to sit at a table in a restaurant and enjoy a meal at leisure. Sea bass, shellfish, crab salad and boiled shrimp were among the delicious food ordered by the five commandos. The waiter had been surprised when McCarter asked for a chilled cola instead of white wine and Manning wanted coffee with his meal.

"Well," Calvin James began as he buttered a muffin, "this is a nice change of pace. Too bad it won't last too long."

"At least we got away from Simms for a while," Mc-Carter muttered. "That rotten bleeder was a pain in the arse when I served under him in Belfast, and he isn't any better now."

"You told us Simms tortured civilians in Ireland to try to get information about the IRA," Manning commented. "At least he hasn't tried anything like that."

"He would if we'd let him get away with it," Encizo stated. "What I can't figure out is why the guy's still with the SAS."

"Actually they transferred him to regular army and reassigned him to the ground forces about ten years ago," McCarter explained. "Unfortunately they've also reassigned him to be attached to Special Air Service from time to time. Lucky us. We got the bastard."

"Simms has experience, and he knows Scotland better than we do," Katz said with a shrug, as he worked at doing justice to the food on his plate. He was quite handy and knew how to use the steel hooks of his prosthesis to best advantage. "He's also a veteran when it comes to fighting the IRA. We don't have to like him or approve of his methods. As long as he doesn't step over the line and does his job, that's all that matters."

"Right now I'm more concerned about meeting the guys O'Flynn sent to get the guns tonight," James confessed, and glanced at his Seiko diver's watch. "It's 8:00 p.m. Dwyer said they'd be expecting the guns to be delivered at eleven. That's 2300 hours to you dudes who are still running on military time."

"Sutherland told me the factory on High Street has been shut down for the past three years," Katz said. "An ideal site for a secret transaction in the heart of Glasgow. More reason for us to believe Dwyer's claims..."

Two young men dressed in the blue uniform and checkered cap of the local constables suddenly approached the table. The policemen looked grimly serious. Katz put down his knife and fork, certain he would not be able to continue enjoying the meal.

"Sorry to interrupt your meal, sir," one of the cops began. He stared at the metal hooks of Katz's artificial limb. "You be Mr. Grey, correct?"

"I fit the description?" the Phoenix commander replied.

"Uh, aye," the officer said awkwardly. "That you do. The superintendent from Edinburgh sent us to fetch you gents."

"Now?" James asked with surprise. "Sutherland knows we've got business later tonight."

"The superintendent is at the docks," the cop explained. "So is about half the Glasgow police. An explosion occurred at a ship in port. Several people are injured. At least two dead. A fire is still raging out of control. That'll have to be contained before they can have a definite body count."

"Could be sabotage," Encizo commented as he started to rise from his chair. "Sutherland must think so."

"We got time to check it out," James added.

"Explosions are my field, so I'd better go, too," Manning announced, and gulped down the last of the coffee from his cup. "You two might as well finish your meal. No need for us all to miss dinner."

"Bloody hell," McCarter muttered and tossed his napkin on the table. "I'd sooner go along than fret about you blokes."

"If this is an act of terrorism, the terrorists may still be at the pier," Katz stated. "Let's dress for the occasion."

The constable waited for Phoenix Force to collect their coats and gear. The commandos had stored their aluminum cases in the hotel vault before they'd entered the restaurant, unwilling to leave the special equipment and weapons vulnerable to thieves in their hotel rooms. They retrieved their luggage and got coats and hats from the cloakroom. In three minutes they were ready to leave.

Phoenix Force followed the policemen outside. Two patrol cars were parked at the curb. One constable moved to the rear of his car and fished some keys from a pocket to unlock the trunk.

"Not sure if there be room in the boot for your bags," the cop commented.

"We'll keep 'em with us," McCarter told him. "Thanks anyway, but we don't have time to spend shuffling about spare tires and whatnot to make room for this stuff."

"Suit yourself," the constable replied with a shrug.

The policemen climbed into the cars and settled in behind steering wheels. Katz, Encizo and Manning piled into the first vehicle. McCarter and James got into the second car. They arranged the luggage as best they could while the drivers started the engines and turned on the headlights. The windows were slightly fogged up by the cold, and a light scattering of snowflakes dotted the windshields.

The cars pulled out from the curb, wipers clicking side to side across the windshields. The streets of Glasgow seemed surprisingly inactive for a major city with a large population. The snowfall was still light, and the Scots were certainly accustomed to cold weather. Yet few pedestrians strolled along the sidewalks, and the traffic was fairly light in the early evening.

The people of Scotland have never been much for nightlife. Nationality does not apply to individual taste and behavior, but, in general, Scots are early risers who work in the day and return to their homes by sundown. Relatively few people seemed inclined to dine at the restaurants, shop after dark or drive in the evening. Only a few cars and lorries competed with the two cop cars along Rottenrow.

The patrol cars headed northeast on the macadam road. They passed rows of shops and pubs. Most were single-story structures and many had closed for the night. The Royal Scottish Academy of Music and Drama towered above shorter buildings in the distance. Phoenix Force barely glimpsed the famous center of Scottish culture as they sped through the streets toward the harbor.

The sirens weren't used, because Phoenix Force urged the constables not to unless they needed them to get past traffic. They were in a hurry but they did not want to draw any more attention than necessary. The constables contacted Superintendent Sutherland by radio and learned the fire at the docks was under control. Several men on the ship and at the pier had been killed or injured, but there was no evidence any terrorists were in the harbor area.

"Oh, hello," James commented in the back seat of the second car. The black commando stared out the rear window at a pair of headlights that seemed to follow the cop cars. "I think we got a tail."

"What?" the constable behind the wheel asked with surprise.

"Been with us since we left the hotel?" McCarter asked as he popped open an aluminum valise.

"Like me-and-my-shadow time," James confirmed, and reached for the long metal case by his feet. "This couldn't be a dumb stunt by Simms and Hutton, could it?"

"I wouldn't put it past him, but I doubt it," McCarter replied as he extracted a compact machine pistol from his valise. The Briton inserted an extended magazine into the well of his KG-99 and pulled back the cocking knob. "Better figure on unfriendly forces..."

The passengers were abruptly jarred when the driver stomped on the brake. The lead vehicle had come to a sudden halt because a large truck had pulled out lengthwise into the street, effectively blocking the police cars. The second vehicle skidded forward, and the front fender banged into the back bumper of the first car.

It was a classic setup for an ambush. Their path had been cut off, and the vehicle that followed them was almost certainly part of a two-pronged attack strategy. McCarter and James quickly opened car doors and dove to the sidewalk, aware the automobiles would be deathtraps in such an ambush. The Briton tucked in his chin and bowed his head as he shoulder-rolled on concrete, the KG-99 cradled to his chest. James broke his fall in the same manner, but he hadn't been able to get his M-16 assault rifle from its case in time. The American reached inside his coat as he rolled and drew a Beretta 92-F pistol from shoulder leather.

The lead car's doors also flew open. Rafael Encizo emerged, Heckler & Koch machine pistol in his fists. Katz had also bailed out from the front door at the passenger's side and held a 9 mm SIG-Sauer pistol in his left hand. Manning tumbled onto the sidewalk near Encizo, aluminum rifle case in one hand and Walther P-5 in the other.

Although Phoenix Force reacted immediately to the threat, the two constables lacked their training and extraordinary battlefield experience. They sat in their vehicles, startled by the behavior of the five foreigners, and until a volley of submachine gun rounds exploded from both ends of the lorry, they thought that Phoenix Force had overreacted. Men, clad in baggy grey coveralls and black pullover ski masks, thrust automatic weapons around the nose of the truck cab and the open back of the rig.

"Get down!" Manning shouted at the constables as he aimed his pistol at the masked gunmen.

James and Katz also tried to warn the policemen, but their voices were lost amid the roar of the enemy weapons. A wave of high-velocity bullets smashed into the police cars. The first vehicle suffered worse damage than the second. The windshield exploded, and a dozen bullet holes riddled the hood and doors. The constable within convulsed as several slugs ripped into his face and chest. Blood splattered the interior of windows and stained upholstery. The constable's body slumped lifelessly in his seat.

The other officer managed to duck behind the dashboard as a salvo of full-auto rounds shattered the windshield of the second vehicle. Another burst of deadly fire sprayed the rear of the car. A dark blue sedan had pulled up behind the police cars, and two more masked gunmen jumped out with their weapons blazing.

Katz braced his left wrist along his prosthesis and fired the SIG-Sauer as he knelt behind the meager cover of a street lamp. The Israeli heard bullets ring against the lamppost and felt his stomach constrict with fear. The emotion was no stranger to Katz. He had lived with fear all his life, and it would not cause him to freeze in an emergency. The Phoenix commander aimed at the nearest opponent, stationed by the rear of the lorry, and triggered three shots.

At least one 9 mm parabellum hit the gunman in the center of the chest. The terrorist recoiled from the impact and pulled the trigger of his Ingram M-10 to slash a useless volley of bullets into the night sky. The orange flame from the muzzle of the compact machine pistol illuminated the man's bloodstained torso. Katz fired another SIG-Sauer round and drilled a 115-grain projectile into the opponent's heart. The man cried out and toppled backward, collapsing beside another masked killer.

The dead man's comrade hardly noticed. He was too busy trying to aim his Sterling subgun at the Phoenix commandos and simultaneously duck low by the tailgate of the truck to avoid a burst of 9 mm slugs from Encizo's MP-5 chopper. Manning also fired his Walther pistol at the gunmen as he bolted for cover at a men's haberdashery. The Canadian swung the rifle case in his other hand and hurled it at the door to the shop. The long aluminum case struck the glass, which burst apart and set a burglar alarm to wailing in protest.

Manning ducked his head and jumped through the shattered window. He landed partially on the aluminum case on the floor, and the Canadian felt the case slide underfoot an instant before he lost his balance and fell forward to the floor. He slapped his hand to the floor to break his fall.

Sharp pain bit into the palm. Manning stifled a cry and rolled onto his back. Broken glass crunched beneath him.

It was too dark in the haberdashery to examine his hand, but Manning realized he had pierced his palm on a shard of glass. The Canadian started to get up when the display window to the shop suddenly burst apart from a blast of automatic rounds. Manning shielded his face and eyes with a forearm as fragments of broken glass slashed through the interior of the haberdashery. A well-dressed mannequin toppled from the window display, its shirt front and suit jacket newly stitched.

Manning crawled to cover along a wall and placed the Walther P-5 on the floor within easy reach. Gripping the glass splinter stuck in his palm, he yanked it free. He winced with pain and felt blood flow from the wound. Manning fished a handkerchief from a pocket and wrapped an improvised bandage around his hand.

"This is turning out to be one hell of a night," Manning muttered as he gathered up his pistol.

DAVID MCCARTER HELD the KG-99 in both fists and fired a long spray of 9 mm rounds at the enemy sedan. One opponent pitched backward as he caught at least one parabellum slug. He fell to the pavement in a dying heap while McCarter blasted a column of bullet holes across the windshield of the sedan. The driver thrashed wildly behind the steering wheel and slapped both hands to his pulverized face. Crimson stained the man's torn ski mask as he slid across the front seat.

Another gunman used the car for cover as he leaned around the rear of the sedan and pointed a revolver at McCarter. Calvin James held his Beretta pistol in a two-handed Weaver's combat grip and snap-aimed at the enemy pistolman. The black warrior squeezed the trigger twice and watched the terrorist topple to the pavement with two 9 mm slugs in his chest.

A fourth gunman at the sedan also used the auto for shelter and tried to swing his Ingram machine pistol at McCarter and James. But the British ace had fired off a volley of parabellums, which sparked against the metal body of the sedan near the terrorist. The KG-99 rounds effectively pinned down the enemy gunman and allowed James to rush to the other side of the car. The black commando ran forward in a crouched stance and positioned himself by the rear tire at the left side of the vehicle.

McCarter ceased fire and the terrorist carefully raised his head to see why. He didn't notice James until the American had the Beretta trained on the top of his ski-mask-clad head. The gunman yelped with surprise when he spotted James out of the corner of an eye and hastily raised his Ingram chopper. The Phoenix commando had no choice. He fired the Beretta and blew off the summit of the terrorist's skull. Brains and bone fragments spewed from the ragged top of the man's mask. The body dropped from view.

Rafael Encizo fired his H&K subgun at the terrorists posted at the front of the lorry while Katz exchanged fire with the opponents at the rear of the truck. The Israeli triggered his SIG-Sauer as he moved to the open door of the first police car and reached inside with the prosthesis to snare the handle of his aluminum case with the steel hooks. Katz pulled it from the car and started to open the case.

A terrorist at the front of the lorry lobbed a bottle at the Phoenix commandos. Liquid sloshed in the bottle, and a flaming rag was jammed into its neck. It shattered against the side of the first police car, and flaming gasoline splashed across the vehicle.

Encizo and Katz ducked low as the fiery shroud draped the roof and hood of the vehicle. Terrorists charged from the front of the truck and attempted to rush the Phoenix pair while the flames kept them pinned down. A 3-round burst of 7.62 mm slugs slammed into the upper torso of one attacker, abruptly knocking him off his feet.

Gary Manning had taken his FAL assault rifle from the case he had thrown through the haberdashery window before he'd jumped inside the shop. The Canadian fired from the shattered window and took out one attacker before he could reach the cop cars. A second terrorist whirled in midstride and swung his Sterling chopper toward the haberdashery. Manning triggered his FAL and got his man in the forehead with a deadly burst.

A third terrorist retreated for the cover of the lorry. Two other enemy gunmen bolted from the rear of the truck. One fired a Skorpion machine pistol at the haberdashery window to keep Manning at bay while the other pointed a pump-action shotgun at Katz and Encizo. The Israeli managed to open his case and take out his Uzi. He hastily raised the subgun and triggered a short burst at the attackers.

The closest terrorist cried out and spun about from the force of two Uzi slugs in the upper chest and right shoulder. The shotgun dropped from the wounded man's fingers, and he dropped to one knee, a hand clasped to his bullet-wrecked shoulder. The other attacker swung his Skorpion toward Katz, but Encizo triggered his MP-5 faster. Fatal 9 mm missiles crashed into the terrorist's chest and throat. The Czech-made blaster fell from the gunman's grasp, and he clutched his bullet-gouged throat and staggered backward. The man wilted to the pavement, twitched weakly and died.

"Heads up!" Manning shouted as he hurled a dark green sphere from the haberdashery window.

Katz and Encizo quickly covered their ears as best they could. The Cuban used his hands and Katz shoved his right shoulder against one ear and covered the other with his left hand. They stayed low and waited for the grenade to explode less than a second later. The minibomb went off at the top of the canvas covering at the back of the lorry. A concussion blast rocked the truck and sent a screaming terrorist flying from the rear of the rig.

"Let's go!" Katz told Encizo as he ran for the rear of the lorry, the Uzi braced across his artificial arm.

The Cuban followed, and they dashed to the back of the truck. A stunned terrorist was stumbling around inside the canvas-cloaked rig. Blood trickled from his nostrils and ears, but the fanatic still held an Ingram machine pistol in his fist. The Phoenix pair couldn't afford to take any chances. Katz raised his Uzi and sent a trio of parabellum rounds into the dazed yet potentially still dangerous opponent.

Encizo charged around the rear of the truck and saw two terrorists run for an alley across the street. One of them turned and pointed a blue-black pistol at Encizo. The Phoenix pro fired his MP-5 and hit the pistolman with the last three rounds from the magazine of his H&K subgun. He saw the terrorist flung backward into the side of a brick building, then slump lifeless to the sidewalk while the remaining terrorist darted into the mouth of the alley.

The Cuban discarded his empty MP-5 because he didn't have any spare magazines for the weapon. Encizo drew his H&K P-9S pistol from shoulder leather and jogged to the alley. He reached the wall and carefully stepped around the corpse of the opponent sprawled on the sidewalk. Encizo slowly approached the mouth of the alley, P-9S clenched in both hands and held ready.

A burst of automatic fire snarled from down the alley. The Cuban stood back and waited for the enemy fire to subside. Then he poked the barrel of his H&K pistol around the corner and fired a single round in the general direction of the unseen opponent.

Encizo hoped the terrorist would instinctively duck for a moment as he leaped for cover at the opposite side of the alley entrance. Encizo reached it just in time, as a fresh volley of automatic fire raked the brick structure. He cautiously peered around the edge and saw the muzzle-flash of gunman's weapon amid the shadows.

The Phoenix commando snap-aimed and fired at the orange glare of the enemy's subgun. The terrorist's fire ceased abruptly, and Encizo retreated for safety. The shadowy opponent did not resume shooting. Encizo wondered whether the gunman had been hit or whether he was simply waiting for a clear target. The Cuban quickly unbuttoned his topcoat and slipped an arm from a sleeve. He swapped the pistol from one hand to the other and pulled his second arm free.

Encizo snapped the coat across the mouth of the alley to try to lure the enemy into firing at the movement. No shots responded to the decoy. He took a deep breath and ventured a quick peek around the corner. It was a blind alley, and another brick wall stood at the opposite end. A man was clawing at a drain pipe along the wall, trying to climb the barrier.

The Cuban entered the alley and aimed his H&K at the man on the wall. He glanced about and noticed a Sterling submachine gun on the ground. The frame was badly dented. The shot Encizo had fired at the muzzle-flash of the terrorist's weapon had struck the enemy's subgun. A discarded ski mask lay next to the damaged Sterling.

"Hold it!" Encizo shouted as he approached the figure on the drain pipe.

The terrorist failed to heed his warning. Encizo raised his pistol and fired a single round. The 9 mm slug sparked on brick above the opponent's head, and the ricochet whined sourly. The man cried out with surprise and lost his grip on the pipe. He dropped to the ground and crashed on top of a set of garbage cans. Two tin containers tipped over and clattered loudly as trash spilled onto the ground. The man stumbled and fell against the wall.

It was William Bruce, and he glared at Encizo with resentment. The Scot was angry and embarrassed by his undignified descent into the trash cans. Encizo pointed his P-9S autoloader at William, but he didn't want to kill the terrorist. The guy was more valuable alive. William felt more outraged than afraid. He believed he was a Scottish prince, blood descendant of his country's first king and thus chosen by God to lead nations. No American commoner would get the better of Prince William.

"Raise your hands," Encizo ordered, his pistol aimed at William's face. "Any tricks and your brains will be all over these walls."

"Damn yeh to hell!" William snarled in reply.

He suddenly kicked a trash can and sent it rolling forward. Encizo tried to sidestep the unexpected attack, but the can clipped him on the right shin. The blow was only slightly painful, little more than an annoyance, yet it served to distract Encizo as William lunged forward and drew his dirk from a belt sheath.

A boot lashed out and kicked the H&K pistol from Encizo's hand. The Cuban glimpsed the nine-inch steel blade in his opponent's fist as William delivered a ruthless thrust for Encizo's stomach. The Phoenix warrior jumped back to narrowly avoid the deadly thrust. William smoothly changed the attack to a sweeping slash, but Encizo weaved away from the whirling blade.

Then Encizo snap-kicked William in the abdomen. The Scot groaned and slashed too late at his opponent's leg. Encizo quickly grabbed William's wrist above the knife with both hands and tried to wrench the dirk from his grasp. William's free hand clenched into a fist and hooked a punch to Encizo's face. The Cuban's head was jarred by the blow, but he held on to the Scot's wrist.

William shoved forcibly and tried to drive the point of the dirk into Encizo's belly. The Cuban didn't resist and moved with his opponent's push. Encizo suddenly dropped to one knee and yanked the terrorist's wrist. William's forward momentum was unexpectedly increased, and he hurtled head-over-heels to the ground.

Encizo jumped up and yanked a Cold Steel Tanto fighting knife from a belt sheath. The thick, six-inch steel blade was designed in the manner of the Japanese *tanto*, a traditional weapon of the samurai. William got to his feet, the dirk still in his fist. He glanced at the shorter, single-edged blade in Encizo's hand and smiled.

"Now this be me sort of contest, laddie," the Scot remarked as he squared off, the dirk held low.

Encizo waited for his opponent to make the first move. The Cuban had been a knife fighter since he was a kid back in his native country, before Castro came into power. He knew the value of strategy in such combat. If William made the first attack, he would reveal something of his knife-fighting techniques, and Encizo would have a better idea how to defend against the Scottish blade man.

The type of knife favored by an opponent suggests probable methods of fighting style. Wililam's dirk was designed for thrusts and stabs more than cuts. Encizo was already aware his opponent also used slashing strokes, but William would probably rely on stabbing techniques to actually take out an adversary.

William raised his dirk in an underhand grip and prepared a thrust. Suddenly he tossed the knife to his left hand and launched the attack from a different direction. It was a tactic intended to catch the opponent off guard, but Encizo was no stranger to the move. He swung the Tanto into the dirk. As William's knife struck the unsharpened spine of Encizo's blade, the Cuban's free fist slammed into his opponent's face.

The Scot swayed from the blow and swung a wild roundhouse stroke with the dirk. Encizo dodged the attack and slashed his Tanto across William's left forearm. The sharp steel sliced the heavy fabric of the terrorist's sleeve and cut into flesh. William cried out in pain, but tossed the dirk to his right hand. He suddenly stepped forward, knees bent, head and shoulders low in a fencer's thrust aimed at Encizo's stomach.

Encizo swerved away from the lunge, but the blade caught him along the left rib cage. The dirk point pierced his jacket and shirt, and he felt the burning pain of sharp steel along his flesh. The blade had grazed him, and the cut was shallow. Encizo had been cut before in knife fights and realized it wasn't serious, although a bolt of terror rode up his spine like an icy dart.

His free hand swooped low and seized William's wrist above the dirk. The Scot had extended his arm too far when he executed the lunge and he failed to draw back before Encizo could grab the wrist. Encizo punched the Tanto into his opponent's midsection and drove three inches of sharp steel into William's stomach. The Scot howled in agony as hot blood splashed over Encizo's wrist.

The Phoenix pro released the Tanto handle and left the knife buried in William's flesh. The terrorist clawed at the knife handle with his left hand and tried to dislodge the Tanto. Encizo grabbed William's right wrist with both hands, raised the arm and ducked under it. Stepping behind the Scot, he pulled the arm back in a hammerlock. Encizo grabbed his opponent's hair with one hand and shoved the wrist with the other. William's own dirk stabbed into his right kidney, and five inches of double-edged steel sunk deep into his flesh.

William Bruce opened his mouth and uttered a despairing wail. A low gurgle terminated the cry, then Encizo felt the Scot's body go limp and allowed him to fall to the ground. Massive shock and blood loss had taken their toll. William twitched slightly and died at Encizo's feet.

"Rafael," McCarter said in a soft voice as he entered the alley. "You okay?"

"Yeah," the Cuban said, and turned to face the Briton. "Tried to take this guy alive, but it didn't work out that way. How are the others?"

"One of the constables is dead, and the other almost had a heart attack," McCarter replied. "He'll be all right when he stops shaking. Gary found a fire extinguisher and managed to put out the fire before the car was completely totaled. Most of the terrorists are dead except for two or three. Hope they can answer some questions."

"That would be good," Encizo said with a weary nod.

10

Scotland Yard Inspector Fellows, SIS case officer Henderson and Davis, the CIA man, arrived in Glasgow shortly after dawn. They deplaned at the airstrip commanded by Major Simms and his troops. Phoenix Force and Superintendent Sutherland waited for them in the hangar.

"Good morning, gentlemen," Yakov Katzenelenbogen greeted, a Styrofoam cup of tea in his left hand and a Camel cigarette held between the hooks of his prosthesis. "We weren't expecting you, Mr. Davis."

"I'm here to deliver a message," the CIA officer said glumly. "Some hotshot in D.C. contacted the Embassy about an hour ago. A 'Mr. Smith' wants you to report to him at 0900 hours on the dot. Sounded pissed."

"That's too bad for him," Gary Manning muttered. The Canadian was in a bad mood because he'd had to drink tea instead of coffee that morning.

"We can find out what he wants later," Rafael Encizo commented. He winced as he shifted his weight and felt the sting of the bandaged wound at his ribcage. "How's your arm, Inspector?"

"Just scratched up a bit," Fellows answered with a thin smile. "I consider myself to be a mighty lucky bloke. After all, few people are ever minorly wounded by a shotgun blast. Speaking of which, I reckon you people saw some action last night."

"You heard about it already?" Katz asked with surprise.

"It's a major news story in London," Henderson replied. "A gun battle in Glasgow isn't an everyday event. Sounded like it might be you chaps."

"We were there," David McCarter remarked. Major Simms had accompanied the arrivals into the hangar. The Phoenix pro exchanged hard glances with his former SAS commander, but neither man prolonged the gaze. The others were aware of their mutual antagonism, and it would only make matters worse to remind them of the friction.

"Well, our search of official records turned up a bit of information on Garrett O'Flynn," Henderson said, taking a brown envelope from his coat pocket. "The fellow who's supposed to be in charge of the IRA cell connected with these terrorists is a proper villain. His name has popped up from time to time ever since 1975. One of Seamus Costello's enforcers with the Irish National Liberation Army in those days."

"The INLA earned the reputation for being the most ferocious Irish extremists in Europe," McCarter explained for the benefit of others less well versed with the IRA. "Conducted a fair amount of terrorism against the Republic of Ireland to the south of Northern Ireland. Accused them of being a bunch of traitors. A bunch of nasty bleeders, and they don't have any qualms about killing civilians."

"O'Flynn certainly doesn't have any qualms about it," Henderson stated as he handed the envelope to Katz. "Got a photograph of him, but it's about ten years old. Savage young man in his early twenties. Oh, he moved back into the mainstream of the IRA by 1979, but we suspect that was more to recruit new chaps for his own splinter group a couple years ago. Interpol claims he's been connected with the German Red Army Faction and possibly the Italian Red Brigade in the past, but there isn't much detail about his activities at the time. Suspected for numerous acts of violence, including murder, sabotage, several bombings and more than a dozen cases of maiming fellow Irishmen he felt were British sympathizers. Knee-capped victims with a power drill, punctured eardrums with a penny nail, smashed fingers with sledgehammers and at least one poor bastard's eyes were gouged out.''

"Disgusting," Sutherland said, shaking his head with dismay. "And this Irish lunatic is working with the Iron Claymore fanatics?"

"Iron Claymore?" Fellows asked, eyebrow cocked with interest.

Katz pointed to the workbench where the miniature emblem of an iron claymore was displayed. The Scotland Yard inspector and the SIS officer nodded in recognition of the terrorist symbol.

"We found this on the body of one of the ambushers after last night's firefight," Katz explained. "Mr. Brown killed the man in a knife fight, but we learned by interrogating three survivors among the terrorists that the fellow with the iron claymore was in fact the team commander."

"Hell," Calvin James began as he emerged from a bathroom and approached the others. "The guys we questioned under scopolamine claimed that son of a bitch was a Scottish prince!"

"What?" Henderson replied with astonishment. "You're joking!"

"I joke better than this," James assured him.

"They told us they belong to an organization, or perhaps a secret society would be a better term, called the Clan of the Iron Claymore," Katz explained. "Some of the terrorists who attacked us last night belonged to the IRA, but none of the Irish terrorists survived the battle. A fellow named Kehoe was among the corpses. Supposedly he was one of O'Flynn's top men. Our friend with the iron claymore symbol called himself William Bruce. He's apparently one of four sons of a man who claims to be a direct descendant of Robert Bruce."

"You mean the first king of Scotland?" Davis inquired. "That's the guy who kept fighting British soldiers and couldn't win until he watched a spider spinning its web over and over again until it succeeded in building the damn thing?"

"You got something against arachnid education?" McCarter replied. "Robert Bruce learned determination from watching that spider—or so the legend goes."

"Yeah, yeah," the Company man snorted. "So these wackos with the Iron Claymore outfit are trying to get Scotland independent so this crazy so-called king can take over?"

"That's essentially right," Katz confirmed. "Of course, they really believe Andrew Robert Bruce—if indeed this is his real name—to be genuine. They're monarchists, but as fanatically devout as any religious or political extremist. In fact, they're a bit of both, since they believe the 'king' will establish self-rule in Scotland and drive out the British to allow their country to be run from within. They also believe they're carrying out a righteous mission to put a man of royal bloodline on the throne. Two of the terrorists insisted this was 'God's will' because their leader is·supposedly heir to the throne of Robert I."

"Rubbish," Henderson snorted. "Scotland doesn't want self-rule. They had it on the ballot a few years ago and rejected independence."

"Not quite," Sutherland stated dryly. "It was a referendum that nearly all Scots found fault with. Less than forty percent of registered voters cast their ballots in favor of it in March, 1979, but that doesn't mean the rest approve of British rule. It simply means they didn't accept the conditions of the referendum."

"I don't think Scotland would like self-rule under a crazy self-appointed king like Andrew Bruce," James remarked. "The prisoners say he'll establish absolute control of goods and services, enforce laws to reaffirm morality and grant the 'agents of the crown' the right to do whatever necessary to carry out these goals. Now, I'm not real sure what all that stuff means, but I kind'a figure it gets down to Dandy Andy setting himself up as a Scottish Hitler, and his terrorist flunkies of the Iron Claymore will be his 'agents of the crown' or something like the Gestapo.''

"Bloody wonderful, isn't it?'' McCarter added. "Blokes who use murder and terrorism for political expression figure they can force 'morality' on other people. Hard to tell what that term even means to them.''

"These lunatics will never accomplish any of their absurd goals,'' Sutherland insisted. "This so-called king isn't a descendant of Robert Bruce, and the people of Scotland are not gullible enough to believe his insane claims. They most certainly will never go along with such madness.''

"Of course not,'' Manning agreed. "Except for the followers of the Iron Claymore, naturally. The odds of Bruce taking over Scotland are nonexistent. The danger lies in what he'll do in the attempt to carry out his plan.''

"What's O'Flynn doing in this mess?'' Inspector Fellows wondered aloud. "Grant it, the man's a political extremist, even by IRA standards, but he doesn't seem to be a fool. Why's his cell helping these Iron Claymore morons?''

"Maybe he thinks it's crazy enough to work,'' Encizo replied. "If it did, Scotland would become a friendly and cooperative neighbor for the IRA in Northern Ireland. O'Flynn probably knows better than to think it will succeed. My guess is he's joined forces with the Iron Claymore clan in order to stir up enough trouble to draw British troops out of Ireland and into Scotland.''

"Okay,'' Davis said with a shrug. "So, why kidnap McGreggor and come up with a bunch of crap about recognizing this senile dipstick as king of Scotland? The U.S. government isn't about to do that, and O'Flynn ought to know better.''

"Some terrorists have lost all touch with reality," Katz stated. "You consider the most ridiculous notion you ever heard, and if you look long enough and hard enough, you can find someone who believes that notion to be true. There are still people who believe the world is flat or that hoop snakes and mermaids really exist. Some think Hitler was a misunderstood statesman and the Holocaust never happened. O'Flynn may or may not believe Bruce's scheme will work. More likely he agreed to the terrorist strikes against Americans because it will eventually reflect on the British government. Scotland is part of Great Britain, so London will start getting the blame for being unable to protect American citizens on her soil."

"That's uncalled for!" Henderson said, clearly offended.

"It still happens all the time," Katz insisted. "At any rate, O'Flynn's motives aren't really important, and speculation is a waste of time. Maybe the idea of kidnapping McGreggor and demanding recognition by the United States for the monarchy of Andrew Bruce was all the demented king's invention, and O'Flynn had to go along with it to remain part of the outfit. What really matters is finding the enemy. We now know who we're up against, but we don't know where they are."

"Those captive terrorists didn't tell you that?" Fellows asked with a frown.

"Nope," James answered. "They were recruited for this cause a couple years ago when King Brucey and his four fun-loving kids were in Edinburgh. They didn't know where the old man got to or where McGreggor might be held hostage. William, the dead son, and his two older brothers—Angus and Duncan—have been the field commanders of the Scottish terrorists, but they haven't told the lower-ranking clan members where daddy hangs out these days. The king isn't making any public appearances until he's sure he can tell the whole world he's in control of Scotland."

"So, what do we do now?" Fellows inquired, clearly baffled.

"Not much point in staying in Glasgow," Katz replied. "The enemy saw us at this airstrip and guessed we might be CIA. To find out, they set off an explosion on a ship in port at the harbor to see if we'd rush out of the hotel to head down to the docks. When we responded, they tried to ambush and terminate us. Apparently the entire Claymore clan and all the IRA stooges stationed in Glasgow hit us last night. None of them got away, so there aren't any opponents left here. The only lead we've got is Edinburgh. Most of the terrorists had been there until recently. Including, I might add, William Bruce."

"You say he was a knife fighter?" Fellows mused. "Perhaps William was the bastard who murdered poor Mr. Macklin. The killer used a dirk, you know."

"That was the same type of knife he tried to use on me last night," Encizo confirmed. "I don't know if he murdered Macklin, but he was sure trying to kill me when we exchanged blades in the alley."

"Too bad you killed him, Mr. Brown," Henderson remarked with a sigh.

"Didn't seem like much of a tragedy at the time," Encizo replied with a shrug.

"We'd better get ready to leave," Katz advised. "I'll contact Mr. Smith in Washington and see what he wants."

"I doubt it'll be good news," Manning said grimly.

"I don't expect it to be," Katz assured him.

DANIEL MCGGREGGOR sat in an armchair and tried to concentrate on reading *Great Expectations*. It was one of several leather-bound books on a single wall shelf in McGreggor's cell. The hostage had always enjoyed the works of Dickens, but it was small comfort under the circumstances.

Aside from denying his freedom, Andrew Robert Bruce and the others hadn't mistreated McGreggor. The cell was relatively comfortable, with a bed, table, chair, sink and toilet. A single electric bulb provided light from the ceiling, and McGreggor had been supplied with books, a deck of cards and a small plastic chess set to occupy his time. Guards posted outside the door would bring McGreggor needed items like clean towels, extra blankets and Scoresby whiskey if he requested them. The American had found himself drinking a fair amount of the 86-proof Scotch whiskey. Scoresby was distilled in Scotland and had long been a favorite brand of his. Though he had never been much of a drinker, he found that in his situation the slight bite and warm caress of alcohol in his stomach brought more comfort than *Great Expectations*.

He had drunk himself into a stupor the night before and regretted it the following day. Scoresby is a fine drink for sipping in moderation but packs a fierce retribution when consumed in excess. McGreggor suffered a throbbing hangover in the morning. His stomach and head were still recovering from the bout of drunken indulgence. He knew better than to repeat that action. Things were bad enough without barfing his guts up every night and waking up with a jackhammer inside his head.

McGreggor wondered how his family was dealing with his disappearance. His wife was certainly worried sick, and the kids were in college, although they may have come home to help their mother cope with the crisis. The businesses were probably doing all right without him, but McGreggor always fretted about corporate takeovers by the competition. The Wall Street stock crash in 1987 had scared the hell out of him, but his businesses had survived the ordeal. It all seemed pretty mild compared to the situation he found himself faced with.

He was afraid of dying. McGreggor had been ruthless in matters of business in the past, and many people had lost their jobs because of his actions. Smaller businesses had folded. People's careers and reputations may have been ruined because McGreggor had been concerned only with his desires for more wealth and power. He was not a particularly religious man, but he now worried about what sort of final judgment God might decree for his soul. Jesus had said something about a rich man entering heaven being as difficult as a camel walking through the eye of a needle. McGreggor hoped it hadn't been a literal statement or that perhaps the eye to the needle was twelve feet high and four feet across and a rather small camel had to pass through it.

McGreggor promised himself he'd change his ways if he survived his current situation. He would give more to charities, help people instead of using them, pay more attention to his family and reject the temptations of greed for money and political influence. That's the reason he had been captured by the terrorists. If that was the price for power, then who needs it? he told himself after taking stock of his abject helplessness.

The cell's door burst open, and Malcolm Bruce appeared in the doorway. His expression was wild, the features of his face contorted by grief and anger. The young Scot unbuckled his belt as he charged into the cell. McGreggor gasped with surprise and fear. He recalled how Malcolm had flogged one of the other men with the brass-studded leather strap. The short-tempered youth looked as though he was ready to do the same to McGreggor.

"Yeh bastard!" Malcolm hissed as he raised the belt in his left fist.

"Hold on!" one of the guards exclaimed as he hastily entered the cell. "We been told no harm should come to the Yank!"

McGreggor started to rise from his chair. Malcolm stepped forward and swung the belt. The American raised his arms to protect his face and head, and the belt slammed across his forearm and elbow. McGreggor yelped with pain and dropped the Dickens book. Malcolm prepared to lash him again, but the guard grabbed his left arm.

"Please, Prince Malcolm!" the sentry urged.

Malcolm drove his elbow back into the guard's sternum. The man groaned and lost his grip, then Malcolm pivoted and whipped his belt across the guard's shoulders. The other sentry stood at the doorway, unsure of what to do, while his partner covered his head with his arms, unwilling to try to defend himself more aggressively against Malcolm.

The youth flogged him across the back and shoulders twice more and stepped forward to deliver a right upper-cut. The guard straightened up from the punch, and Malcolm lashed the belt across his ribs. The blow sent the guard stumbling backward into his partner.

"Ne'er lay hands on me, yeh commoner trash!" Malcolm snarled. "The Yank is gonna pay for what happened to me brother, as God be me witness!"

"No, Malcolm!" Angus declared as he shoved his way through the entrance of the cell. "This changes nothing. Leave the Yank be, Malcolm."

Malcolm glared at his older brother and wrapped the belt around his left fist as if he intended to use it as a cestus. But he refrained from attacking Angus. Malcolm uttered a sound that resembled a cross between a groan and a sob. Then he bolted from the cell, suddenly eager to be away from the others.

"What the hell was that all about?" McGreggor demanded, and backed into a corner, afraid they may have decided to kill him.

"Our people in Edinburgh reported to us this morn with news of an attack on some CIA agents in Glasgow," Angus said grimly. "William, our brother, led the attack. It failed. William was killed."

"I see," McGreggor said slowly, trying to think of how to best handle the development. "I'm sorry."

"Oh, I doubt that," Angus replied. his tone hard. "William and Malcolm were close. He's taking this hard. Malcolm wants revenge. That be a feeling we all share. Me father took this news hard, too. He didn't weep, of course. Not in front of us, that is. A king must grieve in private."

"King?" McGreggor snorted. "You people really think you can get away with this crap? No one is going to recognize your father as King of Scotland. Why don't you try to convince him to give this up before it's too late? Before he gets you all killed—"

"Still your tongue, Yank!" Angus warned, his eyes flashing with anger as he sent a threatening stare at the American. "Me father be head of the clan. The Clan of the Iron Claymore is destined to reestablish the crown of Scotland under the rightful king. We've worked at this goal since I be a wee lad. Me brothers and I swore on the grave of our mother we would ne'er desert our father. He rules the clan and we follow. That be the way of proper sons. They obey their father and remain loyal to the family, no matter what."

"Look," McGreggor began. "You people took me prisoner, but I'm not your enemy. So you want independence for Scotland? That's fine with me. This isn't the way to do it, Angus. Let me go, and I'll help you go about this legally..."

"Yeh do not seem injured by Malcolm's attack," Angus said bluntly. "Perhaps yeh should rest for now."

The guards had already left the cell. Angus followed and checked the man Malcolm had worked over with the belt. The guard nodded to assure Angus he was all right. One of them closed the door and locked it.

"Oh, God," McGreggor whispered and glanced about the walls of his cell. "What's going to happen now?"

11

Major Simms had a small communications section at the hangar. Yakov Katzenelenbogen used the transatlantic transceiver radio unit to contact Washington, D.C. The Phoenix Force commander set the frequency according to the information from Davis and donned the headset before he spoke into the microphone.

"Echo Gray calling Mr. Smith," he announced. "Mr. Smith, do you read me? Over."

The transmission was sent to a special telecommunications satellite designed for use by Phoenix Force and other branches of Stony Man operations. It simultaneously transferred radio broadcasts on specific frequencies and scrambled signals to make it almost impossible to trace the transmissions or identify voices by any radio-tracking devices.

"Echo Gray, this is Mr. Smith," a slightly distorted voice replied from the headset. Katz knew the voice belonged to Hal Brognola. "Read you loud and clear. Are you receiving? Over."

"Affirmative, Mr. Smith," Katz confirmed.

"Heard there was some trouble in the European market," Brognola declared. "Got the news yesterday and this morning. It was on television here. Wondered if it affected your business trip."

"We've been concerned about it," Katz answered.

"The boss is worried, too," Brognola explained. "Talked to him today, and he thinks you should come home if business continues to go badly. Worried about how it might reflect on matters here. You understand, Echo Gray?"

"I understand," the Phoenix commander replied, "but we're getting closer to closing the deal here. Need more time."

"The boss is nervous," Brognola stated. "He thinks you may be making things worse instead of better. I tried to convince him to be patient, but he has doubts about all of us. The entire firm may have to shut down if you can't wrap things up by the end of the week."

"That's less than three days, Mr. Smith," Katz told him.

"I know," Brognola said. "Sure hope you get lucky. Over and out, Echo Gray."

"Over and out," Katz answered, and switched off the radio.

He joined the other members of Phoenix Force and their allies. They knew from his expression that he didn't have good news. The Israeli took out his cigarettes and lit one before he spoke.

"That was our control officer in the States," Katz began. "The message was for my team, but I feel you all have a right to know what he said."

"What's that?" Henderson asked with interest.

"He didn't spell it out," Katz began, "but it's obvious our incidents in London and Glasgow received press coverage in America as well as here. The President is worried about it. He probably thinks we're just piling up a large body-count, with no other results. He wants us to wrap up the mission in the next three days or scrap it and go home."

"Bloody hell," McCarter said, stunned by the news. "He can't put a deadline on something like this! We've made some progress, but there's no way we can be sure of completing the mission in just three days."

"I know that as well as you do, Mr. Black," Katz reminded him, "but that's still his decision."

"The President's worried about a scandal and some bad publicity," Calvin James said with disgust. "That's what it's all about."

"He's new to the office," Rafael Encizo said with a shrug. "The former President had doubts about us from time to time. We still have to break this new guy in."

"We may not get the chance," Gary Manning said with a dour expression. "Isn't that right?"

"Smith said the President may terminate the 'firm,' which I took to mean that our organization may be scrapped," Katz confirmed. "We might be out of business soon, but the mission is still our primary concern."

"For the next three days, at least," James muttered.

"Do we still go to Edinburgh?" Superintendent Sutherland wanted to know.

"It's our only move," Katz answered. "Edinburgh is your jurisdiction, Superintendent. Most of the terrorists from last night had formerly been in your city. They had a base outside of town. It may still be there, although the terrorists will probably abandon it when they realize the team in Glasgow won't be coming back."

"Maybe we'll get lucky and the bastards will still be there," Simms remarked.

"It's worth a try," the Phoenix commander agreed. He turned toward Henderson and Davis. "You two might as well return to London. We'll need someone there, and we can always call you in if we need you here."

"Right," Henderson agreed. "I'll see if SIS can turn up anything on this Andrew Robert Bruce and his demented sons."

"The Glasgow police will supply you with photographs and fingerprints," Sutherland told him. "That may help you get more information about the terrorists, including the late William Bruce. Scotland Yard might also assist in this. Inspector?''

''The Yard will help,'' Inspector Fellows assured him, ''but I choose to stay here instead of going back to London. The case has become a bit personal for me, and I'd rather not handle it from a desk.''

''Let's figure out the details as we get ready for our trip to Edinburgh,'' McCarter suggested.

THE STREETS OF EDINBURGH were no busier than usual. Public transportation in the city is very efficient, and relatively few residents drive cars. No one paid much attention to the blue and white tour bus on Upper High Street. It looked like any other bus, except the windows were tinted to prevent outsiders from peering in.

Phoenix Force was among the passengers. Major Simms, Sergeant Hutton and five other SAS troops were also seated inside the bus. Inspector Fellows, Superintendent Sutherland and six constables comprised the rest. All were armed with automatic rifles, submachine guns or shotguns, in addition to an assortment of side arms.

The bus passed Parliament House. Built in 1632 by order of King Charles I, the majestic building no longer served its original purpose. Edinburgh had once been the capital of the Scottish nation. When Scotland merged with Britain in 1707, the Scottish Parliament had been dissolved. Parliament House remains the seat of Scotland's supreme court, and Edinburgh is still the unofficial capital.

Edinburgh is one of the great cities of Europe. Beautiful and filled with historical sites, it has been called the heart of Scotland. Edinburgh is certainly a center of Scottish culture and education and is the most important financial base in Scotland. Major Scottish banks have their headquarters there. Less industrialized than Glasgow, Edinburgh is still the second largest city in Scotland and is home to numerous manufacturing and publishing concerns.

Yet visitors are most impressed by the monuments of Scottish history that seem to be everywhere one looks in Edinburgh. The Royal Mile in "Old Town" consists of four streets of fascinating history and architectural marvels. The Canongate Tollbooth, a medieval structure with turreted towers, and the High Kirk of Edinburgh, easily identified by a great crownlike spire, are the best known features on the "mile." However, there are also several sixteenth-century houses and museums located here that deserve the attention of any visitor interested in Scottish history.

Indeed, Edinburgh boasts many great museums. The Phoenix Force bus rolled past the Museum of Childhood on High Street. McCarter recognized it and smiled as he recalled his boyhood visits to this charming museum with its unique collections of toys, dolls, games and other items associated with children. In the distance, the National Gallery was visible at the Mound. McCarter could not see the Royal Museum from his window, but he remembered it vividly from the past. The Royal Museum is enormous, and McCarter believed one could acquire a sound education in Scottish history by spending enough time there. Natural history, science, medieval war and craftsmanship were themes covered in remarkable detail at the museum.

"Man, this city is really something," James remarked as he stared out a window at the magnificent Gothic-style spires of the monument to Sir Walter Scott that towered above the East Prince's Gardens.

"You could probably spend a couple years here and not see everything," McCarter told him. "Edinburgh Castle has to be seen to be appreciated. It's been a fortress of one sort or another since the sixth century. The Scottish Regalia is kept there. Royal jewels, crown and scepter."

"I guess Andrew Robert Bruce figures he'll just stroll in here one day and have them hand over that lot to him when he becomes king," Major Simms remarked.

"When we catch up with him," Gary Manning replied as he examined a report form from the Glasgow police, "we'll ask him."

"What's that?" Encizo asked, curious about the Canadian's reading material.

"Analysis of the explosion on the ship back at the harbor in Glasgow," Manning explained. "Apparently the terrorists used regular stick dynamite to set off that explosion. Sort of old-fashioned for modern terrorists."

"IRA uses fertilizer bombs," Simms reminded him.

"Yeah," the Canadian agreed, "but that's improvised explosives. Terrorists only use it when they can't get their hands on military explosives. Plastic RDX compounds like C-4. Stick dynamite suggests they probably got it from civilian sources. Construction crews, demolitions outfits, something like that."

"Well," Superintendent Sutherland began as he took a .38-caliber Colt Police Positive revolver from a coat pocket. He opened the cylinder and checked the chambers. "The place we're headed for is an old food processing plant in Granton, by the Edinburgh port. It's been shut down since 1977. The port is largely concerned with North Sea petroleum these days. Canning fish doesn't make as big a profit as drilling oil. Not for the English, at any rate."

"What's that supposed to mean?" Simms demanded, a trace of accusation in his voice.

"It means we Scots wish you British would either stop off-coast drilling in the North Sea or allow us to share equally in the profits," Sutherland replied, and shoved the Colt into his pocket.

"I seem to recall the drilling is being done by British outfits with British engineers," the major answered.

"They didn't bother to hire many Scots to work those rigs," Sutherland stated. "We've had a great deal of unemployment in East Scotland for a long time. Many a man around these parts could use the work."

"Maybe they don't have the skills," Simms said with a shrug.

"Maybe the English could teach them," the Scot replied.

Several constables expressed their support for Sutherland's position. Sergeant Hutton shook his head as if he considered the Scots foolish to think they could do a job as well as an Englishman. Katz, however, wanted the debate brought to an abrupt end. The unit had been put together in a hurry and would not function as a single, well-conditioned team under the best circumstances. They didn't need any more problems among its members.

"We ought to be getting close to Granton," the Israeli announced. "I want everyone ready before we get there. Weapons loaded, instructions understood and everyone working together to carry this off as smoothly as possible."

Some of the police had not loaded their weapons. They carried pump-action 12-gauge shotguns and .38 revolvers. The constables fed shells into their firearms. The SAS troops were far more familiar with weapons than the Scottish lawmen. Armed with Belgian-made FAL rifles and Sterling submachine guns, the soldiers were ready for combat. Grenades, magazine pouches, fighting knives and holstered pistols hung on their belts and harness straps.

Phoenix Force was armed with their weapons of choice. Katz carried his SIG-Sauer pistol in shoulder leather under his right armpit and kept the Uzi within easy reach. McCarter wore his pet Browning in a shoulder holster, and the .38 S&W was at the base of his spine for back up. The Briton's KG-99 hung from a shoulder strap by his right hand.

Manning's FAL assault rifle was propped against the seat beside him, and he carried his Walther P-5 pistol in addition to a small backpack loaded with explosives. James had an M-16 rifle with an M-203 grenade launcher attached to the underside of the barrel. The black commando wore a Jackass Leather rig with the Beretta pistol holstered under one arm and a Jet Aer G-96 dagger sheathed under the other. He also carried the snub-nosed .357 Colt for back up.

Encizo had his Heckler & Koch machine pistol in his lap. The H&K P-9S autoloader was secure in a hip holster, and a Walther PPK was sheathed in shoulder leather. The Cold Steel Tanto was in a belt scabbard, and a Gerber Mark I dagger was clipped to the top of his boot. All five men also carried spare ammo magazines, grenades, garrotes and other equipment.

Phoenix Force had loaded the magazines of their 9 mm weapons with Federal ammunition. They had chosen 124-grain Hydra Shok hollowpoints and NATO hardball. The magazines were "Dutch loaded"; hollowpoint and hardball cartridges alternately fed into each mag.

"The port is up ahead," Sutherland announced. "We're almost at the Granton area. Shan't be long now, laddies."

THE FOOD PROCESSING CENTER near the Granton port appeared to be deserted as Phoenix Force and their allies approached. They used a heather-covered hill for camouflage as they crept closer. Most of the plant had already been dismantled. Cannery machines, cutting and washing equipment had been removed, as well as furnaces and packing gear. The single structure that remained had no electricity, running water or heat. No vehicles were parked near the forgotten ruins, and no one stirred except two elderly men just beyond the edge of the property.

The pair moved slowly, a little bit stiff with age, their backs bent by the burden of many decades of lives that were often difficult. Both walked with the assistance of a cane, and one man carried a string of fish and a pole. They wore plaid kilts, knee socks, kilt jackets and bonnets. Furry sporran pouches hung in front of the kilts. Neither of them paid much attention to the cold wind that stirred their white whiskers and played with the hems of the kilts.

"Hey, Dave," Calvin James whispered to McCarter as they watched the elderly Scots from the ridge of the hill. "Is it really true they don't wear anything under those kilts?"

"What a question," the Briton muttered with disgust. "Whatever you do, don't ask that question to any of the Scots. They tend to be sensitive about the subject. Figure it's none of your business unless you intend to wear a kilt."

"I'm not asking them. I'm asking you," James insisted. "I mean, in this kind'a weather wouldn't they wear underpants? Otherwise they'd freeze their nuts off . . ."

Katz whispered orders to the men in the improvised assault unit. He told them to wait for the two civilians to get clear of the area, but he asked Sutherland to send two constables after the pair to detain them for questioning and stay with them during the raid. Two old men in kilts were pretty unlikely terrorists, but Andrew Robert Bruce was said to be in his sixties; it was possible some of the older residents might be helping the monarchists or might simply know something about recent activities at the abandoned plant.

There was also the vague possibility that the civilians may not be what they seemed. A clever makeup job and some convincing acting could allow two young fanatics to appear to be harmless senior citizens out for a stroll. Katz warned Sutherland to instruct his officers to handle the situation with equal degrees of caution and tact. If the two were simply a pair of innocent bystanders, the officers needed to stay with them for protection. If they were enemies in disguise, the constables had better be on guard and expect the unexpected.

Katz also told Sutherland to have the rest of the Edinburgh police patrol the surrounding area to both watch for civilians and enemy reinforcements. The Superintendent realized the Phoenix commander's concerns were genuine, but he also knew Katz was giving the constables the tasks that involved the least risk. Katz had assigned the police duties best suited for what they had been trained to handle.

Phoenix Force and the SAS troops were obviously better prepared to take on the primary role of the raid.

Inspector Fellows was clearly miffed when Katz told him to follow orders from Sutherland and accompany the Scottish constables. The Phoenix commander didn't have time to argue and simply told Fellows to shut up and do what he was told. The SAS soldiers who were armed with rifles were instructed to remain at the ridge for backup with Major Simms in command. The other four troopers would accompany Phoenix Force. Sergeant Hutton looked at Simms for confirmation. The major nodded.

"All right," Hutton announced, and unslung his Sterling subgun from a shoulder. "How do we hit them?"

"Front and back," Katz answered. "Use concussion grenades on the doors. Toss them and duck behind cover. Doors might be booby trapped. You know the routine. Watch the windows and stay alert when you get inside. The men at the hill will cover our backs, but when we get into the building we'll be on our own. Be ready for trouble, but not too quick with the trigger. There might be some hobo living in there. We don't want any innocent blood today."

"Those dudes in the kilts are finally out of sight," James announced. "By the way, do any of you know if they wear anything under those things?"

"No," Simms answered with a shrug.

"Is that 'no, they don't' or 'no, you don't know'?"

"How about 'no time to ask silly questions'?" McCarter growled. "Let's get on with our job."

The five Phoenix commandos and the four SAS soldiers headed for the building. There was virtually no cover from the hill to the plant, so they simply advanced in a quick-step, backs arched and heads low, weapons held ready. Encizo lobbed a concussion grenade at the front door. The men rushed to cover at both ends of the building. The grenade exploded, and the door was torn from its hinges. No booby-trap blast erupted in response. Another flash-bang grenade blew open the back door, with the same results.

They entered the building quickly. Phoenix Force and the SAS troops took turns covering each other as they rushed inside. The barrels of their weapons swept from side to side, but there was no one in the old structure to offer any threat.

"Damn it," Hutton muttered with disappointment. "The bastards are already gone."

"We don't know that for sure," Katz told him. "Spread out in 3-man groups. Search every room, closet, and check for a basement."

The interior of the building was even more rundown and ugly than the outside. Cobwebs hung across the ceiling beams and corners. Moldy cardboard lay scattered across the floors. Rats squealed in protest and scurried for cover. Graffiti had been scrawled across the walls, with messages ranging from political protests to graphic obscenities.

Indeed, there was little evidence anyone had been there, until they investigated the other rooms. Katz grunted with satisfaction when he and Encizo discovered a small room with mattresses on the floor and a large metal trash barrel in a corner. The absence of dust on the floor and lack of cobwebs were further evidence it had been recently occupied.

"Cute," Encizo remarked as he carefully stepped over a mattress. "They left the bay area looking like the place hadn't been touched for years in case someone only peered through a window from the outside. Help to prevent rumors about strangers living in this old dump. Not much fun staying here, I imagine, but I suppose it served as a temporary barracks."

"Not likely anyone stayed here for long periods of time," Katz remarked, and gazed up at a large black smudge that stained the wall and ceiling above the barrel. "This appears to be a short-term safehouse, but they probably always had someone here. Different people. Alternate them so they didn't go stir-crazy in a place like this."

"Yeah," Enciso said, "but you know terrorists as well as I do. They generally receive limited training. Crash courses in explosives, firearms, murder and mayhem, with fundamental strategy and tactics thrown in. Most of them like to play spy until they learn how boring it usually turns out to be. You worked for all the major Intelligence networks of the Western world in the past. You know better than I what the run-of-the-mill espionage work is like."

"I know," Katz replied, still examining the soot marks. "Many a terrorist has been captured because he or she couldn't handle the boredom and stress of simply sitting around waiting for something to happen. I was in West Germany in 1974, attached with BND at the time, when the Munich police arrested four members of the 2nd June Movement because they got in a fistfight in their apartment and the neighbors called the cops."

"What was the fight about?" Enciso asked.

"They couldn't agree about where to go for dinner," Katz explained as he leaned over the barrel and inserted the hooks of his prosthesis into a pile of ashes and partially burned papers. "Wonder what we have here."

"Maybe they burned stuff to keep the room warm," Enciso suggested. "Probably freezing in here at night. It's not exactly cozy now."

"No," the Israeli stated. "If they used this thing for a crude heater every night, the walls would be covered with soot instead of only this area. Besides, they'd probably asphyxiate if they burned enough material to keep the room warm. This barrel is half-empty."

"So they burned some stuff in a hurry," Enciso remarked. "Maybe some evidence if we're lucky."

"Maybe," Katz replied as he gingerly lifted a thick multicolored piece of paper. Much of it was badly charred. "This looks like part of a map. I don't want to mess with it. Might destroy something that can only be reconstructed in a lab. Let's see what the Edinburgh police can make of it.''

"Right," the Cuban agreed. "Better check on the others and make sure they don't—"

The blast of an explosion interrupted Encizo. The sound resembled the report of a shotgun—at least a 10-gauge. The Phoenix pair bolted from the room, weapons ready for action. They encountered Manning and two SAS soldiers in the bay section, but they were as puzzled as Encizo and Katz.

"What was that?" Encizo wondered aloud.

"You're asking me?" Manning replied.

James emerged from another room, the M-16 in his fists. He stared at the others, obviously looking for an answer. McCarter appeared from the back door of the building. He displayed a massive shrug to tell the others he was baffled.

"Shit," James rasped. "We under attack or not?"

"Maybe it's a sonic boom," McCarter suggested. "Nothing outside, as far as I can tell. Simms and the others are headed this way, so they must have heard it, too."

"Where's Hutton and the other soldier?" Katz asked as he took a quick head count and found they were two short.

"Sergeant went down into the basement with Miller," an SAS commando answered. He turned to lead the others to the spot even as he spoke.

Manning and James followed close behind the soldier. Katz gestured for the others to stay put and accompanied the trio to the basement. The black commando switched on a pocket flashlight and shone the beam on the stairs below. A figure stirred at the bottom of the steps.

"Miller!" the soldier called out when he recognized his mate.

James descended the stairs, followed by Manning. The flashlight beam danced across Miller's form. The soldier groaned as he tried to move up the stairs on all fours. James jumped down the last few steps and landed next to Miller.

He swung his light and the barrel of the M-16 toward the shadows within the basement. It was drab and dank. Some wooden pallets were lined along the wall. The still figure of Sergeant Hutton lay beside a shattered pallet. Chunks of wood were scattered across the NCO's body. Some crackled with flames.

"Bejesus," the black warrior rasped. "Must have triggered a booby trap."

Manning came down to join his partner. The demolitions expert drew in his breath in a hiss and fished a pocket flashlight from his field jacket.

"Stay back," he instructed as he trained the beam on the smashed pallet and Hutton's body. "Get the soldier upstairs, but check for any chunks from that pallet first. You find any on his clothes or hair, pick it up gently and put it down very carefully."

"What's this about, Green?" Katz asked, managing to remember the Canadian's cover name.

"The pallet . . ." Miller began in a groggy voice. "It just blew up right in front of the sergeant . . ."

"Did he toss a cigarette or a match on it or do anything to cause sparks?" Gary Manning inquired.

"He lit a cigarette," Miller answered with a feeble nod. "Didn't see what he did with the match."

"I think I know," the Canadian declared, and walked to Hutton's motionless form.

"Mind sharing that information?" Katz asked, frustrated with Manning's coy attitude.

"The terrorists probably stored dynamite here," Manning explained as he knelt by Hutton and placed two fingers to the side of his neck. He didn't find a pulse at the carotid. "Hutton's dead."

"I still don't understand what the hell happened," James complained. He inspected Miller's clothing and found no pieces of the pallet. Some small splinters were in the soldier's hair, and he carefully plucked them out and placed the fragments on the stone floor.

Manning didn't reply until he picked up a piece of wood near Hutton's corpse and held it to his nose. He gently lowered it to the floor and glanced over his shoulder to face the others.

"The dynamite was kept here," the Canadian explained. "The basement is cool and dark, and they stacked it on the pallets. Dynamite should always be kept away from metal or stone, anything that might spark. That was okay, but apparently whoever put it here didn't realize stick dynamite needs to be alternated about once a month or so, depending on the type used and what kind of condition it was in when they brought it here."

"I remember a French Resistance fighter in the Second World War who blew himself up while trying to sabotage a Nazi machine-gun nest," Katz remarked. "A demolitions man in the group said the dynamite had been frozen, thawed and unstable."

"Yeah," Manning confirmed. "Dynamite is sensitive. Basically it's nitroglycerin absorbed by wood pulp or porous metal like tin. If you store it long enough and don't alternate the sticks, or if the sticks are damaged or exposed to heat or sudden changes of temperature, the nitro leaks. In this case, it was absorbed by the pallet. Hutton's burning match caused a violent reaction. Nitro, is very unpredictable, you know."

"God in heaven," Miller whispered. "I was just lucky Hutton stood between me and that blast."

"Lucky all the pallets didn't explode," Manning added. "Actually this was a very small explosion. Not much nitro really, and not all of it went up. As I said, the stuff is very unpredictable. Most construction outfits use modern dynamite without a nitroglycerin base. Perhaps the IRA whipped up this batch for the Iron Claymore. Nitro isn't very hard to make, but you have to know what you're doing with it.''

"Nitroglycerin . . ." James said, and wiped his forehead with relief as he thought about plucking the splinters from Miller's hair. "Man, this job gets tougher on the nerves every year."

"Well," Manning began as he strolled back to the stairs. "We'd best leave Hutton here until this area can be washed out to neutralize the nitro still here. One thing is certain: the terrorists didn't use all their dynamite on the ship in Glasgow. That means they're still hauling around some very unstable and untrustworthy explosives—wherever they are."

"What we do know is that they're not here," Katz stated with a sigh, "and that we've got less than three days to find them."

12

A team of forensic experts from New Scotland Yard arrived in Edinburgh in the early evening. Inspector Fellows met them and explained the situation—minus details necessary for maintaining security—and accompanied the scientific team to the Edinburgh constabulary headquarters. They were immediately put to work with the Scottish forensic personnel already involved in trying to reconstruct the ashes and burned papers found at the abandoned terrorist base.

There was little Phoenix Force could do but wait. They ate in a small diner that had a menu consisting of mutton, lamb or pork in limited variations. The Phoenix team returned to the station and learned the forensic people were still working on the evidence. Superintendent Sutherland suggested they go to the rooms in the basement that had been hastily converted into crude billets with cots and blankets. The SAS troops had already taken advantage of the opportunity to get some rest. Katz agreed that it was probably the best thing they could do, as well.

Major Simms stood in a corridor on the basement floor, smoking a cigarette and occasionally drinking from a small metal flask. He saw Phoenix Force descend from the stairs and asked if there were any new developments. Katz answered negatively. The commandos filed into one of the rooms to pick a cot. McCarter allowed the others to go in first and remained in the corridor with Simms.

"Sorry about Hutton," McCarter said, not looking at Simms as he spoke.

"He didn't beat the Clock," Simms replied. "Happens to us all, eventually."

The clock he referred to is the SAS regiment's memorial clock in Hereford, England. The names and dates of SAS soldiers killed in the line of duty are engraved in the walls of the clock. If one "beats the Clock," he lives.

"You probably didn't think much of Hutton," Simms continued as he dropped the cigarette to the floor and crushed it under his boot, "but he was a good soldier. I remember a training exercise in 1982. Some recruits were learning to use their parachutes, and one of them came down on some high-voltage wires. Hutton scrambled up the pole, heedless of the risk to his own life, and cut the boy free. Carried him down, slung over a shoulder. Didn't know until afterward he'd strained half a dozen muscles and dislocated an elbow in the process. There was more to Sergeant Hutton than you had a chance to see."

"I imagine that's true about most men," McCarter said.

"I suppose so," Simms replied, and took another swallow from his flask. "We certainly never got on too well. You and I butted heads the first day you were under my command. Maybe what I did in Belfast was wrong. Maybe I deserved that thrashing you gave me and the transfer out of SAS to a regular army unit. Still, I was always very proud of being SAS. You know what it means to be part of an elite fighting unit. That's why you're with these mysterious mates of yours, right? Finally found an outfit suited for a bloke who's half soldier and half maverick like you."

"It's where I belong," McCarter stated. "I always seem to get in trouble, anyway, so it's best I be with a group where I can do some good by being in trouble."

"Sounds about right," Simms said with a thin smile. "You know, they've never reassigned me to SAS on a permanent basis. Bring me back once in a while when they reckon they need a bloke with my rank and experience. Still, I'm something of an embarrassment because of that Belfast business, and I'll never be accepted again.''

He shoved the flask into a pocket and turned to face McCarter. "I rather envy Hutton,'' Simms added. ''When my time comes, all I really want is to have my name on that bloody clock in Hereford.''

Simms turned and headed into a room where the rest of the SAS troops were already asleep. McCarter stared after him for a second, then shrugged and entered the other room to join his Phoenix Force teammates.

A CONSTABLE AWOKE Phoenix Force at 3:45 a.m. and informed them that they were wanted by Superintendent Sutherland and the man from Scotland Yard. The five commandos hastily climbed from the cots and pulled on clothing, donned pistol holsters and sheath knives and followed the officer upstairs to the conference room. Sutherland and Inspector Fellows were there, along with Major Simms. A pot of hot tea was waiting for them. Manning and Encizo were pleased to find coffee had also been provided. There was even a chilled bottle of Coca-Cola for McCarter.

"You know that American soda pop can eat the insides out of a battleship,'' Simms commented as he watched McCarter gulp down some Coke.

"That tells you how tough I am,'' McCarter replied. He suspected Simms had arranged the coffee and Coca-Cola, but he didn't ask. "So, what did your boys in the lab come up with?''

"Not as much as we'd hoped,'' Inspector Fellows answered as he leafed through some notes. "Most of the material burned in the barrels was just common trash. Paper wrappers, scrap wood, cardboard, that sort of thing. Some other items were burned too well, and the ashes pulverized. Wasn't possible to identify the powdered ashes, regardless of what our forensic people tried.''

"That's not good news," Katz mused, and lighted a Camel cigarette. "I hope you have some for us."

"We found two burned copies of the same newspaper," Fellows continued. "Ran a chap over to the *Edinburgh Gazette*. Publishers weren't too happy about getting out of bed at one-thirty in the morning, but we got them to open up and help our man go through the newspaper morgue until he found the paper with the proper date. Turned out it carried a feature story about your Mr. McGreggor's plan to visit Edinburgh while in Scotland. Sort of a disappointment."

"Kind'a like this conference," James remarked under his breath.

"All right," Sutherland began, beating Fellows to the figurative punch. "We identified that map you found, Mr. Grey. It's of Inverness and the surrounding area."

"Inverness?" Manning asked with a frown. "What's in Inverness?"

"Not much, really," Sutherland admitted. "It's best known for Urquhart Castle and, of course, Loch Ness."

"You mean where the monster hangs out?" James inquired.

"For heaven's sake," Manning muttered, and shook his head.

"The Loch Ness Monster is a silly fairy tale," Fellows declared. "But the fact is every year thousands of tourists and some journalists—if you can call them that—and even some so-called scientists visit Loch Ness with the notion of seeing the monster or taking a snapshot or even catching the bloody thing."

"How do you know the monster is a fairy tale?" Sutherland demanded, genuinely offended by the British policeman's remarks.

"Please, gentlemen," Katz urged. "Unless the Loch Ness Monster is in league with the Iron Claymore terrorists, I don't care if it's real, imaginary or a product of too much

Scoresby on a Saturday night. Inspector Fellows's point is that a lot of tourists and other non-Scots visit Loch Ness. This, naturally, includes a fair number of Americans.''

"So the terrorists may intend to carry out another attack at the Loch or in Inverness," Encizo commented with a sigh. "Sounds like a real long shot. The Iron Claymore knows we're after them and they're not going to make it easy for us. They'll probably stay low or change their targets to hit somewhere we don't expect them. Unless their leaders are dumber than adobe bricks, they'll figure we may suspect Loch Ness by now. This is all central Scotland, more or less. Expect them to hit from the north or the south next.''

"I'm inclined to agree," Fellows stated. "My guess is they'll go after our drilling operations in the North Sea.''

"Those are British operations, Inspector," Katz told him. "The targets have been Americans. It's possible they may change tactics, because Great Britain is still their main opponent, but I doubt they'll hit the oil derricks.''

"They'll never transport the dynamite from Edinburgh that far without blowing themselves to bits," Manning added. "Not unless they get rid of about half of it. Maybe they'll just lie low. They still have McGreggor and they really haven't done much since they got him.''

"By the way," Fellows commented, "we heard from that CIA chap, Davis. He says the Embassy in London received a message from the terrorists. They've warned the American President that they're prepared to kill McGreggor if their demands aren't met. He's got three days to do what they want.''

"So the President still has more time than he gave us," James replied. "Inverness is probably our best bet, even if it is a long shot. We don't have enough time left to just sit around and wait. At least it's following a lead.''

"Well, if we're taking a vote here," McCarter commented, "I'm in favor of going to Inverness, too. Hell, I don't see we have much choice.''

"I suppose we can be contacted by radio and called back if something breaks elsewhere," Encizo said with a shrug. "Inverness is just about the only lead we have right now."

Inspector Fellows looked thoughtful, then nodded. "Very well," he remarked approvingly. "But I don't see any reason for us all to join this same wild-goose chase. Some of us can stay here and try to come up with something more reliable. Perhaps some more details on the North Sea oil drilling and a few other possibilities. There's still a chance extremists in the SNP are involved."

"Yes," Simms agreed. "I don't really see the need to wake up my men for something this farfetched."

A knock on the door drew their attention. Sutherland walked to the door, unlocked and opened it to find a young constable in the hallway.

"It had best be important," the superintendent told him.

"Yeh said we was to inform yeh of anything that might be connected to the terrorists, sir," the constable stated. "Lieutenant Mackintosh told me to report to yeh—"

"Aye, aye," Sutherland said eagerly. "Will you report it then, lad?"

"There was a big explosion reported on the road, sir," the officer replied. "Happened about twenty minutes ago. Truck or something blew up. Not in our jurisdiction, but the lieutenant says I should tell yeh—"

"Where did it happen?" Sutherland demanded.

"On a road outside of Inverness, sir," the young cop answered.

"Inverness," Katz said as he rose from his chair. "Sounds like our goose chase isn't quite so wild, after all."

"I'll go get my troops up and ready," Simms announced.

"We'll grab the rest of our gear," the Phoenix commander declared, already headed for the door. "Sutherland, have transportation ready. We need something faster than that bus."

"Patrol cars will be okay," Manning added, following behind Katz. "The terrorists aren't attacking cops unless they think we're among them."

"Better make it a combination of patrol cars and unmarked vehicles," Encizo suggested. "That way, if this is another ambush scheme, they won't be apt to wipe us out in one fell swoop."

"Need to take more than one route to get there, if possible," McCarter threw in. "Figure it out when you get the cars and drivers."

"I don't know how many unmarked cars we can spare," Sutherland remarked lamely as he stood clear of the door to let Phoenix Force file out of the room.

"Use cruisers if you have to," James told him as he rushed through the doorway. "And make sure you know where the hell we're going while you're at it."

Simms followed them out the door. Inspector Fellows paused to finish drinking his tea, then placed the cup on the table. He smiled at the dumbfounded expression on Sutherland's face.

"Won't you be glad to go back to regular police work at a less frenzied pace?" he asked the superintendent.

"Aye," Sutherland admitted, and glanced at the doorway. "You reckon those lads do this sort of thing all the time?"

"Well, they're certainly good at it," Fellows replied.

"God, I hope so," Sutherland commented. "For everyone's sake."

13

Garrett O'Flynn stood on the catwalk of the parapet surrounding the castle. The Irishman took out papers and tobacco to roll a cigarette. He had to remove his gloves to handle the chore, and his fingers were cold and already becoming numb as he finished rolling a smoke. O'Flynn stuck the cigarette into his mouth and lit it. He gazed up at the dark velvety sky. A few clouds marred the display of wintry stars.

"Another snowfall be coming," Angus Bruce remarked as he mounted the stone steps of the rampart. "A big one."

"You might be right," O'Flynn agreed. "A big storm has been brewing in this part of the world for a very long time."

"Politics," Angus said with a sigh. "Is that all yeh ever think of, O'Flynn?"

"Since 1972," the Irishman replied. "January 30, 1972 to be exact. That was Bloody Sunday, you know. British troops opened fire on Catholics in Londonderry. A civil rights protest rally, not a mob, but the Brits didn't care. They killed thirteen innocent Irish civilians. My brother was one of them. My oldest brother, that is. Protestant bullyboys had murdered my younger brother a few weeks before. Beat him to death in an alley. The loss was too much for my mother's heart to bear. Two sons dead in less than two months. She died in bed on the eve of February 3, 1972."

"I understand family, O'Flynn," Angus assured him. "I know the pain of losing those yeh love."

"Me father was already dead, killed in a factory accident, working for the Brits," O'Flynn continued as if he hadn't heard Angus. "I was already with the IRA before Bloody Sunday. Afterward I had no family, no goals, except the IRA."

"I've a wife and two children, but I won't see them till this be over," Angus said with regret. "Still, a son has duty to his father, and a Scotsman has duty to his country."

"What brings you out here at such an hour?" the Irishman inquired. "I'm a bit of an owl, myself. Sleep in the afternoon and wide awake by sundown."

"Just stepping out for some air?"

"I like to watch the sunrise," O'Flynn explained. "Never know when it will be the last one I'll have a chance to see. Daybreak should be less than an hour from now. So, you up for any special reason and did you just happen upon me, or is there some reason you come up to talk?"

"Me father did not sleep well," Angus explained. "William's death troubles him in his bed. I sat up with him to the wee hours. I was about to go to bed when Stuart tells me Malcolm left with a few of the men. Did me brother speak with you before he departed?"

"Not a word," O'Flynn said with a frown. "Now, don't be taking this as an insult to your family, but Malcolm is a problem. He's too bloody rash. Too short-tempered and apt to charge into things like a drunken lunatic. Hard to say what he could get into on his own."

"Aye," Angus agreed, "but I do not know where he be off to or what he intends to do. Avenge William's death, I am afraid. Yet Glasgow is a long ways to travel. Our clan will cut him off before he gets there."

"Might not be Glasgow he's headed for," O'Flynn warned. "Got a radio message from some blokes at Inverness. Malcolm may be headed there. Message wasn't good news, Angus. One of the trucks carrying dynamite and arms from Edinburgh exploded. Damn fools must have made some mistake with the dynamite. Five more of our men blown to hell. Three of your Iron Claymore comrades, and two of my mates. Bad enough they get killed in combat. Now they're dying from their own carelessness.''

''The Lord does test us fiercely at times,'' Angus said, shaking his head sadly.

''Well, perhaps the Lord is telling us to back off,'' O'Flynn said dryly. ''This operation isn't going well, Angus. We've lost nearly twenty men in the last two days, our offensive strikes against the Yanks and the Brits have come to a halt, and the American President hasn't responded to any of the demands for release of McGreggor. Now Malcolm is loose and probably headed for Inverness in the hopes he can catch up with those five specialists the Yanks sent. CIA or mercenaries or whatever they are, they clearly know how to take care of themselves in a firefight. The Glasgow incident was proof of that. If they capture Malcolm or any of the men from this castle, they may be headed here next.''

''Yeh plan to leave now and return to Ireland?'' Angus inquired. ''Yeh can do that, of course. Scotland isn't your home. Our fight isn't truly yours, O'Flynn.''

''Same fight as always,'' the Irishman insisted. ''Different battleground, but the same enemies. Almost, anyway. Taking on the Americans may have been a mistake.''

''Yeh agreed to it from the first,'' Angus reminded him.

''I figured the Yanks would be preoccupied,'' O'Flynn said with a shrug. ''New President sworn into office, so I figured he would have his hands full trying to adjust to the job. I expected regular CIA or maybe Delta Force to be sent in, but I didn't plan on the Yanks sending a small team of superprofessionals. Whoever they are, they managed to avoid media coverage and arrived here unannounced. They're special, that's a certainty.''

"They still be men of flesh and blood," Angus insisted. "Five men can't change things much."

"They already have," O'Flynn stated. "I have been thinking of getting my men together and pulling out of this operation. A strategic retreat might be the wise option."

"Yeh can withdraw," Angus said. "Yeh have somewhere to retreat to. Scotland be me home and me father's home. I cannot leave."

O'Flynn tossed his cigarette from the rampart and shook his head. He had brought his IRA cell to Scotland to assist the Iron Claymore because he believed this was a chance to embarrass the British and hurt England's relations with the United States. O'Flynn knew the Bruce family and their clan followers would never succeed in putting Andrew Robert Bruce in power as the recognized King of Scotland. Even if they managed to convince the majority of the population the old man really was descended from Robert I, they would never agree to granting the Bruce family godlike power and accept the Iron Claymore as agents of the crown or modern-day knights or whatever Bruce planned to do with them.

It was a fanatic's dream that had managed to gather a small following of deluded and ignorant young zealots who were willing to fight for the Bruce crusade. O'Flynn did not fully understand how Bruce had assembled his clan, but he guessed most were gullible people with romantic notions of restoring Scottish monarchy and becoming part of the ruling class. The IRA had their own reasons for joining forces with the clan. Things had started pretty well, from O'Flynn's point of view. Bombing the American embassy in London, murdering Yankee tourists and kidnapping McGreggor had certainly gotten the attention of the U.S. government and had probably strained relations between America and Great Britain. The plan may have eventually convinced the U.S. to sever relations, but everything had changed when the mysterious team had arrived in Glasgow.

Damn William for launching that attack, O'Flynn thought bitterly. If that bloodthirsty idiot hadn't resorted to violence when the situation called for surveillance, the band of deadly strangers wouldn't have gotten information about the base in Edinburgh. William should have left them alone to fumble about without ample clues, just as the CIA, Scotland Yard and everyone else involved in the investigation had been doing since the operation began.

O'Flynn's reason for participating in the Iron Claymore plot seemed to be dissolving rapidly. Several IRA members had already been killed or captured, including high-ranking men like Dwyer and Kehoe. The Irishman figured the mission was coming apart. The Bruce family and their monarchist followers might believe God would be on their side and grant them victory in the end, but O'Flynn didn't share that optimism.

"The enemy doesn't know about this castle," O'Flynn stated thoughtfully. "As long as they don't learn about our main base, there's still a chance things can come around again in our favor."

"So yeh be staying for now?" Angus inquired hopefully. The Scot realized they needed the IRA. The Iron Claymore followers were more dedicated, but the Irish veterans of guerrilla warfare had far more experience.

"For now," O'Flynn confirmed. "But I must admit the way things are right now concerns me, and I don't intend to get all my men killed fighting a hopeless situation. Could have stayed in Belfast and done that. If I reckon we can't win any more objectives, I'm pulling my lads out before they come here and level this old castle."

"I appreciate yeh telling me," Angus replied with a nod. "If yeh excuse me, I've got to see about stopping Malcolm from reaching Inverness. Can't say what he might do if he gets there."

"To me, it's clear what he'll do," O'Flynn stated with a shrug. "Malcolm's right eager to kill someone. I don't think he even cares who it is. If your brother gets the chance, he'll surely shed as much human blood as possible.''

THE REMAINS of the truck still sent columns of black smoke into the sky as dawn stretched a golden column of light across the billows of gray clouds. Phoenix Force had no trouble finding the burned-out hull of the vehicle. Gary Manning and Rafael Encizo emerged from a patrol car parked on the shoulder of the dirt road fifty yards from the charred debris. Heather swayed in the wind, and snow-flakes once more drifted down on the men as they walked to the wreckage.

''It's sure one hell of a mess,'' Encizo commented.

Chunks of the truck lay scattered across the road and strewn along the hills on each side of the burned pile of junk. One tire was still burning. It had been drenched by gasoline. The stench of the black smoke was unpleasant, but it helped cover the sickly-sweet stink of charred human flesh. Severed limbs and mangled corpses were among the wreckage. Manning glanced down at a battered box-shaped metal object. An extended magazine still protruded from the butt of the pistol grip.

''M-10 Ingram,'' the Canadian remarked, and placed a boot next to the machine pistol. ''I told you that dynamite was unstable.''

He kicked the Ingram and sent it skidding across the road. Superintendent Sutherland stopped it by stamping a boot on the metal frame. The Scottish police officer and Yakov Katzenelenbogen had stepped from an unmarked car parked behind the patrol vehicle. Sutherland looked down at the gun and stared at Manning.

''The terrorists blew themselves up?'' he asked.

''That's not an exhaust pipe under your foot,'' Manning replied. ''The truck must have hit a bump or a pothole or whatever and jarred the dynamite cargo. With leaking ni-tro, it wouldn't take much to set off an explosion. One stick went off, and the others followed. Hard to be sure how big this truck was, but I guess it was about the size of a small beer lorry.''

"Can't be sure how many men were in the rig when it blew," Encizo added, looking at the grisly remains calmly and with no emotion at all. "The corpses are ripped up pretty bad, but I'd say at least four guys were torn apart with their truck."

"Well, I estimate seven to ten pounds of dynamite went off," Manning announced. "I'm just happy it happened on a lonely little road where no innocent bystanders were around to suffer."

"It's terrible," Sutherland stated, looking away from the wreckage. "Murders with axes aren't this gruesome."

"The terrorists would have used the dynamite on other people if they'd lived to carry out another attack," Katz reminded him. "Better they lie splattered across the road than innocent civilians or police officers. Don't forget what they did in Glasgow. They certainly wouldn't feel any remorse if the bodies of their victims lay here instead of their own."

"Aye," Sutherland shook his head. "Nevertheless, it is such a dreadful sight. Does it not bother you, man?"

"I've seen death in worse ways than this," Katz answered. "It was usually caused by men like the ones killed here. Sorry if I sound callous, Superintendent. Terrorists are the personification of destruction. They deliver it to others and, one way or the other, eventually bring it down upon themselves. I've seen too much of the senseless murder and wanton destruction caused by terrorists to feel any grief when one or more of them are dead."

Manning stepped carefully around the wreckage. Upholstery continued to burn, and the engine had been torn apart and strewn randomly across the road like a giant jigsaw puzzle. Two local constables stood by their patrol car. Both men had thrown up and still tried to avoid looking at the carnage. Manning walked past them and examined the road and surrounding ground.

"Tire tracks," he announced. "Another truck, judging by the size of the tread. Deep and wide. It swerved slightly. Driver must have been startled by the explosion."

"Startled?" Encizo snorted. "I bet he had to change his trousers afterward. After all, he probably had dynamite in the back of his rig, too."

"What was that, sir?" one of the Inverness constables inquired, eyes wide with surprise and alarm. "This ain't an act of terrorism?"

"Sort of," the Cuban answered, "but the terrorists themselves were the victims for a change. The bad news is there's more of the bastards on the loose."

Two more police cars and an unmarked car arrived at the scene. David McCarter and Calvin James emerged from one vehicle, while Inspector Fellows and Major Simms appeared from another. Edinburgh police and SAS soldiers were crammed inside the other cars.

The British ace and the black American marched over to Katz. "Our driver took a bloody short cut and got lost," McCarter complained. "Lucky we got here at all."

"Even more lucky there wasn't a firefight in progress," James added. He gazed at the charred ruins on the road and whistled softly. "This was sure the end of the world for somebody."

"Nobody important, except to family members of the Iron Claymore clan," the Phoenix Force commander replied. "What's important is that there are more enemies in the area, and I doubt they'd drive their truck or trucks, as the case may be, very far after what happened to this vehicle."

"How far to Inverness?" Manning asked one of the local cops.

"Less than two miles," the officer replied. "Yeh reckon they be in the town now? With more dynamite?"

"They may have abandoned the rig farther down the road," the Canadian said. "Let's see if we can find it."

They didn't have to go far. Phoenix Force and their police and SAS allies found the second truck less than half a mile from the site of the burned wreckage. The truck had been hastily camouflaged, parked off the road between two trees and covered with loose brush and branches. Manning and Encizo cleared away the foliage from the rear of the lorry. The back of the truck was empty except for a single wooden pallet and a few splintered chunks of wood.

The tailgate had been smashed, and the debris appeared to be remnants of the shattered panels. The canvas along the rear ribs of the truck back had been burned, and one rear tire was flat. Manning climbed into the rig and discovered reddish-brown stains on the floorboards.

"They suffered some damage when the other truck exploded," he declared. "The blast chewed up the rear of the vehicle pretty bad, and at least one person in the back of the rig was injured. There are bloodstains here, about two hours old."

"They took the dynamite with them?" Sutherland asked as he peered into the back of the truck.

"Yeah," Manning confirmed, and climbed down from the rig. He kicked some foliage aside and knelt to examine the ground. "Footprints. Distorted and partially swept by brush. Take a while to tell how many sets of prints are here."

"You don't have to play Daniel Boone," James told him, and pointed at a column of boot prints on the snow-covered ground. "This is obviously the way the terrorists headed. Toward Inverness. Right?"

"Aye, sir," a local constable confirmed. "That be right."

"You think they're carrying the dynamite on foot?" Sutherland inquired, addressing the question to Manning, who seemed to have a better idea of such things than the others.

"I think they must have," the Canadian replied. "Unless they didn't have any dynamite in this truck—which seems unlikely—they would have been forced to either carry the explosives or bury them."

"About a mile away," Encizo mused. "Probably seem like a thousand when they had to haul dynamite they knew was unstable. They sure wouldn't run carrying that stuff."

"But they've certainly reached Inverness by now," Katz said with a sigh. "They have about an hour's headstart. They may have been slowed down by their wounded comrade, but not enough."

"The hospital," Sutherland suggested. "They'll probably take the injured bloke to the hospital . . ."

"Terrorists?" James scoffed. "They'd let him bleed to death first. He'll have to get by with whatever first aid they give him at their safehouse. Unfortunately we don't have any idea where the hell that might be."

"Bloody hell," McCarter groaned, and shook his head. "We track these bastards all this way and now we don't know where to go next."

"Sure we do," Katz corrected. "Inverness. If we can't figure out where they're hiding, maybe we can guess what their next target will be and try to be ready for them when they make their move."

"That's a rather big 'maybe,' Mr. Grey," Inspector Fellows commented as he filled his pipe with tobacco. "I hope you've acquired clairvoyance as one of your many skills. It sounds like that's what you're going to need."

14

Calvin James peered through the Bushnell binoculars as he scanned the quiet waters of the lake. To look at it, there was nothing extraordinary about Loch Ness. Aside from the ruins of Urquhart Castle in the distance, there didn't seem to be anything unusual about it.

"I can't believe this," Gary Manning grumbled as he stood next to James. "You're looking for that damn monster, aren't you?"

"Why not?" James replied with a shrug. "We're at Loch Ness, so we may as well see if the monster is around."

"We're supposed to be watching for terrorists, not fictional sea serpents that don't even have enough sense to live in the sea," Manning told him.

"We're in the role of typical American tourists visiting Loch Ness, and that means we should be looking for the Loch Ness monster," James insisted. "Besides, why are you so sure the creature isn't real?"

"Hey, I'm a Canadian, remember?" Manning began. "Not a city-bound Canadian, but a guy who spent lots of time hunting and fishing in the woods all over a country that is bigger than the United States and has a hell of a lot more forest and a lot less people. I've heard all kinds of weird stories about sasquatch ape-men, and Ogopogo, Canada's version of the Loch Ness monster, which is supposed to be in Okanagan Lake. Well, after years of camping in British Columbia, I've never seen any shaggy giants running around in the woods, and I've done a lot of fishing around Okanagan Lake without seeing as much as a large salamander.''

"So what?" James responded. "I was born and raised in Chicago, but I never saw a raccoon, although other people say they saw the critters getting into their trash cans at night. I was stationed in Nam for three years and never saw any of those elephants and tigers that were supposed to be there. Lived in California for a few years, too, but I never came across a mountain lion or even a coyote.''

"I don't believe this," the Canadian said with a sigh. "You're talking about *real* animals. Everybody knows they're real. You can look them up in encyclopedias and go see them in zoos. The Loch Ness monster is a myth. It's right up there with dragons and unicorns.''

"Just a second," James began as he stuffed a hand inside his coat. "I got a booklet here on Loch Ness with pictures of the monster.''

Manning rolled his eyes. Phoenix Force encountered real monsters all the time. Terrorist outfits, criminal syndicates, conspiracies that could topple nations or trigger nuclear war—all made monsters in lakes and abominable snowmen look like Bambi and Thumper. Still, James obviously found the idea of the Loch Ness monster of interest. Maybe because it was supposed to be a mystery of nature that didn't really threaten anyone. Manning figured James was basically a city kid at heart who still regarded forests and lakes as strange alien terrain where all sorts of unknown beasties could dwell.

While James searched for his booklet to support the "Nessie" theory, Manning glanced about the streets of Inverness. It had an Old World appearance. The shops and cottages seemed very old, and some locals still conducted business with a horse-drawn cart. A chimney sweep, bundled up in greatcoat and scarf with a traditional top hat bound to his head, puttered by on a moped. A few cars and trucks made their way through the narrow cobblestoned streets.

The snowfall continued to drift down from the morning sky, but the sun had secured a spot above the clouds by eight o'clock. Manning noticed a medium-sized fishing boat cruise onto the loch. If the locals were concerned or even interested in the alleged monster, it didn't seem to affect day-to-day activities. If the terrorists struck in Inverness, that would be a very different story.

Manning and James did not move far from the dark blue Volkswagen parked nearby. The M-16 and FAL assault rifle lay in the back seat, covered by a blanket. Grenades and spare magazines were also stored in the vehicle. The men carried their pistols in shoulder holsters under their coats as they stood on the ramp and acted as though they found Loch Ness genuinely exciting.

James didn't have to put on an act. He had found his booklet and showed Manning a grainy photo on the cover. The shape above the water reminded Manning of the shadow of a goose with a long neck and an abbreviated bill. James opened the booklet and found another grainy picture with Urquhart Castle in the foreground and something that looked like a couple of logs in the water near the ruins.

"They'll have to come up with better evidence than that before I'm going to buy this monster crap, Cal," the Canadian told his partner.

"People have been reporting seeing the monster since A.D. 550, and it's been picked up on sonar—or at least some large living objects were," James insisted.

"People have been seeing ghosts for centuries, too," Manning said with a sigh. "Sonar probably picked up a school of fish. Come on, Cal."

"Yeah?" the American replied. "Well, in 1972 underwater cameras photographed a flipper about four feet long. Part of a larger creature, and some scientists think it might be a plesiosaur. That's a large aquatic reptile from the dinosaur era, believed to be extinct for more than seventy million years. Of course, they thought the coelacanth was extinct, too, and it came from the same Mesozoic period.''

"That's the fish off the west coast of Africa?" Manning asked with a frown. "A species found in the open sea is one thing. A giant reptile living in a land-locked lake is quite another.''

"I'm surprised you're so skeptical," James remarked. "You're the guy who thought the prophecies of Nostradamus were coming true when we had that mission in the Persian Gulf.''

"No, I didn't," Manning said gruffly. "Will you forget about Nessie and pay attention to the mission?''

"Sure," James assured him. "What am I supposed to do? I don't see any terrorists. We're to be bait for 'em, and they haven't come for us yet. Maybe they won't. Maybe the police will find witnesses who say the creeps from the truck come stumbling into town on tiptoes because of the dynamite. Maybe one of the other sources will pay off, and we're just killing time here. Until something happens, we may as well look for the monster.''

"Great," Manning said with disgust, and reluctantly raised his binoculars to examine the loch.

DAVID MCCARTER TUGGED a tweed cap low on his brow as he marched along a sidewalk next to Inspector Fellows. The Phoenix commando was not in a good mood. Katz was with Sutherland at police headquarters, checking out records of local citizens who might be inclined to assist a monarchist extremist group like the Iron Claymore clan. Encizo had joined the police in an effort to check buildings in the Inverness area that might be used for a safehouse by the terrorists, and James and Manning were at Loch Ness as a lure for the enemy while Simms and the other SAS troops waited to be called into action.

McCarter reckoned he and Fellows had been stuck with the most boring and least promising job. Their task was to question shop owners, city maintenance personnel and employees at the nearby mills who may have seen a group of strangers wander into Inverness shortly before dawn or after sunup. The Scotland Yard man didn't seem aggravated by the assignment, McCarter noticed. The man's job, after all, was investigating, but the Phoenix commando found such work frustrating and time-consuming. He wanted to face his enemies in combat, and the sooner the better.

"How the hell are we suppose to know which street the bastards strolled down when they entered Inverness?" McCarter complained as they walked along Clachnaherry Row.

"We'll just try the most likely roads from the direction the terrorists were headed," Fellows replied, less than pleased about being saddled with the anxious McCarter. "This is typical information gathering. Fundamental police work."

"I'm not a copper," McCarter said sourly. "Half these shops aren't even open..."

He glanced about at the surrounding buildings and stopped in midsentence when his eyes fell on the legend of a small cottagelike shop with a barn behind it. The sign declared the establishment was MacPherson Ironworks. Yellow letters in the windowpane further stated MacPherson did horseshoes, smithing, fences and curios.

"Well, I'll be damned," McCarter remarked. "What if Inverness is of interest to the Iron Claymore for some other reason than carrying out a terrorist hit here?"

"What are you talking about?" Fellows asked, startled and bewildered by McCarter's question. "Why would the terrorists come here if they didn't intend to launch an attack?"

"Look," the Phoenix commando began, working against his nature to try to exercise patience. "Those blokes had to ditch the truck. It was damaged, and they knew they were hauling a bunch of unstable dynamite. Now, isn't it a bit of a coincidence that this happened less than a mile from where they intended to carry out another hit?''

''They were headed for Inverness,'' the inspector said, rolling his eyes with frustration. ''We found the map at their base in Edinburgh.''

''I know about the map,'' McCarter said with a sigh. ''Seemed a bit unlikely to me they'd burn the ruddy thing without tearing it up first if it was the site for their next attack. Some of these amateurs in the Iron Claymore might make that sort of mistake, but the IRA are too experienced to be that careless. You can bet O'Flynn's people help map out every operation that isn't thrown together in a hurry. As for heading for Inverness, that doesn't make much sense if they wanted to assassinate or kidnap Americans. How many tourists come to Loch Ness in January? Besides, these chaps had just fled Edinburgh at a moment's notice. Figure they planned to immediately rush off to another hit job?''

''All right,'' Fellows allowed reluctantly. ''They were on the run and they headed here because they needed a safe-house.''

''Maybe,'' McCarter said, ''but let's go check out something else while we're here.''

The Phoenix veteran headed across the street, followed by the frustrated Fellows. MacPherson Ironworks was open for business. McCarter opened the door and entered. A four-foot-high iron dragon with metal wings and blunt spines along its arched back stood on a pedestal by the door. Smaller iron figures lined shelves along the walls. Iron masks and decorative reproductions of flintlock pistols hung on a wall above a mock fireplace with an assortment of fancy pokers displayed in a rack.

''Morning, gentlemen.'' A gray haired man whose wire-rim glasses perched on a hawk-bill nose was looking at them with friendly expectation. ''How be yeh today?''

McCarter approached the counter. Fellows stood by the door and glanced about the room, wondering what his strange companion was up to. The commando was carrying his aluminum briefcase with the KG-99 inside, and Fellows was almost afraid that the daffy lout might take out the gun and start shooting like a lunatic.

"We're doing all right, sir," McCarter told the shopkeeper, "but we do need some information. Maybe you can help us."

"This be about the Loch Ness monster?" the man muttered. "I don't know anything about it. Ne'er seen Nessie meself, but I know many a man who claims he has. Can't say one way or another if it be real or not."

"No, we don't want to ask you about the monster," McCarter assured him. "These iron sculptures are very impressive."

"Thank yeh." The shopkeeper smiled with mild pride. "I'm Keith MacPherson. Most of the sculptures be me work. I've two fine sons, and I'm teaching 'em the family trade. MacPhersons have been blacksmiths for centuries. Me father, his father, and the MacPhersons before them. So long be the tradition of me family, none know when the first MacPherson pounded out his first horseshoe."

"Fascinating," McCarter told him as he placed the briefcase on the counter. "A man with your expertise may be able to answer our questions."

McCarter unlocked the case and opened the lid. Fellows tensed, sure that the crazy commando would draw the KG-99. Instead, McCarter reached into the pockets inside the lid and extracted several photographs. He sorted through them and selected three photos of miniature claymore swords found at the scene of two terrorist assaults.

"Now," McCarter began, and handed the pictures to MacPherson. "Can you tell us anything about these?"

"Aye," MacPherson chuckled. "I made these wee replicas of the iron claymores meself. Special order. How did yeh come upon these items?"

"I'm Inspector Fellows from Scotland Yard," Fellows announced suddenly, and showed MacPherson his badge and ID. "We're investigating a series of violent crimes. Murder, kidnapping and more. These swords showed up at the scene of crime repeatedly. You made them for a customer, correct? We need his name."

"I do not betray me customer's right to privacy," MacPherson began. "But I'm a good citizen and try to cooperate with the police. Andrew Robert Bruce requested the swords. Replicas of his family crest. Two crossed claymores. So he claims."

"Iron claymores?" McCarter asked.

"Aye," MacPherson confirmed. "Andrew's family have always claimed to be direct descendants of Robert Bruce. I do not know if there be any truth to this, but most of us reckoned it did no harm for the Bruce clan to believe in something that give 'em a bit of dignity."

"Hold on a moment," Fellows said, surprised by the shop owner's statement. "You mean to say you've known this Bruce chap for some time?"

"Of course," MacPherson answered, putting a briar pipe on the counter and taking a pouch of tobacco from a pocket inside his jacket. "We be from the Broch."

"The Broch?" Fellows asked, frowning.

"That's Fraserburgh, isn't it?" McCarter inquired. "Locals call it 'the Broch,' as I recall."

"Aye," MacPherson replied with a nod. He struck a match and held it to the bowl of his pipe. "Yeh know the Buchan district?"

"I had some relatives who lived near Buchan, so I know a little bit about it," the Phoenix pro explained. "Do you know if Andrew Bruce still lives there?"

"I believe he does," MacPherson answered. "Is he in trouble with the law? This gent says he be with Scotland Yard. What do yeh want with old Andrew? I do not know what crimes he could be committing, half-paralyzed after his stroke and on in years as he be."

"Apparently he's managed to convince a number of people that he's the rightful king of Scotland, and they're causing a lot of trouble right now," McCarter explained. He figured there was no need to give MacPherson any more details about the Iron Claymore clan. "Anyway, we need to find Mr. Bruce. You know where he lives? House, farm or whatever?"

"No," MacPherson answered, and blew a smoke ring across the room. "Mind yeh, Andrew and me aren't friends. I just be a lad from the old hamlet by the Broch. I have not seen the old man for years, but he sent his sons to see about making the wee swords for him. The eldest son, Angus, and William. Got two other lads, yeh know. Duncan was a champion of the caber toss in St. Combs about three years ago."

"Caber?" Fellows raised his eyebrows as he spoke. "That's sort of a log, right? Blokes try to pick it up and throw it as a test of strength."

"Aye," MacPherson stated with a nod. "A very old Gaelic sport. The caber pole must be big and heavy. Contestants hold it by the end and lift it full length before the toss. Takes a man of considerable muscle to toss the caber."

"And Duncan Bruce was a champion," McCarter mused. He made a mental note that one of Andrew Bruce's sons was obviously a physically powerful man. "Is there anything else you can tell us, Mr. MacPherson?"

"Afraid I don't have nothing to add," MacPherson replied. "Ne'er thought much of Andrew Bruce and his clan. Reckoned they be a might daft, but ne'er thought they'd be any sort of threat. Perhaps this is all a misunderstanding, or someone exaggerated things a bit.''

''I hope you're right,'' McCarter told him. ''Thank you for your time, Mr. MacPherson.''

McCarter and Fellows emerged from the shop. The snowfall had increased, and the wind blew harder and colder, but neither man noticed as they crossed the street. Before speaking, the Scotland Yard inspector glanced about as if worried someone might overhear them. ''My God, Black,'' Fellows remarked. ''This might be the lucky break we've been praying for.''

''Yeah,'' McCarter replied, ''but let's not get too carried away. There are terrorists at large in Inverness, and they must be dealt with. And we don't know the exact location of the Iron Claymore headquarters, even if we do have a general idea where to look.''

''Still, we've got more reason for optimism,'' Fellows insisted. ''Don't we?''

''I sure hope so,'' the Phoenix pro replied.

15

Malcolm Bruce pulled back the cocking knob to a Sterling submachine gun and chambered the first 9 mm cartridge. The young Scot hadn't handled many firearms and knew little more about the Sterling than which end to hold. But he didn't confess his ignorance to the eight Iron Claymore followers and the three IRA guerrillas in the cellar of the Inverness Cinema. He didn't intend to do anything to undermine their confidence in his leadership before carrying out the attack.

The youngest Bruce brother also hadn't let on that he hadn't received authorization from his father, Angus or O'Flynn, but had come to Inverness on his own to seek revenge for the death of William. Malcolm knew he could not have convinced Angus or Duncan to agree to his plan. His father was no longer capable of rational decisions, and O'Flynn had no reason to care about the death of a member of the Bruce family.

Malcolm had always felt inferior to his brothers. His father favored Angus and Duncan, the elder sons. They were next in line for the crown, so the old man spent more time with them. William and Malcolm were less important in their father's grand scheme for claiming rule of Scotland. But at least William had been allowed to participate in battles like a man, a warrior prince of Scottish royalty.

They had forced Malcolm to remain at the castle as if he was still a child. He was twenty years old and yearned for the action he had been denied. He desperately wanted to show the others he was as good as any member of the Bruce family. William had been his only true friend, the only person he believed understood him. The men who killed William had to pay, and Malcolm had sworn he would get blood vengeance personally.

He would return victorious. The others would be awestruck by his accomplishment. Father would embrace him and weep with joy that his youngest son had proved himself a man worthy of the Bruce clan and worthy of the title of a prince of Scotland. Malcolm dreamed of such glory, and soon, he thought, these dreams would become reality.

"Prince Malcolm," an Iron Claymore devotee said breathlessly as he staggered down the stairs to the basement. "Yeh be right about those CIA assassins coming to Inverness. I seen two of them out by the loch."

"I knew they'd come!" Malcolm declared with glee. "When they learned about the truck blowing up on the road, they'd figure the rest of the lot would head here and lay low. Just as the explosion at the docks drew them out at Glasgow, the truck explosion attracted those bastards like vultures to a fresh carcass."

"I don't know if charging into battle is a wise decision," an IRA member said nervously. "I still think we should try to contact home base and get instructions . . ."

Malcolm shook his head. "I told yeh before that radio silence is necessary because the Americans and the Brits have ways of monitoring radio frequencies and tracking them to the source of the broadcast. I be in charge here. Me father sent me to command yeh troops and, by the Blood of Christ, I shall not deny me duty nor allow any of yeh lot to do less than expected of righteous men in a just war for freedom."

"None of us will refuse to fight alongside a prince of the blood of Robert Bruce," another Iron Claymore member declared.

"Good lads," Malcolm said. He turned to the messenger. "Now, yeh be sure these men by the loch are two of the murdering scum we're after?"

"Aye," the man confirmed. "One of the five killers be a tall black Yank, and another a big man with lots of muscles and a face like a stone carving. That description fits those two at the loch."

"Then we take 'em," Malcolm announced. "Load the dynamite in the car."

"The dynamite ain't safe to handle," an Irish terrorist warned. "Those poor chaps on the road be proof of that."

"Then drive with care and yeh won't have cause to worry," Malcolm stated. "We need the dynamite 'cause the rest of those Yankee butchers may come a'running when the shooting starts. The Brit soldiers and the coppers may try to stop us, as well, and I want yeh men ready to deal with any enemy forces these scum throw at us."

"At least let us think a bit and come up with a less rash strategy, man," another IRA veteran urged.

"I thought yeh Irish ne'er backed down from a fight," a Scottish fanatic remarked with contempt. "It's been said IRA stands for 'I Ran Away.' Figured that to be Brit propaganda. Hate to learn it to be true . . ."

"You Scottish pig!" the Irishman hissed as he raised his Czech-made Skorpion machine pistol.

"Stop it!" Malcolm snapped, and jumped between the quarreling pair. "Yeh two want to fight, yeh get that wish when we take on William's killers. If yeh live through today's battle, yeh can settle this personal score any way yeh choose."

"Suits me fine," the Irishman said with a shrug.

"Aye," the Iron Claymore flunky agreed, nodding.

"Then let's get on with it," Malcolm told his men. "Time to blow some of these bastards to hell—show them that they can't meddle in the home affairs of Scotland."

GARY MANNING WAS BORED. He stared through his binoculars at Loch Ness and scanned the tranquil waters and surrounding banks. Except for the fishing boat and the castle ruins, there was nothing to see except a dark lake that had spawned a silly legend....

A large gray-brown shape suddenly broke the surface of the water. The humplike shape shifted forward and created a series of large ripples across the lake. Something moved a few feet beyond the hump, an object that looked like a long neck and head.

"Holy shit!" Manning gasped in astonishment.

Suddenly Calvin James grabbed Manning by the collar of his coat and yanked the Canadian off balance. Manning toppled to the ground with a surprised groan when he landed on his back. James had thrown himself to the ground beside his partner. The roar of automatic fire immediately explained the black American's actions.

James had spotted the terrorists approaching the ramp from behind a battered old green sedan parked nearby. Three opponents had produced short-barreled machine pistols and rushed toward the Phoenix pair. Manning hadn't noticed because he was staring at the loch instead of paying attention to the streets from where the enemy was most likely to attack.

"Cal," Manning began, slightly winded and trying to catch his breath. "Did . . . you see it?"

"What?" James replied as he low-crawled to the Volkswagen and yanked open the door. "Hell!"

He reached inside and grabbed his M-16. James shook the blanket aside, thumbed the selector switch to full auto and pointed the barrel at a side window of the VW. He triggered the assault rifle. Glass burst into a cracked pattern around three bullet holes. The 5.56 mm rounds kept going and slammed into the chest of the nearest terrorist assailant.

The man screamed and folded into an inert ball on the pavement. The remaining terrorists returned fire, shattering windows and hammering the metal body of the Volkswagen. James retreated from the open car door to crouch by the front tire. Gary Manning took a similar position at the rear tire, his Walther P-5 in his fist.

"You awake now?" James asked sarcastically as he swung the barrel of his M-16 around the hood and fired another volley at the attackers.

"Did you see that thing in the lake?" Manning asked, but his words were drowned out by the exchange of automatic fire.

One terrorist dropped to the ground and assumed a prone position to fire at James's position. The other bolted toward the rear of the VW. He didn't realize Manning was there until the Canadian poked his pistol around the car and triggered two shots. One 9 mm crashed into the terrorist's upper chest, and the other shattered his front teeth.

James couldn't get a clear shot at the man lying on his belly. A burst of 7.65 mm slugs raked the front of the VW as the gunman blasted another wave of Skorpion projectiles at the black man's position. James ducked low, sucked in a deep breath through clenched teeth and rolled onto his side.

He thrust the barrel of his M-16 underneath the Volkswagen. On ground level with the gunman, James aimed the rifle with one hand and braced the plastic buttstock against his shoulder. The terrorist saw the motion beneath the car a split second before James opened fire. Three 5.56 mm bullets slammed into the gunman's face. His skull exploded, and a geyser of blood and brain tissue sprayed from the wreckage of his cranium.

"Did you see it or not?" Manning demanded.

"We got a firefight goin' on, man!" James replied as he saw two figures emerge from the sedan.

One of the opponents hurled a sticklike object. It sailed over the top of the VW and landed on the ground near James. He glanced down at the tube of pulpwood with a fuse jutting from a crimped blasting cap at one end of the stick. A flame gobbled up the short fuse with a serpentine hiss.

"Blast!" James exclaimed, and quickly grabbed the stick of dynamite.

He swung his arm in a cross-body sweep and threw the dynamite at the loch. It hit the water and exploded along the surface. Water spewed up from the lake and sprayed the banks. Some splashed James and Manning. The Canadian glanced at the loch but didn't see the mysterious hump.

"Damn it!" Manning growled. "I think you scared it away!"

"Jive-ass turkey," James muttered, and shook his head.

The remaining opponents seemed to be using the sedan for cover. One terrorist fired an autoweapon at the VW to keep the Phoenix pair pinned down while his partner raised another stick of dynamite and held a lighter to the fuse.

The flame touched the fuse. It also got too close to beads of nitroglycerin that leaked from the pulpwood stick. The dynamite exploded in the man's hand. The blast tore him apart and sheared off the windows and doors of the sedan. Several more sticks of dynamite were detonated inside the car, and the automobile went up like a miniature supernova. The second terrorist was blown into flying chunks of ragged meat and bone that were hurled twenty feet in three different directions.

The blast rocked the Volkswagen, and a concussion wave knocked James and Manning to the ground. They peered under the VW at the burning crater in the street. Except for a few clumps of debris and mangled metal parts, it was all that remained of the two terrorists and the sedan. Manning whistled softly.

"That was some very unstable dynamite," he observed.

"Yeah," James snorted. "Speaking of unstable, what the hell were you rambling about . . ."

A swarm of full-auto rounds suddenly raked the rear of the VW. Manning scrambled away from his position as sparks erupted from the metal body and bullets tore loose the back fender. Two more terrorists had emerged from an alley farther up Kilmorack Avenue. Sinister figures in baggy gray coveralls and black ski masks, the gunmen carried Soviet-made AK-47 assault rifles and tried to train their weapons on the Phoenix commandos.

The wail of sirens announced several police cars heading for the battleground. James returned fire with his M-16 and drove the enemy back into the alley. Manning took advantage of the lull to reach inside the VW and get his FAL assault rifle. A bullet struck the open door close to his head as he pulled the weapon from the car.

"Son of a bitch," the Canadian rasped as an icy tingling crept up his spine. "There's a goddamn sniper with a high vantage point somewhere over there."

He gestured with the FAL rifle to indicate the buildings to the east of their position. The enemy had caught them in a cross fire. If the guys in the alley could drive them into the sniper's line of fire or pin them down long enough for the unseen gunman to get a clear target, the Phoenix pair would be figurative fish in the proverbial barrel.

The first patrol car swung around a lorry that had come to a halt in the middle of a side street. Sirens wailing and red light flashing, the car swung onto Kilmorack and raced past the burning wreckage of the sedan. A volley of AK-47 rounds slammed into the hood and windshield. The driver convulsed behind the wheel, and the car whirled out of control. It skidded sideways and crashed into a lamp pole. The vehicle came to an abrupt halt as two more patrol cars rushed to the scene.

A masked figure darted out from the side door of a pastry shop. The terrorist hurled a stick of dynamite at the approaching patrol cars. The first vehicle swerved to try to avoid the dynamite, but it exploded the instant it struck the cobblestones. The police car tumbled over on its roof from the force of the blast. The automobile skidded upside down and crashed into the one immediately behind. The second car came to a sudden halt, but the impact sent the upside down patrol car sliding across the sidewalk to slam into the front of a pub.

Glass shattered with a roar as the disabled auto smashed through the plate glass window, crushing two tables and several chairs and finally bashing in the side of the bar inside the pub. Fortunately the establishment was not open for business, and no customers were harmed. The two Inverness police constables and a pair of SAS soldiers inside the vehicle were not so lucky. The driver was already dead, his throat crushed against the steering wheel and his skull split open. The other constable had sailed face first into the windshield twice and hammered a crack in the thick safety glass with his forehead. Suffering from a fractured skull and a broken neck, he wasn't going anywhere except the morgue.

One SAS trooper managed to crawl from the back seat. His right arm was dislocated at the shoulder, and he had sustained numerous bruises and sprains. His mate was less fortunate. The man's foot had been literally broken off at the ankle. He shrieked in agony as blood spurted from the ragged stump at the end of his calf.

The two terrorists at the alley redirected their fire at James and Manning. The masked pair had assumed the police car that had slammed into the lamp pole no longer presented a threat. They didn't see Rafael Encizo kick open a rear door of the car and emerge from the vehicle. The Cuban had been slightly dazed and shaken by the car crash, but he had recovered from the effects enough to force open the dented car door and step outside with his Heckler & Koch MP-5 held ready.

Encizo spotted the two terrorists at the mouth of the alley and snap-aimed his submachine gun. The Cuban fired a long burst at the pair. One man pitched backward from the impact of three parabellum slugs in his upper torso. One or more bullets sang against a stone wall behind the second gunman. The terrorist ducked and triggered a hasty burst with his AK-47 as he retreated deeper in the alley. The 7.62 mm rounds chopped into the patrol car that Encizo used for cover. He glanced around the rear of the vehicle and saw the opponent had vanished.

"You'll have to do better than that, *bastardo*," Encizo remarked as he took an M-26 fragmentation grenade from his belt.

The Cuban pulled the pin and hurled the grenade. It bounced from one wall and fell inside the alley. Encizo fired another short burst of MP-5 rounds to discourage the terrorist within from trying to get rid of the grenade. The M-26 exploded, hurling battered trash cans, flying pieces of garbage and human body parts from the mouth of the alley.

A bullet chipped a chunk of brick from a wall near Encizo's position. The Cuban ducked low behind the patrol car, and another slug smashed the only window that had not already been shattered when the vehicle met the lamp pole. Encizo held his fire, aware the bullets came from above. A man with a rifle was obviously trying to take him out, and the Cuban battle veteran realized the sniper was beyond the range of his submachine gun.

Manning and James were already aware of the sniper and knew his general position. When the rifleman fired at Encizo, the muzzle-flash of his weapon betrayed his exact location. Gary Manning quickly raised the buttstock of his FAL to his shoulder and aimed at the orange glare at the edge of a rooftop. The shape of the gunman's head and shoulders loomed above the muzzle-flash of his rifle. Manning saw the front sight of his FAL assault rifle in the center of the sniper's ski-mask-clad face.

The Canadian squeezed the trigger. A 3-round burst spat from the barrel, and the trio of 7.62 mm projectiles blasted the sniper's skull. The terrorist dropped his rifle. It fell four stories to the concrete below. His corpse was draped across the lip of the roof, the arms dangling limply and his head hanging down.

YAKOV KATZENELENBOGEN emerged from the patrol car that had slammed into the unlucky vehicle now upside down. The Israeli held his Uzi across his prosthetic arm and pointed the weapon at the pastry shop. Superintendent Sutherland sat dazed in the back of the car. He had banged his head against the ceiling of the vehicle when it had collided with the other car. The driver was sprawled across the steering wheel, unconscious. Blood seeped from the constable's mouth. His upper jaw had slammed into the steering wheel with enough force to break two teeth and render him senseless.

Thanks to training and mental discipline, Katz had kept his body loose when the crash had occurred and he had been spared the muscle sprains and dislocated limbs others had suffered. The Israeli had also obeyed the most fundamental rule of travel in an automobile—he had buckled his seat belt. Sutherland would not have rammed headfirst into the car ceiling if he had done likewise.

Katz crouched alongside the car and trained his Uzi on the door where the dynamite-throwing terrorist had come from. A shoulder and part of an upper arm appeared at the door frame. The Phoenix commander rapidly considered his options even as he glanced about at surrounding doors and windows in case more opponents lurked in different directions. There was little doubt the exposed limb belonged to an ambusher, but it was a small target. If he expected the man to attack with a firearm, the best choice of action would be to wait for the enemy to offer a better target when he made his move. However, Katz knew the terrorists were armed with dynamite. The man probably wouldn't expose more than an extended arm to hurl another explosive stick at the patrol car.

The Israeli opened fire. The Uzi sprayed the doorway with 9 mm rounds. Bullets splintered wood and tore into the sleeve at the exposed triceps. A scream responded to the counter-attack, and blood squirted from a severed artery. The arm disappeared from sight as the terrorist retreated inside the shop.

An explosion bellowed from the doorway a moment later. Windows burst and glass spewed into the street. A broken table and part of a chair—minus the backrest—flew through one gaping window frame. Crimson spray and chunks of human flesh arced from the doorway. The remains of a liquidated terrorist splattered the cobblestones outside.

Obviously the opponent had lighted the fuse to another stick of dynamite and was preparing to throw it when Katz shot the man. The guy had dropped the dynamite or had failed to get rid of it before the stick went off. The Phoenix commander jogged to the doorway and peered inside. The pastry shop was a shambles. Smashed furniture littered the floor. Bits of cakes and cookies—some shaped in a crude dinosaur image and sold as ''Nessie cookies''—were scattered across the room. Glass from a display case had shattered, and shards were embedded in the frosting of an assortment of cakes. The top of a tall wedding cake had been sheared off by the blast.

Two men lay among the debris. One was dead, his chest ripped open and his face reduced to a ghastly crimson pulp, teeth visible in red-stained gums no longer covered by lips. The second man had survived the explosion because his comrade had taken the bulk of the blast. The young man slowly rose. He shook his head to try to clear it and glanced about for the Sterling submachine gun he had dropped when the explosion had occurred.

"Freeze!" Katz ordered as he stepped closer. He knew the man's eardrums may have been ruptured and the terrorist's ears were certainly ringing, at the very least. It was unlikely the youth could hear him, so he moved in to allow the opponent to see the Uzi.

Malcolm Bruce clutched his belly with both arms and stared up at Katz. He was surprised to see a middle-aged man with an artificial limb and a submachine gun. Malcolm was aware that one of the mysterious five commandos from America fit this description, but he had assumed the senior member of the team would not participate in combat. The gray-haired amputee may have caught them off guard, Malcolm thought, but he was certain he could take a man almost three times older than himself if he could disarm the Israeli.

"Me guts is on fire!" Malcolm cried. His head felt as if an air raid siren was trapped inside it, and he could not hear his own voice as he spoke. "I'm dying, yeh bastard!"

The young Scot hugged his belly and doubled up. Malcolm unbuckled his belt and allowed Katz to take one more step. The youth suddenly stood erect and lashed out with the brass-studded belt in his fist.

The unconventional weapon struck Katz's Uzi. The unexpected blow sent the subgun flying from Katz's hand. Malcolm immediately followed with another swing. The leather strap slashed at the Israeli's face. Katz barely raised his prosthesis in time to block the attack. Brass studs clanged on the metal limb.

Malcolm's right fist shot out and delivered a hard jab to Katz's jaw. The Israeli's head bounced from the punch, but he glimpsed the belt in his opponent's left fist as it swung in a high arc aimed at his skull. He ducked, and the leather-and-brass weapon flogged him across the right shoulder. Katz hissed from the sharp pain near his collarbone.

"Son of a British gutter slut!" Malcolm snarled, and swung a vicious kick at the older man's torso.

The side of Katz's left hand chopped across Malcolm's shin to stop the kick from making contact. Malcolm lashed out with his belt once more. Katz's prosthesis rose like a solid bar in the path of the strap. A flesh-and-blood limb may have been broken by the force of the belt stroke, but the artificial arm blocked the leather weapon. The belt curled around Katz's prosthesis like a pet boa constrictor.

Malcolm swung his right fist at Katz's face. This time the Israeli was ready for the attack and blocked Malcolm's forearm with the back of his left fist. Katz delivered a short left hook to the Scot's jaw and simultaneously stamped his boot into Malcolm's kneecap. The youth was taken off guard by the combination attack. This allowed Katz a moment to step forward and thrust the steel hooks of his prosthesis under Malcolm's chin.

The Scot gasped as metal claws closed around his throat. The belt was still draped around the prosthesis as Katz applied pressure. The tips of the trident hooks bit into flesh and crushed the thyroid cartilage at the center of Malcolm's throat. The youth flopped his arms in useless protest as Katz literally tore his throat out. Malcolm Bruce staggered backward three steps, blood flowing across his shirt front. His eyes opened, and his mouth formed a large black oval—the expression of astonishment at facing one's mortality. Malcolm's knees buckled, and he collapsed to the floor. Death was his final reality, and he sprawled lifeless at the Israeli's feet.

"Oh, hell!" David McCarter exclaimed as he appeared at the doorway, KG-99 in his fists. "I missed the whole bloody battle. Took us a while to get across town . . ."

"There may be more of them," Katz declared. He gazed down at Malcolm. "Help the others search the area in case some of these bastards haven't been taken out yet. Have Mr. Blue check out the wounded. Our people get first consideration unless one of the terrorists is right at the brink of death and no one from our team faces a life-threatening situation.''

"Right," McCarter replied with a nod. "After a bit I'll tell you what Fellows and I learned about Andrew Robert Bruce."

"I hope it's good news," Katz said as he took one final look at Malcolm's corpse. "He was very young."

Katz shrugged, aware he had done what he had to in order to survive. He retrieved his Uzi and headed out the door.

16

Superintendent Sutherland placed the felt tip pen to a map on the conference table and drew a red circle around a portion of the east coast of Scotland. Katz, McCarter and Major Simms leaned over the table and examined the marked area.

"The Buchan district is here," Sutherland stated. "There be good farming land. Sheep and such are raised in the area. Yet the standard of living isn't as good for most residents in this area as elsewhere in Scotland. People tend to be a wee bit distrustful and clannish here. Buchan Doric be more common than English. Many villages and such in the district. Not many tourists or non-Scots venture here. Not many outside the Buchan lot among Scots visit there, for that matter."

"And Andrew Robert Bruce is supposed to be somewhere in this area," Major Simms said with a sigh. "That's a lot of ground to cover with no idea where to start."

"Maybe not as much as you might think," McCarter mused as he stuck a Player's cigarette in his mouth. "Bruce fancies himself to be a king, right? Now, where would a king choose to live?"

"In Jordan?" Katz replied.

"I'm serious," McCarter insisted.

"A king would plan to live in a castle," Sutherland said thoughtfully. "A castle. Of course! There be several small castles in the district. Most are near Fraserburgh. Some are located in towns like Inverallochy and Pitsligo."

"These aren't tourist attractions or historical sites protected by law and guarded from vandals?" Katz inquired, familiar with castles in other European countries.

"No," Sutherland explained. "These castles once belonged to feudal lords. Petty tyrants who treated their peasants like cattle. Many were Jacobite supporters, which angered the local Buchan population. Peasant uprisings caused angry mobs to storm these castles. They drove out the feudal lords or killed them. The castles are burned-out ruins. Ugly reminders of a rebellious period the Buchan folk still take great pride in."

"So, no one actually owns these castles or even cares what happens to them?" Katz said thoughtfully. "If the terrorists decided to use one of these for a base, they'd select a castle as far away from towns and villages as possible. No way they'd want to draw attention to the construction and renovation necessary to make an old ruins a livable dwelling."

"Somebody would have noticed," Simms said. "Hunters, hikers, shepherds—someone must have noticed some new activity at even the most remote site."

"Not necessarily," Sutherland replied. "Still, there's a chance someone may have noticed some odd goings on. The folk in the district don't talk much to outsiders. A non-Scot cannot even comprehend the Buchan Doric tongue, and even Scottish Gaelic-speaking folk have trouble understanding them. I'll contact some constables in the district. Ask 'em if they've heard anything that might be a lead. Probably just rumors, but that may be enough if we get lucky."

James and Manning entered the conference room, followed by Encizo. The black man shook his head as the Canadian asked whether he was absolutely sure he had not seen anything at Loch Ness.

"Aw, man," James groaned. "I told you before, I didn't see a damn thing. You're the one who said the Loch Ness monster was bullshit..."

"But I saw this big hump and something that looked like it could be a head and neck," Manning insisted.

"Maybe there's a muddy floor at the bottom of the lake, and logs, debris or even sunken boats can be trapped down there for years until a current works it loose," Encizo suggested. "You probably saw something like that. It came up to the surface, and you just got a glimpse at it before Mr. Blue pulled you to the ground."

"Sure didn't look like anything like that," Manning replied.

"What's all this about?" Sutherland asked.

"Never mind," the Canadian said with a sigh. "You guys come up with anything?"

"Hopefully," Katz answered. "It's a bit of a long shot, but we've had more than one pay off in this mission."

"I'd like to find the bastards' main base," Simms commented bitterly. "One of my men is dead, and two others are in the hospital. This mission is becoming personal."

"Just don't get carried away with emotions," the Israeli warned. "That can get you or others with you killed. Remember, we're not here for revenge or to execute anyone. Unfortunately we weren't able to take any of the terrorists alive today. If we had, perhaps we could have learned where their headquarters is located instead of having to search for a king in a castle that may not even exist."

"What?" James asked with surprise. "Who came up with this idea?"

"It's not as farfetched as it sounds," McCarter replied defensively.

"I never like your ideas," Manning told the Briton. "Oh, sometimes you're right and sometimes your plans work, but they're always dangerous and crazy as hell."

"Dangerous and crazy is an apt description of Andrew Robert Bruce," Encizo reminded the Canadian. "Let's hear the theory."

INSPECTOR FELLOWS and Superintendent Sutherland contacted the police in the Buchan district while Phoenix Force and the SAS troops took advantage of the opportunity to relax for a few hours. Katz took a nap on a cot as McCarter and Encizo inspected weapons and equipment. James consulted with the unit medic of the SAS team to make certain he had ample supplies.

Manning borrowed the Loch Ness monster booklet from James and managed to find a copy of the *Dinosaur Dictionary* in a bookcase in the day room. He studied drawings of extinct aquatic reptiles and asked several Inverness constables whether they had ever seen the creature in the lake. None of the cops cared to discuss it. One muttered something about "bloody Yanks" as he walked from the room.

Sutherland and Fellows assembled Phoenix Force and Major Simms in the conference room again. The policemen explained they had made several telephone calls and talked to a number of police officers of various ranks in Fraserburgh, Cairnbulg, Inverallochy and other towns and villages. Most had no information to offer, but four different officers from two separate communities had heard similar stories about a group of strange men who had moved into an old castle nicknamed the Hermit's Palace.

A remote ruins, miles from the nearest village or farm, the castle had been uninhabited for centuries. Many locals believed it was haunted, and a host of bizarre tales revolved around the Hermit's Palace. No one knew the origin of the old castle, so many stories were made up about it. One true story, however, concerned the bands of wild dogs that roamed the area. This was reason enough to stay away from the Hermit's Palace, warn children not to play there and keep herds of sheep far from the site.

Nonetheless, occasionally someone would venture close to the mysterious old castle. A pair of hikers had recently told a Fraserburgh constable they had seen trucks parked at the old ruins and several men who were busy restoring walls with stone and mortar. An Inverallochy officer recalled three children's tale of seeing men armed with military rifles at the castle. Two other constables mentioned similar stories. These included a hobo's claim that the Hermit's Palace was indeed haunted because he had heard wails and shouting from the castle and had seen lights at the windows of the crumbling palace.

"They may have installed electrical generators," Encizo remarked after hearing about the last item. "The rest sounds fairly convincing, especially the kids' story about men with military arms."

"Any idea how big this castle is?" Manning inquired.

"Fairly large by the standards of most of the old castles in the area," Sutherland answered. "The locals reckon it has enough rooms within to house fifty or more men. Has a twelve-foot-high wall around it. May have been quite a fortress once."

"Maybe it still is," Katz mused. "I think we may have located the base. That means we have to move quickly if we hope to raid the place before the terrorists abandon the site. It won't take long for the enemy to learn the second attempt to get rid of us failed. They're not going to hang around after they realize the last hit team won't be coming home . . ."

"That means we have to stop them tonight," Encizo added. "McGreggor may or may not be held captive there. If he is, we'll find him, and if he isn't, we'll find someone who can tell us where to look for him."

"McGreggor may already be dead," Fellows said grimly.

"We've known that from the start," Katz assured him. "All we can do is carry out our mission and see it through to the end. There's no way to bring back the dead, but we can prevent the terrorists from claiming any more victims."

"The bastards can't be much of a threat in a prison cell," McCarter commented as he ground out his cigarette in an ashtray. "Even less if they're in a grave."

ANDREW ROBERT BRUCE hammered the armrest of his throne with his fist and trembled with rage and grief. Tears crept from his squinted eyes and flowed down his cheeks. Duncan stood beside his father and placed a huge hand on the old man's shoulder. He tried to comfort the senior Bruce, but his father continued to sob and muttered "No, no," over and over again.

Garrett O'Flynn watched the self-proclaimed Scottish king and shook his head. Sean and Jamie, his personal bodyguards, waited for the IRA commander to decide what action to take in response to the news of the gun battle in Inverness. O'Flynn turned to his men, nodded and led them from the hall.

Angus met the three Irishmen in the corridor. He saw his brother and father at the opposite end of the hall. Even from a distance, Angus saw Andrew Bruce was overwhelmed with sorrow. He asked O'Flynn what happened, although he already suspected what the answer would be.

"Your brother Malcolm got to Inverness before anyone could stop him," O'Flynn replied. "He must have ordered radio silence, because we couldn't get through to the temporary base there. A news broadcast on the radio just announced there was a big gun battle and explosions near Loch Ness this morning. So-called terrorists clashed with the police. Three peelers were killed, a couple others injured and two British soldiers are in the hospital. The 'terrorists' were all killed in the battle. Eleven, total."

"Me father..." Angus began.

"He knows," O'Flynn confirmed. "I'm sorry about Malcolm. I'm sorry about all of it. Some of the men who died in Inverness were IRA comrades."

"Yeh be leaving then?" Angus asked, his throat constricted with passion and his voice half-choked.

"There's no choice left for us," the Irishman replied. "We've lost too many men. Half the members of my cell have either been captured or they're off to join St. Patrick. The Iron Claymore clan has suffered even greater losses. This castle is all you've got left, and you can bet your last shilling they'll be closing in on this place within the next forty-eight hours."

"I see," Angus said with a nod. "What do yeh suggest we do now?"

"Cut and run," O'Flynn answered. "There's nothing left to do except try to survive to fight another day."

"Father will ne'er leave," the Scot stated. "Not now."

"Carry him out if you must," the IRA commander insisted. "The operation is over, mate. Kill that American bastard and get out while you still can."

"Not for me to make that decision," Angus told him.

"Your father is coming apart at the seams with grief," O'Flynn stated. "He's in no shape to command the clan. You have to decide if you want to obey your father and die—along with the rest of your clan—or take command and save yourself along with the rest."

"Ne'er wanted to be a leader," Angus said with a sigh. "That be me father's dream, not mine."

"Like it or not, it's on your shoulders now," O'Flynn declared. "I'm getting my men together, and we're pulling out tonight. We're Catholic, you know. Suicide is against our religion."

"I'll talk with father," Angus said.

"Whatever he says, the decision will still be up to you," O'Flynn told him. "I know William and Malcolm were your brothers, and I don't mean to belittle their memory, but they both died because they were bold and reckless when they should have watched and waited. Avenge them later. You got to stay alive to do that, Angus. That's a lesson I learned long ago in Northern Ireland.''

"Aye," Angus replied. "God be with yeh, Garrett."

"I'll just settle for getting back to Ireland in one piece," O'Flynn stated. He glanced at his wristwatch. "It's six twenty-five. We'll be ready to leave by seven. If you care to come with us, best be ready, as well."

"We can be in Glasgow around midnight," Sean added. "Board a fishing boat that belongs to a chap sympathetic to our cause and we can cross to Ireland. Eat breakfast in Belfast."

"Think it over, Angus," O'Flynn urged, "but do it now. We're running out of time..."

Two Iron Claymore followers ran into the corridor from another hallway. Both men clutched weapons in their fists, and their faces were white with fear. They breathed heavily, and beads of sweat had appeared on their brows. O'Flynn instinctively gripped the frame of the Sten submachine gun that hung from a shoulder strap near his hip. His stomach knotted, and he felt icy eels swim up his spine, aware the news these men brought them would be as final as nails driven into the lid of a coffin.

"Prince Angus," one of the terrorists began, panting from stress and the effort of running through the halls of the castle. "The sentries...upstairs sentries...they have seen a helicopter approaching from the south. It hovers in the air as if observing us..."

"And Jesus wept," O'Flynn whispered, his voice tense with fear. "It's too late for all of us now."

"Prince Angus?" the other Iron Claymore flunky inquired hopefully.

"Prepare to defend the castle from invaders," Angus replied in a stern voice. "If this be an assault on us, by God we'll make a fight of it!"

"Sean! Jamie!" O'Flynn barked at his bodyguards. "Fetch me that American. Maybe we can use McGreggor to bargain with the enemy. If not, we'll make damn sure the bastards don't take him out of here alive."

17

The Westland Whirlwind HAR-10 hovered in a wide circle in the twilight sky. The RAF chopper was usually assigned to coastal duty for sea rescues in the North Sea. Thanks to the political pull Phoenix Force exercised due to White House authority, it had not been difficult to get the British prime minister to order the RAF to loan the helicopter to the commando team.

The Royal Air Force had even included a pilot and offered to supply extra manpower if needed. Phoenix Force had declined the offer because speed was more essential to success of their mission than the number of men involved. The HAR-10 cabin was not large enough to carry a big assault force, anyway, and the aircraft was not designed for combat. A single SAS trooper was in the cabin, armed with a mounted machine gun, but the helicopter was not intended to participate in the battle itself unless circumstances forced it to get involved.

Phoenix Force, Major Simms and five other SAS commandos approached the so-called Hermit's Palace on foot. There was limited camouflage available to cover their movement. The sparse brush and heather would not conceal the unit, but the circling helicopter assured them the enemy would be distracted while they closed in. The aircraft remained well out of range of any weapon apt to be among the terrorists' arsenal except a land-to-air anti-craft rocket launcher. Everyone hoped the Iron Claymore was not equipped with such firepower.

Two sentries stood at the top of the ramparts. They watched the helicopter with consternation, but failed to glance down at the real attack approaching the walls on foot. Phoenix Force and the SAS soldiers were clad in black night-camouflage uniform and were heavily armed for combat. However, they were far from invisible and realized the enemy might spot them at any moment as they approached the heavy oak gate.

Three more terrorists joined the sentries at the wall. An alarmed shout warned the commando unit someone above had seen them. Gary Manning and Calvin James immediately raised their automatic rifles and fired at the figures on the ramparts. High-velocity 7.62 mm and 5.56 mm slugs ricocheted off stone. The high-pitched whine startled three Iron Claymore fanatics and convinced them to duck low. Another man screamed and toppled forward to plunge over the edge. He kicked wildly and lashed out his arms in a wild windmill motion, as if trying to swim in the air.

The man's screams ended abruptly when he crashed into the hard ground near Gary Manning. The Canadian heard the bone-crunching thud and muscle-tearing rip when the body hit. The Phoenix pro felt his stomach quiver, but he did not stop moving. Manning barely glanced at the fallen figure as he headed for the doors of the gate, making sure the terrorist was either dead or too badly injured to present a threat.

The fifth terrorist at the rampart aimed his AK-47 in the general direction of the muzzle-flash of James's M-16 and opened fire. A column of 7.62 mm slugs tore into earth near the black commando's feet as he dashed for the wall. He raised his rifle to return fire, but an SAS commando had already fixed the sights of his Heckler & Koch G-3 sniper rifle on the enemy gunman and squeezed the trigger. The terrorist's head snapped back as a bullet plowed through his brain and blasted an exit hole at the back of his skull.

Manning reached the gate. He removed a packet of C-4 plastic explosives from a jacket pocket and placed it at the narrow crack between the two thick doors. The demolitions expert turned the timing dial on the detonator and signaled to the others that the charge was set. Manning dashed along the wall approximately twenty feet from the gate and turned and pressed himself against the stone surface, one arm draped over his head.

The C-4 exploded with a sound like a furious clap of thunder worthy of a medieval dragon. The gates flung open, and the castle trembled from the force of the blast. McCarter and Enzico rushed forward and lobbed concussion grenades through the gaping entrance. The Phoenix warriors heard the grenades explode, and two voices shrieked within the walls.

A terrorist at the rampart dared to raise his head and lean over the stone summit to point an FAL rifle at the Cuban commando. James was watching the wall and spotted the gunman through the sights of his M-16. He triggered the weapon and blasted a trio of 5.56 mm messengers into the throat and jawbone of the would-be killer. Bullets shattered bone and pierced the soft flesh under the man's jaw. A slug burned through his tongue and smashed the roof of his mouth to find a resting place in the center of his brain. The terrorist dropped his rifle and slumped lifeless across the catwalk beside a terrified Iron Claymore comrade.

Enzico and McCarter charged through the open gates. Two terrorists lay motionless on the stone pavement. A third was on his knees, leaning on the barrel of a rifle he used as a crutch as he tried to rise. The man saw the Phoenix pair and grabbed the trigger mechanism. Enzico promptly shot him point-blank in the chest with a trio of MP-5 rounds.

The slain terrorist flopped on the ground beside his fallen comrades. Other terrorists opened fire from windows of the castle. McCarter and Enzico ducked behind the stone framework of a well. Bullets cracked against the rocky shelter, and one smashed the wooden bucket that hung from a rope at the top beam.

"I sort of wish somebody else had been first through the gate," Encizo rasped as he unslung a H&K M-69 from his left shoulder.

"Why's that?" McCarter inquired, but he flinched when a ricocheted bullet whistled a few inches from his head.

Encizo held the M-69 in both hands. The compact weapon resembled a giant flare pistol with a huge muzzle. He swung it around the edge of the well and squeezed the trigger. A 40 mm grenade belched from the stubby barrel and sailed into the stone wall of the Hermit's Palace itself. The grenade exploded on impact between two windows. The blast drove stone fragments in all directions. There was no glass in the windows, so stony projectiles pelted the terrorists inside the castle.

Manning and an SAS rifleman opened fire from the open gate. Twin streams of automatic bullets blasted windows, driving the terrorist gunmen back. One opponent dropped his weapon and slapped both hands over his bullet-shattered face. The man dropped from sight, but two more Iron Claymore triggermen appeared at the doors to the archway of the castle entrance. The terrorists opened fire. Manning jumped back for cover at the edge of the gate. The SAS trooper was less fortunate. He staggered backward as bullet holes formed a diagonal line across his chest. The British soldier fell against the framework of the gate and slumped into a seated position on the ground. He stared down at the blood on the front of his field jacket and died.

"Sons of bitches want to play hardball," Calvin James growled as he moved next to Manning by the gate. "Okay. Let's do it that way!"

He thrust the M-16 around the corner and pointed it at the doors to the castle. The black warrior triggered the M-203 grenade launcher attached to the underside of the barrel. A 40 mm shell bolted from the barrel and hissed through the air to slam into the entrance of the castle. The grenade exploded and blasted the door into flying splinters. The bloodied and dismembered remains of two terrorists also spewed from the blast.

McCarter fired his KG-99 at the windows while Encizo broke open his M-69 and loaded another grenade shell. It was vital to keep the enemy too busy trying to keep from getting killed so they wouldn't have an opportunity to retaliate by lobbing grenades back at the raiders. The Briton triggered short bursts at the windows and ducked behind the well. James and Manning also fired at the enemy and added to the terrorists' concerns.

Encizo aimed his H&K launcher and fired the second shell. The grenade arced neatly through a window and burst in a sizzling cone on the floor within the castle. Billows of dense green fumes ejected from the projectile. Terrorists coughed and backed away from the tear gas, fluids running from eyes and nostrils.

James reloaded his M-203 and fired another tear gas grenade through the doorway. More noxious fumes formed a green cloud inside the Hermit's Palace. A confused terrorist stumbled blindly across the threshold, pawing at his eyes with one hand and holding an Ingram machine pistol in the other. Manning aimed his FAL rifle and blasted a trio of bullets into the unlucky gunman's chest. The man tumbled down the stone steps to the ground.

Each commando carried an M-17 protective mask in a case attached to his belt. They tore open the canvas containers and took out the masks. Phoenix Force and the SAS troops donned the M-17s. Faces covered by rubber and plastic filters, eyes circled by Plexiglas lenses, they resembled an assault force from another planet.

Yakov Katzenelenbogen and Major Simms went up to Manning and James at the gate. The four men charged through the entrance one by one, covering each other as they advanced. Katz fired his Uzi at the windows as he ran in a crouched position. Manning fired above the Israeli's head at the third-story windows, and James concentrated fire on the doorway.

McCarter and Encizo joined the others and covered them as they filed through the archway into the castle. The only remaining terrorist on the catwalk by the outer wall sprawled across the walkway and pointed his Kalashnikov rifle at the figures entering the building. Simms glanced up and saw the gunman about to fire down at them.

"Sneaky bugger!" he growled within the trappings of his M-17 mask. The major swiftly raised his Sterling submachine gun and squeezed the trigger.

The terrorist swung his AK-47 at Simms, aware he presented the most immediate threat. Flames spat from both weapons simultaneously. The Iron Claymore gunman screamed as four 9 mm slugs smashed through his ribcage and burrowed into his heart and lungs. The terrorist dropped his rifle and slid from the catwalk, falling lifeless to the ground.

"Nice shooting," McCarter commented. "That was close."

"Very close," Simms replied with a groan.

The major turned to face McCarter. Blood leaked from two bullet holes in the left side of his chest and another at the solar plexus. Simms's knees buckled, and he collapsed across the stone steps to the castle door. McCarter gasped and knelt beside the fallen officer.

"Calvin!" McCarter shouted as loudly as the mask allowed. He forgot to use James's cover name. At that moment, it hardly seemed important. "The major's been hit bad!"

"Not that bad," Simms said, his voice strained, yet he seemed oddly calm. "Not really so bad. My name will be on the Clock now. Won't it, Sergeant?"

"Hold on, sir," McCarter urged as he gripped one of Simms's hands between his palm and squeezed.

Simms did not respond. The officer's chest did not move, and the lenses of his mask were not fogged by labored breathing. James knelt next to the two Britons and picked up Simms's other arm. It was already limp, and James knew he would not find a pulse even before he placed two fingers on the man's wrist. To be certain, he checked for a heartbeat.

"He's dead," James told McCarter.

"Bastard died like a real soldier," McCarter said softly. "SAS to the bone, Major. You bet your arse your name will be on that clock in Hereford."

"We still got a little war here, man," James remarked.

"Right," the Briton replied as he rose. "Let's do it."

DANIEL MCGREGGOR heard the shooting and explosions. There was no window in his cell, but he guessed the sounds of battle meant someone had finally come to rescue him. The President hadn't forgotten him, after all. The businessman rubbed his palms together in expectation and smiled. The goddamn terrorists were not going to get away with this shit, after all.

His glee ended suddenly when he realized that the terrorists might not be willing to surrender their hostage and would rather kill him than allow the rescuers to take him out of the castle alive. McGreggor heard voices outside his cell. He was familiar with the sound of most of his guards' voices. These were different, and the accent was Irish instead of Scottish.

McGreggor had worried about the IRA captors more than the Iron Claymore clan from the beginning. He doubted Andrew Bruce and his sons would be as inclined to kill him as the Irish terrorists would be. Except for that young lunatic Malcolm, of course, but he had overheard the guards mention that the youngest Bruce brother had sneaked off on a personal crusade against the men who had killed the fourth Bruce brother.

The American glanced about his cell for some sort of weapon. McGreggor was no fighter and he didn't try to fool himself that he had much chance of defeating even one of the terrorists, let alone three or four at the same time. Still, he wasn't about to let them just walk in and murder him without at least trying to put up a fight.

His eyes fell on a glass of whiskey on the desk. McGreggor heard the jingle of keys and knew they were about to unlock the cell door. He quickly grabbed the glass as the key turned in the lock. The door opened, and Jamie appeared at the threshold, a cut-down double-barreled shotgun in his fists.

"Come on, Yank," the Irishman ordered. "You're—"

McGreggor tossed the Scotch whiskey in Jamie's face. The IRA flunky had not expected any trouble from the docile American businessman, and McGreggor's tactic caught him completely off guard. The Irishman roared with anger and pain when the whiskey splashed in his eyes. McGreggor charged into Jamie and collided with the younger man.

Both men staggered through the doorway and slammed into Sean. The bellow of a shotgun blast thundered in the corridor. McGreggor felt something ram into his stomach and he gasped in terror. For a split second, the American thought he had been shot, but he realized the blow to his belly was just the shotgun barrels when the weapon recoiled in Jamie's fist.

One of the guards crashed to the floor, his lower chest torn into a crimson crater of bloodied pulp. Jamie's shotgun had blasted a barrelful of buckshot into the sentry. The IRA thug shoved with the shotgun held in his fists like a bar and pushed McGreggor into the doorway. The other guard grabbed the American by the shoulder and shirt front.

McGreggor reacted and rammed an elbow into the man's breastbone before he realized he had done it. The guard staggered backward, surprised by the prisoner's action. However, Jamie swung a rock hard fist to McGreggor's jaw. The American's head seemed to explode in a flash of white-hot pain, and he dropped to the floor at Jamie's feet.

"Goddamn Yankee bastard!" the Irishman hissed, and pointed his shotgun at McGreggor's head.

"You talking to me, Jack?" a voice asked from the end of the hall.

The startled terrorists turned to see Calvin James at the head of the stairs, M-16 in his fists, barrel pointed in their direction. Jamie swung the shotgun toward James, and the black man triggered his weapon. Three 5.56 mm slugs split open the Irishman's face from the bridge of his nose to his hairline. Brains sprayed from the exit wounds at the back of his skull and splattered the surviving guard's face and chest.

"Mother of God!" Sean exclaimed as he saw his partner fall dead beside the dazed figure of McGreggor.

The Irishman stared into the muzzle of James's M-16 and dropped his sawed-off shotgun to the floor. Sean raised his hands in surrender. The unnerved guard followed his example and stuck his arms in the air. James slowly stepped forward, rifle trained on the pair.

"Get into the cell," he ordered. "No bullshit, or you're both dead."

They obeyed instructions and entered the cell. James shooed them away from the door, pulled it shut and locked it. He pulled the key out as McGreggor began to pick himself up from the floor. The right side of his jaw was swollen, but he still smiled as he looked up at James.

"What took you so long?" he asked.

"Missed the bus and couldn't get a cab for hours," James replied. "Stay behind me and don't wander. This isn't over yet."

"Why are you wearing that thing?" McGreggor asked, referring to the M-17 mask.

"Lots of tear gas downstairs," James answered. "Not enough to fill the whole castle, and it hasn't gotten up here yet. Sorry I don't have a spare mask, but the stuff won't kill you. Might make you sick. Sort'a like the last election."

GARY MANNING encountered two Iron Claymore clanners as he prowled through a cloud of tear gas in a massive den. Both opponents were half-blind and coughing from the effects of the fumes, but both were still armed. The Canadian shot each man through the heart with the last six rounds of his FAL rifle.

Manning placed his back against a wall and ejected the spent magazine. He heard more shooting throughout the castle. The remaining members of the SAS team had joined the battle and they were engaged in combat somewhere in the west wing of the building. The clouds of green gas had become so thick that he had wandered away from the others before he realized it. The Canadian took a fresh magazine from an ammo pouch and prepared to reload his weapon before he backtracked to find his teammates.

Suddenly a large figure emerged from behind a wet bar at the opposite side of the room. Duncan Bruce had poured some bottled water over a cloth for a makeshift protective mask when Manning had entered the den. The big Scot had ducked behind the bar while the other two confronted the Canadian Phoenix pro in the one-sided battle. When Manning paused to reload, Duncan saw his chance to strike.

He hurled a stool at Manning. The Canadian raised his rifle to block the unusual projectile. The stool struck the frame of his FAL, and the weapon hopped from Manning's grasp. Duncan charged forward, lower face covered by the damp cloth mask. The Scot's eyes were misted by tears, but he saw Manning well enough to lunge at the Phoenix fighter.

Manning sidestepped the attack and swung a hard right cross to Duncan's face. The Bruce brother hardly seemed to notice and lashed an arm at his opponent. The bottom of his fist hammered Manning in the gut. The Canadian groaned and hooked a short left to Duncan's breastbone. Furious and strong as a young ox, Duncan seemed to ignore Manning's blows and promptly drove an uppercut to the other man's abdomen.

The Phoenix commando doubled up from the punch and lashed out a backfist that completely missed his opponent. Duncan seized the back of Manning's collar with one hand

and the belt at the small of his back with the other. The Scot whipped a bent knee into Manning's chest and drove the wind from his lungs. Then he swung the Canadian off his feet and hurled him like a bag of grain across the room.

Manning slammed into a leather-backed chair and toppled to the floor, taking the furniture with him. He rolled away from Duncan and sprang to his feet. The Scottish hulk raised his big hands in a wrestler's stance and approached his opponent, confident he could tear the Canadian limb from limb.

Manning raised his right hand in a quick feint to distract Duncan and jabbed his left fist to the Scot's jaw. Duncan's head bounced from the punch, and Manning tagged him with another left jab, following with a right cross. He realized his mistake when the Bruce son ducked. Manning had swung too hard, and his weight was behind the stroke. He nearly threw himself off balance when the punch failed to strike its intended target.

Duncan weaved slightly and moved behind Manning in a low crouch. His arms slipped under the Canadian's armpits, and he clasped his hands at the nape of Manning's neck in a full-nelson hold. Duncan growled as he swung Manning toward the wall and prepared to hammer his face into the stones.

Manning raised a boot and planted it on the wall to check the motion before Duncan could smash his forehead into it. He pushed hard and sent them both reeling backward. Duncan crashed into the bar, the small of his back striking hard. Manning bent his elbows and snapped them down forcibly to break Duncan's grip. The fingers slipped from his neck, and Manning quickly jabbed a back elbow-stroke to Duncan's face.

The cloth around the Scot's lower face was stained with blood from a split lip. He whirled a wild left hook at Manning's head, but the Canadian dodged the fist and delivered a left jab to Duncan's nose. The Phoenix commando followed with a right cross to his opponent's jaw, and Duncan slid awkwardly along the length of the bar.

Manning followed him and snap-kicked Duncan in the abdomen. The Scot doubled up from the blow, and Manning chopped the side of his hand across the back of Duncan's neck. The big man fell to one knee, stunned by the barrage of punishing blows. Manning clasped his hands together, raised them overhead and swung his arms as if wielding an ax. He hammered his fists into the base of Duncan's neck and heard the sickly crunch of vertebrae give way. Duncan Bruce collapsed face first to the floor. His neck broken, spinal cord severed, the powerful Scot trembled briefly and died.

GARRET O'FLYNN wiped his eyes with the back of his hand and coughed violently as he stumbled into the kitchen. He spat angrily and pushed his way past two fellow IRA troopers who seemed about to throw up. O'Flynn moved to the wood-burning stove and reached for the cabinet above it. The Irishman opened the door and hauled out a cardboard box. It contained several GP-1 Life Masks with goggles.

"Here," he instructed, taking one mask from the box and handing the others to one of his comrades, "put these on."

"What?" the man asked, confused by the order.

"Put it on your face, you idiot!" O'Flynn snapped as he slipped a mask over his head. The device resembled a dark duckbill over his nose and mouth. "It has a charcoal filter, which will offer some protection from the tear gas."

O'Flynn donned a pair of goggles, as well. The two IRA underlings followed his example and slipped on the GP-1 masks and glasses. O'Flynn considered what options they had left. Fight or surrender seemed to be the only choices. There was no way to escape, he realized. Even if they could get beyond the castle and the outer walls, the helicopter would surely spot anyone who tried to flee across the open ground.

Suddenly an egg-shaped object hurled through the doorway, hit the floor and rolled between O'Flynn's feet. It bounced against the base of the stove and skidded under a table. One of the IRA stooges reached under the furniture and made a desperate grab for the grenade. O'Flynn jumped to the end of the stove farthest from the table and crouched low. He covered his head with his arms a fraction of a second before the grenade exploded.

Just outside the kitchen, Rafael Encizo and Yakov Katzenelenbogen took stock of the blast's effect. Chunks of the table, a skillet and the box with the GP-1 masks were hurled through the doorway by the concussion blast. The Phoenix pair entered the room and found one terrorist sprawled on his back, his face and chest shredded by wooden splinters. Another lay on his side, curled up in a ball of terrible pain, both hands clamped around ruptured eardrums.

O'Flynn had also suffered a ruptured eardrum, and his nostrils bled into the charcoal filter of his mask. The Irishman glanced up at Katz and Encizo. His arms moved like the limbs of a lead puppet as he started to raise his Sten subgun.

"Give it up," Katz warned, and pointed his Uzi at the Irishman. Encizo did likewise.

"Fuck you," O'Flynn replied as he shifted the Sten toward the Phoenix commandos.

Katz and Encizo opened fire.

DAVID MCCARTER STOOD at the entrance to the great hall. A frail-looking old man sat on a throne, his body rigid, eyes open and motionless. The British commando stared at the paintings behind the throne. He recognized Robert I and David II, but the third painting hardly resembled the broken, aged figure that seemed frozen in the armchair.

The Phoenix fighter stepped into the hall. Movement from the right flickered at the corner of the lens of his M-17 mask. McCarter turned sharply, but the long iron blade of a claymore sword chopped across the frame of his KG-99 and struck it from his grasp before he could point the weapon and squeeze the trigger.

Angus swung the sword in a rising sweep, the hammered and sharpened edge aimed at McCarter's neck. The Briton dodged the whirling blade. He mentally chided himself for not making certain the old man in the throne was alone before he entered the room. If Angus had been armed with a gun, McCarter could have been killed on the spot.

The last of the Bruce brothers slashed a diagonal sword-stroke at McCarter. The Briton jumped back and narrowly avoided the iron blade. He reached for the grips of the Browning pistol in shoulder leather, but Angus stepped forward and swung the claymore again. McCarter felt the blade strike under his left arm. The blow lifted him off his feet and sent him tumbling onto the floor.

The sword had struck the shoulder holster. Leather and the frame of his Browning autoloader had spared McCarter the deadly sharp edge of the Scottish weapon. But the blow had dislodged the pistol and sent it skidding across the floor. Angus raised his claymore high and stepped forward to swing a murderous downward stroke that was intended to split the Briton's head.

McCarter shifted aside, and the blade rang against the stone floor less than an inch from his head. The Briton swung a boot high and slammed the steel toe under Angus's ribs. The kick propelled him several feet, but the Scot managed to keep his balance. McCarter rolled away from his opponent and jumped to his feet. Angus faced him once more, claymore held ready.

"Damn yeh to hell!" Angus hissed. "Yeh destroyed me father's clan! Destroyed his dream forever!"

"Christ, I hope so," McCarter replied as he glanced about the room for something to use to defend himself against Angus's blade.

He spotted the Bruce coat of arms on the nearest wall. One sword was missing, obviously the weapon Angus wielded. The other still hung on the wall. McCarter ran for it as Angus bellowed with rage and attacked again.

"Kill him, Angus!" a voice cried out.

The Scot's head turned with surprise when he recognized his father's voice. The old man leaned forward in his chair and watched the battle. His eyes were open and glassy, drool hung from his quivering lips and his entire body trembled.

Angus had been distracted for less than a fourth of a second, but that was long enough for McCarter to reach the wall and draw the other claymore sword. He was unfamiliar with the weapon. It was long and heavy. The sword felt awkward in McCarter's hands and it seemed far too clumsy to use in combat.

Angus Bruce did not seem to have this problem, McCarter observed. The Scot swung his claymore in a rapid figure-eight pattern. As he closed, McCarter swung his sword like a cricket bat, having little other experience to draw upon. The iron blades clanged in violent contact.

McCarter immediately swung a boot and nailed Angus between the legs. The Scot howled with pain as the kick mashed a testicle. The Phoenix warrior shoved as hard as he could with his claymore to push Angus's sword back. Angus pivoted with the movement, despite the agony in his groin, and whirled in a full circle to slash a sword stroke at his opponent.

The iron blade whistled above McCarter's head as he dropped to one knee. The sword brushed the black beret from the Briton's head, touching his hair. McCarter felt the terror well inside him as he thrust his claymore like a lance. The iron point pierced Angus's solar plexus, and the blade sunk deep in the Scot's flesh.

Angus stumbled backward and glanced down at the long dark blade lodged in his stomach. His arm quivered as he raised his claymore. Angus's fingers lost their strength, and the sword slipped from his hand to clatter on the stone floor. The Scot opened his mouth to speak, but blood rose from his throat as he vomited across his shirt. Angus Bruce turned slightly and fell forward. The hilt of the claymore stuck in his body jammed against the floor, and the blade was driven deeper.

"No!" Andrew Robert Bruce exclaimed as he watched his eldest son crumple to the floor in a lifeless heap.

The old man started to rise from his throne. Bruce stiffened and fell back into the chair, his face contorted with pain. His fingers clawed at the armrest, one leg twitched forlornly. Then he moved no more. McCarter heard someone behind him and turned to see Katz approach.

"We wondered what happened to you," the Israeli remarked. "The terrorists are finished, McGreggor is alive and relatively well and we managed to wrap up this mission in time to assure the new President we're reliable."

"Hal will be pleased," McCarter replied as he stepped to the platform and checked the motionless figure seated on the throne. "He's dead. Heart couldn't take it, I reckon."

"The man who would be king of Scotland," Katz commented as he glanced down at the corpse of Angus. "This was one of his sons?"

"Yeah," McCarter confirmed with a nod. "I think he was the last one."

"Foolish old man," Katz said with a sigh. "He lost his family, his sanity and his life in pursuit of a crown he wouldn't have known what to do with. What a waste."

"We see a lot of it," McCarter agreed. "Let's get out of here. This place is bloody depressing."

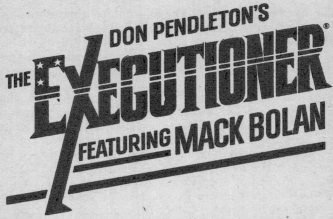

DON PENDLETON'S

THE Executioner®

FEATURING MACK BOLAN

Baptized in the fire and blood of Vietnam, Mack Bolan has become America's supreme hero. Fiercely patriotic and compassionate, he's a man with a high moral code whose sense of right and wrong sometimes violates society's rules. In adventures filled with heart-stopping action, Bolan has thrilled readers around the world. Experience the high-voltage charge as Bolan rallies to the call of his own conscience in daring exploits that place him in peril with virtually every heartbeat.

"Anyone who stands against the civilized forces of truth and justice will sooner or later have to face the piercing blue eyes and cold Beretta steel of Mack Bolan . . . civilization's avenging angel."
—*San Francisco Examiner*

GOLD
EAGLE®

Available wherever paperbacks are sold.

MB-2RR

TAKE 'EM NOW

FOLDING SUNGLASSES
FROM GOLD EAGLE

Mean up your act with these tough, street-smart shades. Practical, too, because they fold 3 times into a handy, zip-up polyurethane pouch that fits neatly into your pocket. Rugged metal frame. Scratch-resistant acrylic lenses. Best of all, they can be yours for only $6.99.

MAIL YOUR ORDER TODAY.

Send your name, address, and zip code, along with a check or money order for just $6.99 + .75¢ for postage and handling (for a total of $7.74) payable to Gold Eagle Reader Service. (New York and Iowa residents please add applicable sales tax.)

Remove from pouch

unfold once

unfold twice

and they're ready to wear

GOLD EAGLE

Gold Eagle Reader Service
901 Fuhrmann Blvd.
P.O. Box 1396
Buffalo, N.Y. 14240-1396

GES-1A

Offer not available in Canada.

Illegal nuclear testing in Antarctica sends Phoenix Force Down Under when a maniacal plot threatens global destruction.

SUPER PHOENIX FORCE #3

COLD DEAD

GAR WILSON

The two superpowers suspect one another of illegal nuclear testing in Antarctica when the bodies of two murdered scientists show high levels of radiation in their systems.

It's a crisis situation that leads Phoenix Force to New Zealand, where a madman's growing arsenal of nuclear weapons is destined for sale on the international black market....

Don't miss the riveting confrontation in COLD DEAD when it explodes onto the shelves at your favorite retail outlet in April, or reserve your copy for March shipping by sending your name, address, zip or postal code along with a check or money order for $4.70 (includes 75¢ postage and handling) payable to Gold Eagle Books:

In the U.S.
901 Fuhrmann Blvd.
Box 1325
Buffalo, NY 14269-1325

In Canada
P.O. Box 609
Fort Erie, Ontario
L2A 5X3

Please specify book title with your order.

SPF3-1